Double Magick in the Falls

by

April Hollingworth

The Candi Reynolds Series

Double Magick in the Falls

Cover Art by *Debbie Taylor*

The Wild Rose Press, Inc.
PO Box 708
Adams Basin, NY 14410-0708
Visit us at www.thewildrosepress.com

Publishing History
First Black Rose Edition, 2015
Print ISBN 978-1-62830-735-1
Digital ISBN 978-1-62830-736-8

The Candi Reynolds Series
Published in the United States of America

"Who are you?" I ask this time.

No point in demanding, as it obviously doesn't get me anywhere.

"I am Victor Harlow and owner of Vlad's Bar. Why were you spying on me and for whom?" he demands while tracing a gentle circle on the velvet skin of my wrist.

Pulling my wrist out of his grasp, as his fingers are doing funny things to my stomach, I turn to look him full in the face. My God, he is gorgeous.

Short, jet black thick hair, I want to run my fingers through. Ebony black eyebrows arched over silvery green eyes, which are unfairly surrounded by long, thick, black eyelashes. Seriously, if a girl had those, she would never need to buy mascara!

A long straight nose and full sensuous lips, which look so kissable, high cheekbones and a strong square jaw. He has a beautiful neck and an image of fangs sinking into it flashes before my eyes making me gulp, I drag my eyes lower to his broad shoulders and a large ever so muscled body in a lean tall package. Wow, he is scrumptious.

Biting my lip, I suppress a moan at the thought of exploring every inch of his delectable body and kissing his sensual mouth. I suddenly realize he'd been saying something, but I have no idea what.

Praise for *DOUBLE MAGICK IN THE FALLS*

"Candi, a powerful witch, is sharing steamy nights with a glowing-eyed vampire, Victor, while they hunt a murderer and try to save themselves. Romance. Mystery. Murder. Find it all!"

~Linda Joyce, author of Bayou Bound

"In this fabulous book about a witch, we are drawn into a world full of intrigue, murder, magick and love. I loved this book! It was action-packed and full of surprises. April, you are my new favorite author!"

~Anne Gonsalves

"A unique paranormal, romantic, mystery filled with witches, vampires, and shifters. It grabbed my interest with its quick pace and snappy dialogue. I loved the characters, especially Victor and his effect on Candi."

~Christine Elaine Black, author

"Immediately you know you're in for a wild ride when the young protagonist reveals that her parents were murdered and she herself is a witch. Candi starts off in this mystery-thriller bound and determined to find out why a group called The Protectors killed her parents."

~Lori Lesko, author

"Immediately, I was drawn into the gruesome death of Candi's parents and her dark journey to find the group who killed them and why. The author spins this tale in a clever way, with a great blend of characters, leaving you hanging onto the pages waiting for the mysteries to be unveiled."

~Verusha Singh

Dedications

To Marian and David Hollingworth AKA Mum and Dad for always believing in me and encouraging me with my writing.

To my sisters Christine Simpkins and Tracey Mitchell, for your support. Thanks, Tracey, for helping me come up with the title.

To my nieces Mia and Laila, and all my aunts, uncles, and cousins for your support and best wishes.

And especially Roisin Hollingworth, younger sister extraordinaire and my personal cheering squad and greatest believer.

~*~

I would also like to give a special thanks to my editor Lill Farrell, editor extraordinaire. Without your help and guidance, this book would not have reached its fullest potential.

And to The Wild Rose Press for giving me this opportunity to join the family of Roses in the Garden.

And finally, thank you Debbie Taylor from DCA Graphics for my wonderful cover art.

Prologue

October 31st 1999

Dear Journal,

My heart breaks every time I think of my mother's death. I try not to, but it's only been a couple of weeks, and my feelings are still so raw. It doesn't help that I've been uprooted from my home and sent to live with my grandmother at Paradise Falls. Seriously, where do people get these names?

It doesn't help when my father died three years ago in exactly the same way. And the worst part is, I was the one who found them. Propped in a sitting position against the wall, their arms crossed in the front as if trying to hold their intestines in. Except their intestines were carefully arranged around them, looking like gone off sausages. Hearts ripped from their chests.

Worst of all, was their smiling faces. I learned later their mouths had been stitched in that position. But I can't get the image of their grinning corpses out of my head. For me, this is the most horrific part of their deaths. It is bad enough someone could kill both my parents, but why in such a horrendous fashion?

Grandmother Eve has a shop called Magick of Old; she said I can help out on the weekends. Seriously? I'm uprooted from my home and dragged to Timbuktu, and now forced to work in a magic shop. She probably sells those crappy kid's magic boxes and stuff. Again, what is with the funny spelling? There is no K in magic.

I just want my life back, and my mum, God, I miss her so much. I'm thinking of joining the army, of starting a new life.

Every time Grandma Eve looks at me, she gets sadder. My pain is bad enough to deal with. I can't handle hers as well. Maybe I'm being selfish, but I just can't.

Let their spirits find each other in the great beyond, and let them move on to somewhere better. Until I meet them again. Mom and Dad, I love and miss you. I hope you are at peace in each other's arms. Help me with my decision and convince Grandma Eve to let me go.

Candi Reynolds
P.S. Happy seventeenth birthday to me
****

October 31st 2000

Dear Journal,

I've been living with Grandma Eve for a year. Tomorrow I am leaving to join the army. I know Grandma Eve is upset with my decision, but to be honest, this is something I must do for myself. Something I have wanted for over a year. Today is my eighteenth birthday, and I no longer need permission to join. I'm glad for the year I've had with Grandma Eve. She has taught me so much about the craft. The K in magick is the way witches spell it to differentiate it from witchcraft, or those who mess about with magic.

Anyway, I now spell magick with a K. I wonder why Mum never told me we were witches. The only thing I'll be taking with me is the camera my mum gave me before she died. I don't need anything else and don't want anyone to read you. God knows how they would react to what I've written. I won't be writing to you again for a long time, if ever. Well, let's just leave it at a long time.

Candi Reynolds
P.S. Happy eighteenth birthday to me

Chapter 1

October 31st 2012

Dear Journal,

It's been twelve years since I left Paradise Falls, twelve years since I wrote in you. A lot has changed. I joined the veterinary corps, and they became my family. But after so many years, it is good to be home. I brought Jasmine back with me. She's a beautiful Alsatian and she's my friend, we've been together ever since I joined the army. Though I have to admit, Grandma's face when she saw her was hilarious. I've never seen her look so flabbergasted.

I'm a photographer now, specializing in night shots of wildlife. I still use the camera my mum gave me. Though technically with all the enhancements I've done to it, it's only the shell that's left of the original. I just can't say goodbye to it. It's like my lucky talisman. I'm selling to magazines and getting my name out there. It isn't mega bucks, but I love it.

I do some daytime shots, too, but since returning to Paradise Falls, I've been helping Grandma in the shop in the mornings. It is a good way to get back into the scene and meet people. I can't believe I ever thought

Grandma's shop was a cheap joke shop, instead of a true witch's magick shop filled with ingredients, tarot cards, and so much more.

I can't believe my mum has been gone for thirteen years. At times, the pain is so raw it seems like it happened yesterday. Other times it's like a lifetime ago. I've changed so much, hopefully for the better.

I finally found out why my parents were killed, and to be honest it just seems so pointless.

My mum, as I told you long ago, was a witch. And my dad was a werewolf. In the supernatural world, you don't mix with those outside your own kind. Obviously my parents did, which is why they left Paradise Falls.

They were hunted, and my dad caught and murdered. My mum took me and we fled, but they caught up with her, too. What I don't understand is the three year gap between the killings, or the ritualistic way it was done. Or truthfully, why I am still alive. Don't get me wrong. I am thankful, but...it doesn't make any sense.

Anyway, I am back in Paradise Falls, this time for good.

It still hurts my parents were taken from me, and I want to find out who killed them. They had left, why hunt them down over so many years?

I have to go. Jasmine needs to go for a walk, and it's a full moon tonight. Everything always looks so much more enchanting and otherworldly under the light of a full moon. Time to take some photos.

Candi Reynolds.

P.S. Happy thirtieth birthday to me

****

Taking a deep breath, I close my journal. I'd forgotten how good it felt to write in it. As if writing to an old friend. Stretching, I stand and cross the room to the door. Changing my mind, I return to the desk.

Sliding my fingers along the side, I feel for the slight knot in the wood. A hidden drawer pops open. Placing the journal inside, I remove the hidden cloth covered bundle. I don't have much time, but feel the need to do a three card spread, with my Midnight Mystic Oracle Cards.

Card 1: MOONLIGHT.

Mystery

It's time to examine your dreams, and remember them as well. As the answers you seek, are there.

Card 2: BLOOD MOON.

Caution

Have faith and work hard, but don't become self-obsessed. Ask for help to achieve your goals, if required. Always be yourself.

Card 3: WOOD SPRITE.

Spirit of Nature

It is time to get back in touch with nature. Explore woods and wildlife. Experience new things, and open your mind to different things. Seek adventure. Rebuild your life and live it the way you desire.

Huh, okay, ask for help if I need it? Why would I need help? With a puzzled frown, I quickly write down the cards and their translations.

Quite often, things become obvious later. Putting the cards back into the draw, I close it and leave the room. A full moon is not something to waste, especially when you're a photographer who prefers taking photos at night.

I leave Grandma's house and call Jasmine to me; we walk to the East Bridge where we cross over. Witches do not like their surrounding areas to be photographed. Mainly, I believe, in case they're up to some hocus-pocus.

Once we cross over the bridge and car park, we head toward the woods. I hear wolves howling and feel disappointed I can't photograph them. They're across town, and most likely werewolves. A full moon, though wonderful, can make werewolves a higher risk than normal. The call of the moon is too strong, and so is the hunt for prey. I sure as hell don't want to become part of their hunt.

As Jasmine and I slip into the woods, she suddenly goes still. In the army, you learn to sense danger and always trust your instincts. My instincts scream out a major predator is near. I spot a group of men outside a bar. I don't know why I can differentiate major predators from simple humans. Witches and werewolves obviously, but humans, though they can be vicious, don't normally cause this strong a reaction.

However, my senses keep telling me danger is near, and I need to take care. Suddenly one of them turns and stares directly at me, or at least in my direction. I don't think he sees me. My senses go on high alert and lust shoots through me. He is gorgeous. Built like an Adonis come to life, he looks dangerous as hell, his glowing blue eyes pull me in, while his full sensual snarling lips, drawn back over huge fangs, assure me I'm right. He most definitely is a predator.

I have always assumed vampires were myth. Stupid, since I am a witch and I've worked with werewolves and shifters, you would think I would have realized, there are, or could be, other supernaturals as well. But hey, you learn something new every day.

I just learned I'm attracted to a very hot vampire with huge fangs and glowing blue eyes. Who knew? I sure as hell didn't!

Keeping low, I quietly ease back, making my way to the other side of the woods with Jasmine securely at my side; I hurry across the car park and over the bridge.

On the other side, I let out a breath I didn't know I was holding. With one final look back, I scan the trees, but see nothing, though for just a second, I sense someone watching.

A sense of change washes over me, as if nothing will ever be the same again. With a shake of my head, I brush away my thoughts and retreat to Grandma's house. I'll ask her tomorrow about the vampires, and if she knows of any houses up for sale.

I need my own space, and I don't think it's wise to use the woods across the bridge for any more photo shoots.

Thinking of the woods brings the vampire to mind. I bite my lip hard to clear my thoughts. I need a run, that's what's wrong with me. I'll have to go for a decent run tomorrow, to burn off the extra energy from

8

tonight.

I love running, and my body needs it as well. The army was great, all the exercise regimes helped keep me focused, and solutions to problems became clearer.

I do my best thinking while running, and get a serious case of bad attitude and total bitch when I don't find the time for a regular run. And hopefully, it'll get the lust-filled cravings out of my system, too.

Cutting across the grass, I smell a storm coming.

"The elements are gathering. It's going to be a rough night," I whisper.

My mum always said that, when my dad smelt the coming storm. She was always right, too.

"God, I miss you, Mum, and you, Dad, as well," I say on a breath of a sigh.

Reaching Grandma's, I sense she's back, so I call out a greeting and quickly hurry upstairs so I can get my trainers off.

Grandma does not appreciate dirty trainers in her clean house. She also cannot understand my need to run. She also believes an Alsatian is not the right pet for a witch, and surely, she can take herself for a run without me! My grandmother has many opinions!

Quickly putting my camera down, I lament not having taken any photos, but I have a feeling I probably would have been caught by the vampire if I had.

"I'll be down in a minute, Gran. I need to ask you something," I call out.

Quickly removing my trainers, I run a brush through my long red hair and clamor downstairs to the sitting room, where my gran is waiting, relaxing in front of a blazing fire, the book she'd been reading closed on her lap.

"Hey, Grandma Eve, I've decided that I'm staying put in Paradise Falls. Do you know of any houses that are for sale or rent?"

Where my gran is concerned, it's best to just get to the point, she prefers it. Come to think about it, so do I.

"I'm glad you're staying, child." Giving a nod of her head, she continues as if coming to a satisfying conclusion.

"The old Winters' house is up for sale, not too pricey since it's been abandoned for a while. I think you will be well suited to it. There's even a dog flap in the back door you can use for that dog of yours." Eve gives a puzzled shake of her head, as if saying why a dog?

"Thank you, Grandma," I reply with honest relief. "What do you know about vampires?" I ask with some hesitation. It feels so strange to be wondering. I mean I love reading and watching films about them, but who knew they were actually real?

"They're dangerous, and you should stay away from them," was Eve's definite, but non-helpful reply.

"Yessssss, but..."

"No buts, child, stay away from them, and that's final. Now I'm tired, and going to bed." Shaking a finger at me, as if to emphasize her point, Eve rises and strides out of the room, without a backward glance or another word.

I gape in surprise at her unusual behavior. The wagging of her finger at me and the sharp tone of voice was normal enough. The year I previously lived with Eve after my mum's death had me on the wrong side of her plenty of times. But the lack of any information, and the finality of the conversation, surprised and troubled me.

Looking thoughtfully out the door, I wondered if Eve could be scared. Could vampires be so dangerous? A quick flashback to the vampire in the parking lot has me thinking yes, especially with how I reacted. I decide to go to bed as well.

Tomorrow I'll look at the old Winters' house, but if it's in my price range, I'm taking it. Situated on the border of the woods, it is just what I'm looking for. As I climb the stairs, the rain starts, and I hear the sound of distant thunder.

Waking up to the annoying sound of singing birds, I growl in frustration and stick the spare pillow over my head. With a start of surprise, I sit up and brush my hair out of my face, letting the pillow plop back onto the bed. Looking toward the window, I stare in confusion. The curtains and the window are thrown wide open.

What the hell? I mutter, knowing I always close the window and keep the curtains tightly shut. A morning person I am most definitely not. Even after so many years in the army, or maybe that's the reason I like to sleep late.

"Grandma, did you open my window and curtains this morning?" I holler, as I scramble out of bed.

"Yes, I've booked you an appointment to see the old Winters' house before work today, hence this treat," Eve replies.

I watch in surprise as my grandmother enters the room, carrying a large tray full of sausages, crispy bacon, fried eggs, hash browns, grilled tomatoes, buttered toast, black and white puddings, and a large mug of coffee with plenty of milk. Nose sniffing in delight, I quickly take the tray off her and set it on my bed.

"Wow, thanks, Grandma. I'll just freshen up." I give her a quick kiss on the cheek and rush into the bathroom.

Back in my room, I tuck into my breakfast. With a groan of happiness, I finish the last bite of my toast, grab my mug of coffee, and set the empty tray on the floor.

"That was wonderful, thank you. What time is the viewing?"

"Ten. You have forty minutes to get ready and get to the house to meet Alex Higgins, the local estate agent."

"No probs, that's loads of time. Thanks Gran...for everything." I give her a quick hug.

"Go on, get yourself ready, girl, before you're too late." I watch Gran's face as it lights up from the impromptu hug.

I know Gran missed me and worried *The Protectors* would find me and kill me, just as they had my parents. It was a silly fear, as children I learned are never harmed. However, the loss of my mum is still raw for her, and the thought of the last connection to her being murdered terrified her.

She knew I was determined to follow my own path, and I think she is proud of the strong woman I have become.

She will always worry, and with me living nearby she will know I'm safe. Though she'd never understand my affection for my dog.

Why a witch would ever have a dog was beyond her. In her old-fashioned way of thinking, if you're going to have a pet at least make it a cat.

****

Quickly I scramble into my tracksuit bottoms and tank top and put my hair into a scrunchy. Grandma does not like people wandering around in their pajamas, even if it is only for a couple of minutes.

Jogging downstairs, I fill two dog bowls with food and fresh water. A quick woof of hello and a happy tail wag is my greeting before Jasmine devours her food.

Running back upstairs, I get into the shower. A quick wash, brush of my teeth, and change into a pair of jeans and a light jumper. Pulling on a pair of boots, I pick up my jacket and car keys, before heading back downstairs.

"Grandma, I'm going now, I'll see you at lunchtime," I yell out as I leave the house.

Seeing Jasmine I call her over. I climb into the front seat and she hops in beside me, and I head to the old Winters' house.

My first glimpse of it takes my breath away. Through the windy trail and trees, I catch sight of the two-story house. The paint is fading and peeling, and some branches are brushing against the upstairs windows, gently scratching the glass. The upstairs balcony has a dead plant in a cracked pot on it, and the wrap-around terrace has a sad apologetic look, as if embarrassed to be caught in such disarray. The estate agent standing in front of the house wears a defeated look on his face.

I for one have already fallen in love with it and can see so much potential. But no way am I letting him know that!

Climbing out of my car with Jasmine on my heels, I cross the area of the drive to the estate agent.

"Mr. Higgins I presume," I inquire, while offering my hand.

"Ah yes, but call me Alex please. Eve Allhallows said you were looking to buy? Miss Allh—"

"Reynolds, Candie Reynolds," I interrupt.

"I do apologize, and you wanted to look at this house?" Alex asks, as if I had gone crazy, or he had misunderstood.

"Apparently. May we look around since I'm here?" I request, since it does not look like we're going to move. Doesn't the man know how to walk and talk at the same time?

"We, ahhh you have a dog? Yes, of course you can," replied Alex, sounding highly flustered.

"Yes, I have a dog. Now we've figured that out, can I look at the house please," I reply a note of warning and irritation in my voice.

I know exactly what he was thinking; it didn't take a genius to figure out since it was written all over his face. A dud indeed, and even if I was, why should it matter one way or another?

"Yes, yes, of course, this way please. As you can see the house has been abandoned for quite a while, and ah, yes, this way please," answers Alex, gesturing toward the locked front door.

"If you would unlock the door, I can walk around the house by myself if you prefer. How much did you say it was going for?" I casually inquire, as if I don't care one way or another.

"Yes, well, it's going for €175,000, though if you are interested, it could probably be negotiated. To be honest, I think the owners just want to get rid of it."

"What land comes with the house?" I ask, hiding

my smile and wondering how many times he's tried to get rid of the property.

"Well, the land is very extensive. Most of the woods are part of the land. There's a trench around the boundaries. Old Mrs. Winters wanted to make sure no animal would be harmed if they crossed over to her land, but wanted it apparent to people they were about to trespass. There is also an old ruin and small graveyard," Alex replies, muttering the latter part under his breath. With a defeated look on his face, he turns to leave.

"I can't look around the house if you won't unlock the door!" I exclaim in annoyance. Good god what is with this man, for crying out loud! What, did most people feel unsettled on hearing there was a graveyard on the land?

"Oh you still want to look at it?" gasps Alex, quickly unlocking the door before I change my mind.

"Of course I do," I huff, giving him a strange look.

****

Entering the house, I see high ceilings and spacious rooms. Three doors lead off the hallway. Opening the first, I find the sitting room with a huge open fireplace.

The second door reveals a cupboard under the stairs is in fact a bathroom with toilet and sink. The last door at the end of the hall is the kitchen and dining room.

The dining room also has a large marble fireplace and an alcove leading off to a sunroom. The kitchen has a large wood stove and another door leading into the utility room with the back door, and as Grandma Eve had promised, a dog flap.

Upon opening the back door, I notice a nice bit of

garden, not too big, with a shed and a small fence around it, the woods surrounding the fence.

Feeling pleased I reenter the house, lock the back door, proceed back into the hallway and upstairs. I notice four doors leading off the upstairs landing.

Inside the first room is a big, old-fashioned, claw-footed tub, toilet and sink to the left, and a shower to the right. If I hadn't fallen in love with the house already, the bathroom would have made me fall for it in an instant.

Wow, I'm in love!

Leaving the bathroom, I open the next door, which is a bedroom with a veranda. Seeing a long wardrobe, I cross the room and open the doors to find not just a simple wardrobe, but a walk-in one with shelves and two rails.

How are you still empty? Seriously, the house is gorgeous.

Leaving the bedroom, I move to the next room, which is another large bedroom, and then upon opening a door to the left of the room, I find an en-suite bathroom.

Very nice, I murmur, thinking this would do as a guest bedroom.

Entering the last room, I decide I can partition it off, and build a darkroom, and still have plenty of space for my computer desk and chair, a couple of book cases and maybe even a comfy chair.

I head back downstairs and out the front door, where I spot Alex impatiently waiting for me.

"Is there anything you're not telling me about the house?"

"She died in the house," Alex blurts out, as if he

can't hold the information in any longer.

"Who did, old Mrs. Winters?"

"Yes."

"Did anyone else?"

"I don't think so," Alex replies.

"Natural causes or murdered?" I might as well know, though to be honest, it still wouldn't stop me from buying the house.

"Natural, of course," gasps Alex in shock, as if the idea of murder is a foreign experience.

"Of course," I say with irony, thinking of my parents.

"Okay, there is a hell of a lot of work needing to be done to the house. I'll offer €125,000, but obviously I'll need to get a surveyor out to look over the place, if the owners are interested in my offer. Also, anything in or on the grounds as of this moment, is part of the sale. Contact me at Eve's when you receive an answer.

"You're interested in buying it?"

"Haven't I just said that? Look, let me know when you have an answer. I have to go to work now. Thank you for letting me look around. Come on, girl."

I open the car door, and Jasmine squeezes in ahead of me giving her tail a happy thump. Climbing in, I fasten my seat belt and drive off.

"You like the house, too?" I ask with a feeling of excitement.

"Woof."

"It's gorgeous, and thankfully most of the work seems to be surface, though it will still take time as well," I mutter thinking of all the sanding down which needs doing inside and outside, the painting and building of the dark room. The branches from the trees nearest the house need to be cut back so they don't overshadow, and cause future damage and dampness.

"The drive will need tarmac put down, too, and the porch needs support beams, or something done to it to stop the sagging. Yeah, there's a lot of work needing to be done." I sigh, and so does Jasmine in answer.

Chapter 2

A grin spreads over my face, as I hang up on Alex Higgins. The owners accepted my offer. I haven't even been at work for an hour. I'm a bit surprised as the offer was so low, but it just means I don't need to scrimp on repair work. I can hire someone outright to get it all done. I call a recommended surveyor, who agrees to come out tomorrow to look over the house and lands. Next I contact my solicitor to get the paperwork started.

****

A feeling of excitement and the Earth settling comes over me. It is as if things are coming back to their rightful position in life.

"Are you listening to me?" demands a little old lady, with bright blue hair, and a rather ferocious scowl on her wrinkled face. "I demand you pay attention to me this minute!" she screeches, at decibels the deaf can hear.

"I can hear you, but sadly…" Huh, how to put it politely, so the little old dragon won't explode from anger?

"My attention was on another matter at the time. But you now most definitely have my attention, and everyone else's as well," I reply with utter politeness, seriously, I have done myself proud. Or not, going from the look of furious irritation on the lady's face.

"Why, you insufferable child, I ought to teach you

some manners, you and your beast. Now, get out of this shop at once. I know the owner, and she won't permit the likes of you in here," cackles the old lady, pointing a bony finger imperiously at the door.

Politeness forgotten, I stand up to my full height of five foot nine, so I nicely tower over the little hag in front of me.

"Do not, under any circumstances, threaten me or mine again, old woman," I growl, my green eyes narrowing, and sparks flitting off my fingertips.

"As for knowing the owner, you are not the only one who does. Obviously I know her, since I'm working in her shop, and she's my grandmother. Now, behave yourself or leave this place, but never presume to speak to me or treat my dog with anything other than politeness again. You may not like us, but tough shit on your behalf. Now, is there anything I can help you with, or are you ready to leave yet?" I demand in a controlled voice.

Hearing gasps of surprise, I look at the other customers, most of whom seem more shocked at seeing me standing up to the old lady, than at sparks shooting from my fingers. That's the way of things when surrounded by witches!

"I hadn't realized you were a witch, or that you were Eve's granddaughter. With you having a dog, how am I supposed to know?" the little old lady answers huffily.

As if that explained things. She did look nervously at my fingers, probably terrified the sparks would strike her.

"Ah well, that's okay, I mean, obviously it's okay to speak to anyone else with complete lack of respect, just because they're not witches," I reply with a major amount of frustrated sarcasm. What the hell was wrong with people?

"Well, I need help with a spell," whispers the little old lady as she looks shiftily around to see who's listening.

"What kind of spell?" I demand, knowing I'm not going to like the answer, by her attitude.

"Well, it's, hmmm, I've been wronged, and I want someone punished," answers the lady with a quiver in her voice.

"You want a revenge spell. Sorry, I don't help people with them."

"You mean you can't," sniffs the old lady with disdain in her voice.

"I mean exactly what I said. I DON'T HELP PEOPLE WITH REVENGE SPELLS," I state loudly and clearly, in case the nasty old cow can't understand me.

"Well, how rude," gasps the woman, as her jaw drops in shock.

"I'll be sure to pass on a message to Eve you were in, if you give me your name."

"Eve? Oh no, that's okay, no need to. I'll…I'll speak to her myself, at some point when I have time," she replies, quickly scampering away, as she looks around as if expecting Eve to suddenly pop up out of nowhere.

"Hello, can I help you?" I inquire of the nearest gaping-mouthed customer.

"What? Ah yes, I would just like to get this crystal please," answers a surprised-looking customer. "You're very brave, standing up to Ms. Hayes. She scares me and most people actually."

Smiling gently at the petite woman in front of me, I take her crystal from her and wrap it up in tissue paper.

"That's €5, then please. Most people don't scare me," I admit, handing back the crystal and taking the money.

"Oh, you are lucky. Most people scare me. I'm Beatrix, Beatrix Sullivan. Ms. Hayes is my neighbor sadly." Beatrix sighs in resignation.

"Nice to meet you, Beatrix. I'm Candi Reynolds."

"Reynolds? Oh, I presumed you would have your grandmother's surname. Well, I had better go. Nice to meet you, Candi." With a little wave, Beatrix leaves.

A man approaches me next, with a swagger in his step.

"Hi, Candi was it?" he asks leering at me, as if I'm an item to be procured. "How about I pick you up at seven p.m. for dinner and drinks, maybe dancing if you're lucky," he states as if it is a foregone conclusion.

"No, thank you. Now what can I help you with?"

"What? What do you mean no? No one says no to me. Do you know who I am?"

"No. Why, is it important?"

"My name is George Seabast the Fourth," he pompously replies, taking hold of his jacket lapels and standing straighter with his head slightly to the side, as if to enhance his magnificence.

"Oh, okay. Well, my answer is still no. Now are you buying or leaving?"

I feel totally perplexed at his weird stance. Seriously, I am trying to be polite. But what is with these people? Or is it me? Am I so different from everyone else?

"What? Did you say no to me? Well, I never!" a very shocked George Seabast the Fourth explodes before flouncing out of the shop.

Shaking my head in exasperation at the idiotic man, I know there is no way I'm working in Grandma Eve's shop again. I just can't deal with people. Glancing down at Jasmine, I notice her huffing and snorting gently at me.

"It's not funny, so stop laughing," I scold in exasperation.

The remaining customers carry on with their shopping and have the sense not to ask me for revenge spells or anything personal.

And thankfully the rest of the morning flies by uneventfully. Looking at the time, I finish up, closing the shop for lunch. I'm meeting Grandma Eve in The Olive Tree Café. I'll also tell her I'm not working in the shop anymore. Anyway, she doesn't need me; she has enough staff already, thankfully.

****

Quickly walking around the shop, to make sure no one is left inside, I close and lock the front door then put away my till, set the alarm, and leave. Giving Jasmine's head a quick scratch, we cross the road heading toward The Olive Tree Café. Noticing The Witch's Brew bar, I stifle a groan. I could really do with a drink right about now.

Entering the café, I spot Grandma Eve. Leaving Jasmine, I head inside, order lunch, and a bowl of water and head back outside.

"Hey, Grandma. Look, I am ever so sorry, but I can't work at the shop anymore. Seriously, I think some of your customers are stark raving mad," I state with obvious frustration. With a laugh, Eve pats my hand.

"Yes, I have heard of what happened with Evelyn Hayes and George Seabast the Fourth. Though apparently, you handled yourself with finesse. But you never did enjoy working in the shop. What will you do instead? I can ask about to find you a job if you like?"

"I have a job already. I'm a freelance photographer."

"Well yes, but it's not a full-time job. How will you survive financially?" Eve asks, with worry lacing her voice.

"Grandma, my photos sell, and they bring in the money. There's no need to worry about me," I answer with a smile. "Anyway, I forgot to tell you my news; I'm buying the old Winters' house." The sudden sound of dishes crashing interrupts our conversation. Quickly standing, I help the waitress collect ruined food and coffee.

"I'm so sorry," gasps the shaking waitress.

"That's okay."

"I'll be right back with your lunches, I'm sorry."

Watching the waitress scamper back inside, I turn and give Eve an exasperated look.

"So much for keeping buying the house a secret," I state with exasperation.

"It'll be old news anyway in another hour. It must still be making the rounds of the gossipmongers in town," laughs Eve with satisfaction. "I'm glad you decided to buy it, you suit it, and the house needs love. Anyway, it was probably seeing that dog of yours, which made her stumble and drop the tray!"

"I'm just surprised it hasn't been snapped up before now. It's such a gorgeous house." I ignore her final comment as there's no point in arguing.

The waitress returns bringing our coffee and food. Taking the plate of rare steak, I chop it up giving it to Jasmine, to the shock of the waitress.

"Thank you that's lovely," I say with a polite smile.

"If you need anything else, just let me know. Your dog is beautiful," replies the waitress with a wistful smile.

A pleasant change. Giving Jasmine a smile, I'm delighted at least someone in this town is happy to see her.

"Thank you, her name is Jasmine, and I'm Candi. What's your name?"

"Sally Jenson. Hi, Candi, I met you before when you first lived here. We were in class together."

"Wow, you have a good memory. Sorry I don't remember." Embarrassment flushes my cheeks.

"I only remember you because you were living with your grandma, and because of what happened to your parents. *The Protectors* did the same to my cousins," Sally answers, not realizing the distress she leaves my grandmother and me in, as she walks back inside the café.

"*The Protectors*, they are a group? You knew didn't you? Oh my God, you've known all this time they killed my parents! How could you not tell me?" I angrily demand. Feeling like I'm about to cry, I stand up and fling a quick, "I gotta go," at my grandma, leaving with Jasmine on my heels.

****

Heading back toward the shop and my parked car, I retrieve my keys so I can jump in before I burst into tears. Once in the safety of my car, I drive to the old Winters' house, soon to be my home, parking around the back. Exiting, I head into the woods to look around, so I can cry without anyone seeing me.

Chapter 3

With Jasmine at my side, I haven't even scrambled halfway through the woods, before I realize I can't see, due to the tears streaming down my face. With a sob I collapse in-between broken branches and bracken, finally succumbing to my distress, I cry my heart out.

The pain of my loss swiftly rushes to the surface. Surrounding me, as if it'd just happened. I curl my fingers through Jasmine's soft fur as she half sits on me, giving me comfort.

"When will their loss ever be less painful." I sniffle as I hunt for a tissue to blow my runny nose.

Her only response, a soft whine before placing her head on my shoulder.

"I'll figure out somehow, how to help you as well. You've been my best friend since the first day we met, when we both joined the army. I blame myself for you being stuck in this form. If I hadn't begged you to transform before finding out all the answers, you wouldn't be stuck. And the fact no one senses you're a shifter terrifies me the most, because I wonder if I've lost you." I promise, as tears stream down my face, while my heart feels like it's breaking all over again.

"Even if it means asking my grandma, though to be honest, a shifter would be more helpful," I add, hugging her. With a sad woof, she stands shaking herself.

"We will find an answer, even if it means going to

the other side of town, though after the moon cycle calms the werewolves down of course," I hastily add.

With a grunt of agreement, she looks at me. With a final sigh, I scramble to my feet and walk farther into the woods to explore the land I'm buying. Breathing deeply, I feel peace enter my body the farther we go.

Eventually I arrive at the ruins and come to a stop. Glancing down at Jasmine, I catch her staring intently at the ruins. Stealthily we move forward with me in the lead.

Walking around, I notice the building from the outside seems sound enough. Watching where I step, I enter the old house. I spot uprooted floors and some fallen bricks. The inside of the house looks like it was ripped apart rather than abandoned.

As I step into what would have been the kitchen, it becomes obvious the house has been gutted. A sense of sadness and expectation lingers in the building. As if the house is holding its breath, waiting to see what I'll do next.

Jasmine moves toward the stairs and climbs them with purpose. Following her, I ascend the stairs to the first landing and stare in shock at the destruction. Someone has smashed through some of the walls and ripped apart what little furniture left in the house.

"What on earth happened here?" In horror, I stare at the destruction before me.

Deciding I've seen enough, I descend the stairs and leave the house. Finding a spot in the sun, I plop down and wait for Jasmine to come out. I must have dozed off as I suddenly realize she's sitting beside me, her tongue lolling out the side of her mouth, in a big doggy grin.

"Hey, you like it here, don't you?" I haven't seen

her look so relaxed in a long time. "If you want, when we get you back to yourself, you can have the house!" I get a happy tail wag and a gentle bump of her head against mine in answer. With a laugh, I clamber to my feet.

"Come on. Let's get back. I need to take some photos."

Retracing our steps, we arrive back at the old Winters' house and my car, with only a few scratches to show for our adventure. Climbing in, I put my car in gear and head back to my gran's house. I park and enter the house to collect my camera. Jasmine plops herself down on her bed, and with a grunt of contentment falls asleep.

I enter the woods at the back of the house. I eventually become aware of the stillness and absolute quiet. Not a rustle or chirp of a bird disturbs the silence.

While I'm taking photos, a feeling of uneasiness washes through me, and that's when I spy the shoe. Moving at a stealthier pace, I advance taking continuous photos. An ankle appears followed by the cuff of a jeans-clad leg, and I know deep in my heart I am about to find the body of another victim of *The Protectors*.

Confirmation comes when I see hands folded in front of the body, as if attempting to hold in the intestines, which are displayed around a grinning corpse.

Taking as many photos as possible, I retrace my steps, exiting the woods as quickly and quietly as possible. I don't want to bump into the killer if he is still around. Once out, I phone the police. The officer answering the call informs me to stay put. I quickly hurry home and make a copy of the photos on my computer, transferring them to a USB, which I hide in my desk's hidden drawer. I hurry back to the edge of the woods with Jasmine at my side.

****

An hour and a half later, a detective finally turns up, and I am furious. As he exits his car, my internal magick tells me he's a werewolf. Supernaturals meeting for the first time can immediately sense each other's species. After that, we can sense the magick in each other, though most of us dampen down our powers, which make it harder to know exactly what species someone may be, making it feel like a low-level vibration, humming silently along a wire.

"Sorry about the delay. So you found a body then?" he asks, as if he was talking about the blooming weather.

"Yes, yes, I did. You can come see it, if you're not too busy."

"Excuse me?"

I notice the detective standing straighter, taking a closer look at what I presume by his expression is an "impertinent witch" standing in front of him. His eyebrows shoot up into his hairline when he notices a dog sitting calmly beside me.

"I said if you're not too busy, since apparently it takes an hour and half to get from one side of town to another. Or is murder on this side of town less important than elsewhere?" I demand, practically spitting fire.

With that comment left hanging in the air, I storm off into the woods. I sense the detective following, as he walks too quietly for me to hear him. The further I walk into the woods, the stealthier I become. If the murderer is still here, I would rather he didn't surprise me due to my temper.

I'm positive the detective can scent the body. Being a werewolf, he would have to be a complete failure not to, with their heightened sense of smell. When we finally arrive at the scene, I move out of the way so the detective can see the body.

Scavengers had started to eat in the period of time it'd taken him to get here, which isn't surprising, as the victim was human. If it had been a supernatural, the animals would have stayed away for another couple of hours, if not longer.

With a quiet curse, which I have a feeling he thought I shouldn't be able to hear, he steps closer to the corpse.

Looking at the destroyed crime scene, I feel sorry for the dead man. The probability of the murderer being caught is slim to none. Glancing at the detective, I'm glad to hand over my digital card with the photos of the crime scene, before the animals disturbed it. The detective looks like he takes his job seriously and will do everything he can to solve the murder.

"I took photos of the crime scene when I arrived," I inform him, handing him my card.

"What?" Shock flickers across his face.

"I'm a photographer, and was out taking photos when I found your John Doe there. Hence I took photos of the scene as I found it." Seeing his expression I get annoyed. "Mind you, if you had bothered coming quicker, this poor man would not be in such..."

With a growl, I shove my card at him and turn and walk off back the way we'd come. I don't get far before a large hand drops on my shoulder trying to drag me to a halt. Quickly grasping his wrist, I flip the detective. With a gasp of surprise, he lands flat on his back with a *thunk* and a string of curses.

"I would advise you to never grab me again Detective...?" I practically growl.

"Kheda McKnight."

I notice the shock on the detective's face and guess he wasn't flipped often due to his impressive six foot two inches, broad powerful shoulders, muscular chest, narrow hips, and long muscular legs. He would make most male werewolves nervous with their superior strength, let alone other species or even humans.

"Sorry, I shouldn't have grabbed you. Why is the shapeshifter staying in animal form?" Kheda inquires with curiosity lacing his voice.

With a start, I turn to look at Jasmine. With hope blossoming in my heart, I move toward the detective as he gingerly rises to his feet.

"Jasmine's stuck in her dog form, and I don't know how to change her back." I pace in agitation before coming to a stop in front of him. "She's been like this for just over a year. I don't know what to do to bring her back."

A whine comes from Jasmine. She's flopped onto the ground, head on her paws and a sorrowful expression in her blue eyes.

"Oh, sweetie, we will find out how to get you back again." Kneeling down beside her, I scratch her behind the ears in the spot she likes best.

"What happened for...Jasmine, was it? To make her stay so long in her animal form? Look, find out what trauma caused her to enter her dog form for protection. As she's still in it, a part of her mustn't feel safe yet."

He stares thoughtfully at Jasmine. "I need to get the coroner down here to collect John Doe. I also need to check out these photos and take your statement. Can you come down to the station now please? I'll also need your contact details."

"Sure, I'll meet you there."

"If you want I can give you a lift, and I appreciate you meeting me here, otherwise the body would have sat a lot longer. Normally a witch detective would come out to the scene, but no one else was available, which is why the long wait for me to arrive."

At my confused expression, Kheda carries on. "Other supernatural species are not allowed in the witches' woods unless escorted by a witch. So normally a witch detective would investigate to make things easier."

"Okay…let's go," I reply feeling more puzzled than anything, as we continue through the trees back the way we'd come.

Chapter 4

An hour later, we finally leave the police station. By this time I'm starving and decide to grab a burger from Hal's diner. Situated across the river on the East side, it's known for serving the best burgers in Paradise Falls. As it's just around the corner from where I'd seen the vampire last night, I know it probably isn't the best idea I've had in a while, but hunger wins out. Was it really only last night? Damn, a lot has happened in the last, no…not even twenty-four hours!

"Come on, girl, I'm starving," I say heading toward the University on West Avenue.

Crossing over West Bridge, we bypass the tattoo parlor named Tattoo Parlor, no imagination from the owners, which makes the fact they do the best tattoos I have seen even more surprising.

I dash past the car park. I hate walking past car parks when it's dark. They give me a serious case of the heebie-jeebies. Just because I can take care of myself, does not mean I like to take careless risks.

Continuing along Brokers Walk, we turn left at the Pawn Shop toward Sterling nightclub, where I hear the first sounds of life since crossing East Bridge. The sounds of dance music flitting through the night, barely penetrates the quiet before fading, startling me.

Glancing down at Jasmine, I notice she seems just as surprised, cautiously I look around. Complete silence. No breeze, nobody jogging or walking. Nothing. It's like I've entered a silent cocoon, where the nightclub's music can barely be heard.

It feels wrong and confusing. I hadn't sensed anything, let alone noticed how unnatural it was. But now that I have, I want to be off the streets, fast. Without saying a word, I hurry toward the club and cross to Hal's Diner.

Entering Hal's, it's like someone's pierced the sound bubble, letting it all in, a sudden excruciatingly painful, sonic boom of full blown volume. The rush of noise wrenches a gasp of pain from my mouth, almost bringing me to my knees.

Sheer determination and willpower alone keep me from collapsing. My poor ears are ringing and the sudden volume brings on the beginnings of a migraine.

Jasmine is having similar problems, judging from her whine of pain. With her sensitive ears, this isn't too surprising. Grimly we make it to the nearest empty table, situated on the far side of the diner by a window. With a relieved moan, I finally manage to collapse into the booth.

"What can I get you?" asks the waitress who appears five minutes later.

Thankfully, I've gotten my breath back, so I order a M50 burger, taco chips, and a large diet soda for myself and a bowl of water and a rare steak for Jasmine. The waitress, whose nametag reads Savannah, gives her a friendly ear scratch before leaving with our order.

Glancing out the window, I see people on the streets looking confused and a little frightened. One pedestrian, on seeing Hal's makes a dash for the door.

Upon entering, he lets out a scream and promptly passes out. Customers who are closest to the man lift him, bringing him to the nearest booth, which is still occupied by a woman I presumed was sleeping, but in fact is probably also unconscious. Savannah returns to my table carrying a tray of delicious smelling food.

"What is going on out there?" I ask as I stare at the man in the booth in confusion. "Why did he pass out?" I cut up the steak and put it on the table in front of Jasmine.

"I'm not sure; it's been like this for the last couple of hours." Glancing at the man passed out in the booth, Savannah continues. "Those of weaker magick are having a rougher time. If you need anything else, let me know." She smiles before walking off.

I pick up my burger and with a groan of satisfaction bite into it; mushrooms, tomatoes, beef, bacon, Gouda cheese, lettuce, and special sauce all in a sesame bun; pure heaven. With the flavors bursting in my mouth, I feel good for the first time since leaving the police station.

****

Halfway through my meal, the door to Hal's opens again. The man entering looks vaguely familiar. With a grimace of distaste, he scans the room and heads in my general direction. Not surprising since the only empty booths are near me. I carry on eating until a shadow falls over the table. Assuming it's the waitress, I look up and am surprised to see the man standing beside me.

"Can I help you?" I ask puzzled.

"You can move over so I can sit down," he answers with a voice like rich velvet.

"Why?" Blimey, I could listen to his voice forever.

36

But I don't recognize it, so where have I seen him before? If I had talked to him, I would definitely remember, so why does he want to sit with me?

"We need to talk you and I." Then looking toward Jasmine he adds, "And you as well, shifter. Now may I sit?"

Scooting over, I glance at Jasmine, who stops eating long enough to give the man a look of puzzlement, her head tilted sideways as steak juice dribbles from her muzzle. With a quick lick of her chops, she carries on eating, though she continues to watch with interest.

For six months, no one had realized she is a shifter. Now twice in one day it has been noticed in a very matter-of-fact way. So why hasn't anyone else noticed?

"Who are you?" I demand as Mr. Rich Velvet Voice sits down so close to me I move over again just to have some personal space between us.

"I am the one who caught you two spying on a very private conversation last night. Why would you spy on me?" he inquires, lowering his voice.

With a start, I realize as he's talking I've been leaning into him, and am now leaning so close to him I could kiss his jaw line, if I just stretch a little bit. I feel my body stir to life at his close proximity.

My breasts feel heavy and my nipples tighten in anticipation, but it's the desire shooting to the core of my femininity and pooling in liquid heat that makes me twitch in shock. I've never had such an instant reaction to a man before, even if he is gorgeous with a voice like rich dark chocolate.

With this realization I bolt away from him and in the process smack my head against the window

Concentrate, I mentally chastise myself. *God, could you imagine having phone sex with him?* Giving another involuntary moan at my last thought, I catch him giving me a knowing look, and I pull myself together. Taking a quick gulp of my soda just to give myself a second more, I turn back to him.

"Who are you?" I ask this time. No point in demanding, as it obviously doesn't get me anywhere.

"I am Victor Harlow and owner of Vlad's Bar. Why were you spying on me and for whom?" He demands while tracing a gentle circle on the velvet skin of my wrist.

Pulling my wrist out of his grasp, as his fingers are doing funny things to my stomach, I turn to look him full in the face. My God, he is gorgeous.

Short, jet black thick hair, I want to run my fingers through. Ebony black eyebrows arched over silvery green eyes, which are unfairly surrounded by long thick black eyelashes. Seriously, if a girl had those she would never need to buy mascara!

A long straight nose and full sensuous lips, which look so…so kissable, high cheekbones and a strong square jaw. He has a beautiful neck and an image of fangs sinking into it flashes before my eyes making me gulp, I drag my eyes lower to his broad shoulders and a large ever so muscled body in a lean tall package. Wow, he is scrumptious.

Biting my lip, I suppress a moan at the thought of exploring every inch of his delectable body and kissing his sensual mouth. I suddenly realize he'd been saying something, but I have no idea what.

"Sorry, what did you ask?" *Fuck, I'm drooling over a vampire,* I realize as I wipe the saliva from my mouth with my napkin.

"Why, were you spying on me, and for whom do you work?" Victor patiently repeats his question.

I notice he looks intrigued, as if he's tempted by my obvious attraction to him, though I am trying, granted unsuccessfully, to hide it. I have the distinct feeling he doesn't normally have patience for other supernaturals. The thought gives me a slightly warm fuzzy feeling, which I try to crush.

"We weren't spying on you. I was going for a run with her," I explain, indicating Jasmine, who rolls her eyes at me. "I was planning to take photos which I didn't," I hastily add. "I'm a photographer and…look I didn't even know vampires existed, so when I saw you snarling, I got the hell out of there. We weren't spying, we were only trying to go for a run, and do some work!" I feel rather like a naughty schoolgirl caught doing something wrong.

"Look, what is going on out there?" I suddenly ask Victor.

"I don't know. I thought it had something to do with you two," admits Victor grudgingly.

"Why did you think it has something to do with us?" A frown furrows my forehead, and I can feel my nose scrunching up, probably giving me the look of a confused rabbit, as I try to figure out why he would think we were involved.

"I thought it had something to do with the pair of you because all this started happening when you two turned up."

"Oh, umm, well, huh, I don't know what to say," I finally get out feeling very perplexed.

With a sad whine, Jasmine rests her head on the

table beside her plate. With a quick look at her plate, her tongue swipes clean any remaining meat juices. With a glance at Victor, she gives a contented sigh.

Giving her an exasperated look, I turn back to Victor and feel like sighing myself. Man, he is gorgeous. What was I going to say again?

"You didn't seem to be very affected when you came in. How come?" I ask remembering Victor had only grimaced slightly, toward the man in the booth, who had passed out on the floor.

"I'm a vampire. I'm stronger than most," Victor replies as if it's obvious. "How about you two?"

"We were, well…we were better than the man who came in before you obviously and some others as well." Listening to the curiosity in his voice, I gather he's remembering we were eating when he entered.

I look at the other customers and take in their confusion, and wonder what caused it, and why it affected everyone differently?

"Mind you, going by what Savannah was saying, it's affecting the weaker supernaturals the most," I helpfully add.

"Look we have to go." I quickly scribble down my phone number and give it to Victor. "Call me if you find out what's going on." I get up to leave.

Feeling a tingle in my fingers from where they brushed Victor's, I think nothing of it. Going by his reaction, you would think I had slapped him.

"Sorry, I generate a lot of static," I explain as he quickly gets up to let me pass.

"I'll call you if I hear anything, or if things get worse," Victor says as he carefully folds the napkin and places it in his pocket.

"One more thing." Victor stops me from going any farther, by the simple act of placing a cool hand on my arm. "What is your name?"

"Candi, I'm Candi Reynolds," I reply extracting my arm and putting the money for our food on the table. I leave with Jasmine at my heels. The sound is slowly coming back outside which to be honest is a relief. Quickly I hurry back to my grandma's. I can't wait to go to sleep, as I'm exhausted.

It has been a long day with viewing the Old Winters' House, working at the shop, finding a dead body, the weird soundproof streets, and finally the vampire, who turns me into a puddle of lust just at the thought of him!

Chapter 5

Upon waking up, I'm surprised to find myself still in yesterday's clothes. I must have fallen asleep in the process of taking off my shoes. Looking down, I change it to shoe, as I still have one on, though at least my laces are undone.

Dragging myself up from my bed, I half land on the floor. Since I'm down there, I decide to remove my other shoe. Clambering to my feet, I scramble into the bathroom for my morning routine. Once washed and dressed, I collect my keys and shoes, and head downstairs. Coming to an abrupt halt, I stare in awe.

Jasmine is halfway between human and animal form. Letting out an involuntary gasp, I startle her and disrupt the transformation. Giving an exhausted whine, she returns to her dog shape. Bending down to scratch her behind her ears, I give her a quick hug.

"You almost changed back. I'm so sorry...I was shocked and disturbed by your change...I'm so sorry," I stammer, my words running into one another.

With a huff and a gentle nudge, she heads toward her empty bowl and gives me another look as if to say, "Where's my food?"

Quickly removing yesterday's bowls, I fill two clean ones with fresh water and food. Leaving her to eat, I enter the kitchen to make my breakfast. Selecting a bowl, I add cereal and milk, make coffee, and sit down to enjoy. After finishing, I grab a banana and munch while finishing my drink.

I phone the surveyor to find out when he's coming, but I'm left frustrated, as I can't get hold of him. All I want is to buy the house and move into it. I decide to get my run in, as I need it badly.

Decision made, I return upstairs to change and collect my camera. Slipping the camera into my left pocket, I call Jasmine, lock the front door, and put my keys in my right pocket. Slowly we start jogging toward the woods behind the house. Once in the woods we start to run.

I love running, the feel of the wind in my face, dodging low-hanging branches, the snap of twigs and the pounding of my feet, my heart rate increasing and all worries slipping away, as if cobwebs swept aside by a gentle hand.

Liberating, calming, and peaceful. I carry on running, until I finally arrive on the other side of the woods. The view from the top of the cliffs is magnificent. The sea like a heartbeat I can visibly see, pulsing against the bottom of the cliffs before retreating.

Carefully descending to a ledge about halfway down the cliff, we sit just relaxing, as our breathing becomes even. Taking my camera, I snap a couple of photos of the general view and some more of the waves crashing against the jagged rocks below. Spotting a gray heron flying overhead, I capture some photos of him.

For such a lanky bird, they are extremely elegant.

With a contented smile, I head back up to the edge of the trees. Putting my camera away, I take a final look at the glorious scenery, before retreating back into the woods, this time slower, taking photos of the surrounding greenery, of squirrels running up the trees and eating nuts, and birds washing themselves in a puddle left over from the rain. The sunlight changing direction in the trees makes me realize how long we've been out. I suddenly notice I'm hungry, so we head back to the house.

****

On arriving back, I knock my trainers against the side of the wall to rid them of clinging mud. Unlocking the door, I remove them, before climbing upstairs to put them away. Taking my camera from my jacket, I place it carefully on my desk, and then I put away my jacket.

Selecting fresh clothes, I enter the bathroom for a quick shower to freshen up. Dumping my dirty clothes into the laundry basket, I switch on the shower and climb in. With a happy groan, I let the hot spray beat down on me, my muscles relaxing under the steady pressure washing off the sweat from my run. Finally, I dry myself before cleaning the shower and adding my towel to the laundry.

Crossing to my dressing table, I apply moisturizer and brush my hair, then picking up my mobile, I shove it into my jeans pocket, collect my laundry basket, and head downstairs to put in a load of washing. I feed Jasmine, who's gently snoring, and make a quick sandwich and a glass of water for myself. Entering the sitting room, I eat in front of the TV while channel flicking.

Finding a murder mystery, I devour my ham salad sandwich. It's only after cleaning my dishes I think to check my phone for any news from the surveyor. To my surprise, I have four missed calls from Detective Kheda McKnight, one from the surveyor, and one from an unknown number.

I listen first to the surveyor's message and am delighted. It's good news. Everything's fine, thankfully the only work needed is what I'd noticed myself. I ring my solicitor to arrange for signing the property deeds on Friday at two p.m. and the closing the following week.

Feeling frustrated as Friday is three days away, and I'm expected to wait another week! I demand to know why we can't do the closing and signing on Friday. *Hello, cash buyer*, why the delay? He informs me he'll contact the seller's solicitors and get back to me. Apparently they hadn't realized I was paying in cash.

Next, I listen to Detective Kheda's messages. With each message, he's obviously getting more and more pissed off at not being able to contact me. Quickly, I phone him back.

"I've been trying to get in touch with you all morning. Where have you been?" Kheda testily demands.

"Hello to you too, Detective. Sorry for taking so long to get back to you, but I've only just checked my messages. Now how can I help you?" I politely ask.

"I need your help; I need to go back to the murder scene and…"

"Don't tell me, you a werewolf, can't find the crime scene?" I jokingly interrupt him.

"With the crime scene on witches' land, I can't enter unless escorted by a witch, which as I explained to you yesterday, is why normally a witch detective would be solving the murder, and why it took me so long to get there. I had to be sure that I was the only detective available and that a witch was staying to meet me," Kheda replies with obvious frustration.

"What? That's ridiculous, you're trying to solve a murder, not hunt witches for dinner! Look, meet me at the edge of the woods where we met yesterday." How stupid! Now I understand why it had taken so long for him to arrive yesterday. I feel a little guilty for being so snarky. Not much, but a little.

"How soon can you be there?" Kheda asks with relief in his voice.

"Two minutes."

"Make it ten, and thank you."

"No problem, Detective, see you then.

My final message turns out to be from Victor Harlow, vampire most scrumptious. Hearing his rich as velvet voice vibrating down the phone line, I feel my stomach muscles tighten and my toes curl.

"Hello, Candi, this is Victor Harlow. I need you to meet me today at one p.m. on the East Bridge please. Until then, have a nice afternoon."

A shiver of desire ripples through my body as his voice washes over me like a waterfall of decadence, just begging me to come out and play. *Until then*, I parrot. *I haven't even agreed to meet him. Well, at least he said please,* I think as I save his number in my phone. I quickly switch off the TV and hurry upstairs to put back on my trainers and jacket and collect my camera and keys.

****

Switching my SD card over, I secure my card in the secret drawer in my desk. Work photos are just too damned important to misplace. Running downstairs, I explain to Jasmine what's going on as I lock up behind us. I drive the short distance as quickly as possible so I won't keep Detective McKnight waiting.

Two minutes later, we sit waiting for the detective to turn up. With her nose pressed up against the window, Jasmine leaves a wet smudge on the glass, as her breath fogs the windowpane.

"You really like him, huh?" I ask.

With a sigh, she turns around and looks at me, and for the first time in a long time, I see her human side just under her fur. Today's the closest I've seen her return to her human form. I feel a jolt of excitement ripple through me, the thought of having my friend back completely making me happy.

"I miss you," I suddenly blurt out.

Giving me a sad look, she puts her head on my shoulder and sneezes on me.

"Ewww, that's gross." I laugh, thankful no snot landed on me. "Ah, this could be him." I nod toward a car coming toward us. As he parks, we clamber out of the car and cross over to join him.

"Thank you so much for coming, ladies," Kheda says, gratitude lacing his voice.

"No problem, Detective. Shall we head in?"

Walking in, stillness descends upon us, and the scent of the woods becomes almost alive. The moss on the trees, mud, and disintegrating underbrush, rainwater dripping through leaves, and a brook babbling on its merry journey nearby, all seem to tell a story of life and death. The three of us carry on toward our destination, while something scuttles past nearby.

The farther we head toward the crime scene, the closer we move toward each other. I'm plastered to

Jasmine's side, and she in turn is plastered to Detective Kheda's, and none of us mind the contact.

"So what are we doing here?" I whisper.

"I need to see the area without the body and to see if I can trace where the killer came from and went. It's routine follow-up," Kheda whispers back.

"Okay, but I gotta say this is seriously creepy."

"Woof," Jasmine barks in agreement.

****

Reaching the crime scene quiet surrounds us. As if every living thing is holding its breath, not even the birds ruffle their feathers. At first, it looks as if a tornado has descended upon the area. Boot prints and broken branches are scattered about the place. None of this destruction was present when I'd taken the photos and going by the gasp of anger from the detective it must have occurred after he had left as well.

"Bloody hell, what the, ahhhh, I'm going to kill someone," Kheda growls, grinding his teeth, in obvious frustration.

"I might be able to try something. Take my camera and keep taking photos if anything happens," I instruct him as I set my camera up for him to use before passing it to him. I kneel in the mud.

"Try what? What are you doing? Look, Candi, get up, you're messing up an already destroyed crime scene," Kheda snarls in annoyance.

"Step back, keep quiet, and do not under any circumstances touch me. Jasmine, please make sure he stays back."

Immediately she starts to round Detective Kheda back a safe distance, growling in warning when he tries to object. She'll make sure I'm not disturbed while I'm practicing magick.

****

Sitting cross-legged on the ground with my hands resting palms upward on my knees, I clear all thoughts from my head and take a deep breath. Feeling it expand my lungs, I let it out and take an even deeper breath, focusing on what has taken place here. Releasing the breath, I think of how I'd found the dead man. Dragging in another breath, I hold it and demand to see what happened.

"Hecate, Goddess of darkness and the crossroads, please hear my cry. Help us see the past just gone. Crone, mother and child, I beseech you. Help us see so we may deliver justice to the wronged, so they may find peace in the afterlife," I call, allowing my voice to fill with power.

"This isn't going to work," Kheda mutters quietly, to which he gets a growl for his trouble.

The wind picks up and starts swirling in front of me, as if a mini tornado has decided to pop in. I hear Kheda give a startled gasp and sense he's just about to move forward as if to grab me out of harm's way. Jasmine blocks his path again, this time baring her teeth at him in a very clear threat.

A shadow-like mist of a woman with two huge black dogs appears in the middle of the mini tornado. I notice Kheda stumble back as he stares in shock at the sight before him. As the tornado calms, the clearer the woman and dogs become until they are all that is left.

"Daughter of mine, you may rise and come forward," Hecate instructs with power in every word, but a gentle smile playing across her mouth.

Gracefully rising to my feet, I move forwards.

Cupping my hands together, my right palm in my left hand, I place my hands over my heart and bow my head in respect to my Goddess.

"Thank you, Goddess Hecate, for answering my plea." When dealing with Goddesses, it is best to always keep it simple and to the point.

"*My child, as always you ask for others not yourself, so I shall grant you your request, but only if you join the quest to find the murderers of my sons and daughters. Do you accept?*"

"I accept."

"*And you daughter and son of mine, do you accept this quest for justice, a quest much bigger than you can ever imagine, do you accept?*"

"Yes," Kheda answers, determination lacing his words.

Jasmine shimmers, her hind legs elongating and her body stretching, until she transforms back into her human self. With a gasp, she comes forwards on shaky legs, her long jet-black hair rippling down her back, a few wisps falling over her shoulders and covering her naked breasts as she bows deeply.

"I accept, Goddess," she answers, her voice hoarse from lack of use.

"*And what of you, vampire, do you accept this quest?*" Hecate asks, her voice carrying through the woods, to the East Bridge where Victor stands waiting for me to join him. In a blink, Victor stands in front of Hecate. I feel my heart stutter in shock at his abrupt appearance, and notice the others flinch in surprise.

"I also accept, my Goddess," answers Victor, giving a deep bow his cupped hands placed over his heart.

"*Good. You shall find others on your quest who serve me, but you will find more who are serving themselves. Listen to your hearts to know whom to trust, and don't trust unwisely as it's not just your lives on the line, but the souls of those gone before you and those to come. Good luck, my children. Be wise in your decisions. Now please stand back so you may see what has come before.*" Hecate and her dogs vanish.

No wind, no nothing, just gone.

"Holy shit," whispers Kheda.

"Everyone get back. Detective Kheda, my camera please," I instruct, my hand stretched out to take it from the detective's limp grip. "Jasmine, I am so glad you're back. I have missed you so much. Hey, Victor, sorry I was late but as you can see…Okay, guys, get ready, here it comes," I call out, finally getting to take a breath. I lift my camera and start snapping photos as images appear in a rush.

****

A form appears, dressed all in black and shrouded in darkness, carrying a large backpack and a man over his shoulder, before unceremoniously dumping him on the ground.

With great care, he starts to arrange the man. Gently sitting him up and leaning him against the tree, he removes his backpack. Lovingly he withdraws a bowie knife, an exceptionally long tube, and a sewing kit. The tube he unfolds, brings one end to the nearby stream and places it in the water, then returns to the man.

He sits and begins talking. He picks up his knife and makes an incision in the man's skin. Quickly he places the tube in the area he's cut, and blood flows out of the body, through the tube and into the stream, where it's washed away. The man twitches, letting out a pitiful cry, so faint only the killer in front of him can hear it, and us, silent witnesses helplessly watching, unable to do anything, as we realize the man is not in fact dead, but dying before our horrified eyes.

As the man's life slips away, the murderer starts threading his needle, and I realize exactly what he is about to do, just before he reaches for the man's face.

He forces his gloved fingers into the man's mouth, pulling one side into a smile and stitching the inside to keep it in position, cutting the excess thread with the tip of his knife before repeating the process.

After finishing, he puts the needle and thread back into his backpack. A sigh escapes the now dead man's lips, as the last of his blood seeps out of his body and down the tube.

The murderer removes the tube, rolling it up into a neat circle and returns it to his backpack. Finally picking up his knife, he cuts through the man's body, as easily as cutting through hot butter.

He slips his hands into the man's torso and with brutal force, rips open his chest. I can hear the breaking of bones so piercingly it's as if a gun has gone off. Picking up his knife, he carefully removes the dead man's heart and once again places his knife on the ground.

Holding the heart in both hands, he lifts it as if in an offering before eating it and licking his gloved hands clean. He picks up his knife, slits open the dead man's stomach, licking his knife clean before putting it in his backpack, and zips it up.

As the intestines spill from the body, he

meticulously arranges them about the cadaver, finally crossing the dead man's arms in front of him, as if he's trying to hold them in. Picking up his backpack and slinging it over his shoulders, he calmly walks away, leaving behind the smiling corpse.

Two minutes later, we watch as I come on the scene. I had only just missed him! Time speeds up until all crime scene investigators have finished, everything's removed and everyone's gone home.

That is when he comes back, furious the body is gone, screaming in outrage and ripping through the area, destroying everything he can reach, only snapping out of his tantrum when a twig pierces his glove. With a final snarl, he grips the twig and storms off, back the way he came. Leaving behind one tiny drop of blood!

"We have got to find the blood," Kheda says as he carefully moves forwards, crouching down and crawling to where we'd seen the blood drop.

"They're alive," I whisper. "When he kills them, I mean."

"I know, honey, I'm so sorry." Knowing how my parents died, Jasmine gives me a much needed hug.

Clever man Victor is, he realizes quickly I'm not thinking of the murder I just witnessed. "Who do you know who was murdered in this way?"

"My parents," I reply.

Giving myself a shake, I look at Kheda crawling on the ground trying to find the drop of blood from the killer.

"Detective, stand up. You won't find the blood that way," I inform him thinking of the wind and other activity that's disturbed the ground since the murderer left.

"I've got to try. It's our only clue," Kheda replies in obvious frustration.

Giving Detective Kheda an exasperated look but understanding his desperation perfectly, I fish a clean tissue from my jacket. Dragging in a breath, I let it out and suck in another, filling my mind with the killer, remembering and focusing on the single drop of blood.

With the drop shining like a beacon in my mind's eye, I exhale and a beacon of light exhales on my breath, shining on a tiny spot five feet to my left. Carefully I walk toward it, and using the tissue, I pick up the leaf with the blood drop on it.

"Your DNA sample, Detective."

"Huh, thanks. Look, please, will you all call me Kheda? I had better get this tested. Thank you again." Kheda carefully puts the blood sample into a little plastic zipper bag he removes from an inside pocket of his jacket.

"Kheda, be careful. Don't forget what Hecate said about who you can trust, this is the only sample we have," Jasmine reminds him.

"I will. Do you want to borrow my jacket? I should have asked you earlier, I do apologize," Kheda answers giving her an admiring glance.

"No, you're fine, thanks. I'll change back into my other form before we exit the woods. I think it's best if I stay that way as much as possible…for now at least." She watches Kheda retreat back the way he'd come until she can't see him anymore.

Turning toward the sexy vampire, I drink him in. Remembering he'd wanted to meet me, I quickly ask, to cover my gawking, "So, Victor, why did you want to meet?" Going by the look on his face, I think he'd forgotten as well.

"It was about the, for a lack of a better word, 'soundproof streets,' " Victor replies. "Look, what just happened there?

"I mean, that was the Goddess Hecate, and the whole murder being relived. How? I don't understand. The Gods and Goddesses, they don't come to Earth any more, haven't for centuries but..." Trailing off into silence, Victor stares off into the distance looking rather like a child who was told there is no Santa, only to find out there is not only a Santa but the Easter Bunny, too. Shaking his head Victor refocuses his attention on me.

"How did...why did...Sorry I can't focus," Victor admits, while rubbing the back of his neck as if to relieve tension.

"The Gods and Goddesses never went anywhere. Most people stopped worshipping them and stopped believing in them." Holding up a hand to stop whatever he's about to say I carry on.

"I said most people. Some of us like me, have always believed and talked to them. I am a daughter of Hecate, as were my mother and all the women of my family. What you saw was a mother coming to her children's aid. And what we saw, well, I'd requested to see what had happened, and so we were shown. These killings are done by a group called *The Protectors*. Supposedly to keep bloodlines pure, but this victim was human. I don't think anyone ever knew the victims are alive when..."

I trail off unable to voice the last part as my throat clogs up with unshed tears. In my mind's eye, I see my mother bled to death, stitched, and ripped apart instead of the unknown man.

"It's laughable them calling themselves *The Protectors* for they don't protect anyone. Why not call themselves the killers or idealists. What are they afraid of anyway?" I demand as anger rolls inside of me.

"The prophecy," replies Victor in a distracted voice, as he gently pulls me into his embrace.

Feeling content, I allow Victor to hold me until his words penetrate my brain.

"What prophecy?" I ask, feeling as if finally the answers are coming. Would I finally find out the real reason my parents were killed, why everyone knows about *The Protectors*, and yet no one does anything about them?

"I'm not sure, but my sire knew of them, though he never got to tell me what it was. However, I do know it's written down somewhere. My sire was the keeper of the book of prophecies, but I don't know what he did with it. Sorry I probably shouldn't have mentioned it at all," Victor answers with an apologetic shake of his head as he looks down at me and gently rubs his hands in circles on my back.

"It's okay, I just thought we were finally getting somewhere," I reply with a deep groan. "Where were you created?"

"I was created here in Ireland. My creator was from Transylvania, but he lived in America, Scotland, and many other countries. To be honest, if you wanted to look for the book, we would have to look everywhere.

"I don't even know when he last had the prophecies or if he gave them to someone else. I only know he was the keeper in the first place, because he was around when they were written and given into his charge," Victor replies in frustration, dragging his fingers through his hair and leaving it standing on end, making it look like he had just climbed out of bed.

"Look, guys, we gotta get back," Jasmine pipes up.

I know she's right, there are too many people who know about the murder, and we don't want to be caught here especially with a vampire! Also if anyone caught Jasmine naked, it would be difficult to explain her state of undress and sudden appearance.

If no one has realized she's a shapeshifter yet, for safety, I'd definitely rather not let them find her nude in human form. It's going to be strange enough introducing her around. There would be tons of questions with my dog disappearing suddenly and the appearance of a friend with the same name.

"Okay, guys, we should head home." I reluctantly step out of Victor's arms. "Victor, call me when you remember what you wanted to tell me, about the soundproof streets and also if you remember anything that could help us find some answers." Unwilling to lose contact with him I reach out and place my hand on his arm. "Be safe."

"Nice meeting you, Victor, and like Candi said, stay safe."

"And both of you be careful, too. We're living in these dangerous times. You can't take any chances especially with a killer on the loose. This guy is even sicker than we originally thought," adds Victor with a shake of his head. "I still can't believe they're alive when…"

I guess he remembered my parents were murdered in the exact same way.

"Don't worry, we'll be safe. At least we're together. Look after yourself and phone us if you feel anything out of the ordinary, especially if it's a feeling you can't explain." I remembered the amount of times such feelings had saved my comrades and me when we were in the army.

"I will, and if you need me, call me and I'll be there. Otherwise, I'll see you tomorrow. Oh, wait, the soundproof streets…apparently it was done by magick to cover a kidnapping. Two vampires have gone missing, though I don't know them. They were meant to have an interview at Sterling Nightclub and never showed up. It could be nothing, but to be honest it seems too much of a coincidence, to have them disappear on a night someone uses magick to soundproof the streets." Victor flits away leaving us gaping in shock after him.

"He's right, it is too much of a coincidence," I mutter as I wonder what witch would have enough power to cause such a spell, let alone kidnap two vampires. "Come on, Jasmine; let's head back to Grandma Eve's."

In silence we retreat. Glancing over at Jasmine, I can't wait to move into the old Winters' house, then she can stay in her human form whenever she wishes.

"I better change back," she says, as if following my train of thought. "I really don't want to, but…"

"I know, but for now it's safer. But the moment we move into the old Winters' house, you won't have to unless you want to. I'll start introducing you to a couple of people at a time. Mind you, I only know a couple of people." I laugh.

"What's happening tomorrow that you're meeting

Victor?" She transforms back into her dog form leaving me standing, staring in surprise. He had said he'd see me tomorrow, hadn't he?

****

Following the werewolf detective, down to the basement of the hospital where the morgue and the technician's lab are kept, the cloaked figure watches, as red-hot anger boils and licks through him. Consuming him in its intensity. He'd spilled one drop of blood...one; and he had found it! How? Lips thinning into a straight line, he forms a plan to retrieve his blood. Revenge will be sweet and a lesson will be learned. Silently he retreats up the stairs to return at a more suitable time.

****

We finally arrive back at my grandmother's and to my great disappointment, there is no message from my solicitor. My grandmother is in, and I decide to have a chat with her, update her on matters of my new home and apologize about well—to be frank—being a complete bitch about the whole *Protectors* thing.

Just because I was upset about her not telling me what she knows, doesn't mean she cares less, and after what I'd seen in the woods, I wonder how much everyone's silence is related to fear? Still, if Grandma Eve knows anything about the prophecy, she's going to tell me whether she likes it or not.

Walking into the sitting room, I'm shocked at how old she looks. It's as if she's aged ten years in less than a day.

"Oh my god, are you okay?" I demand as I rush to her side. Kneeling beside her chair, I reach toward her and grasp her hands in mine. "What's happened?

Are..."

"I'm fine, Candi. I am so glad to see you. I thought you'd gone. I thought I had driven you away like your mother," sobs Eve, distressed at the thought of history repeating itself.

"Like my mother? What do you mean?"

"I drove your mother away, because I wouldn't support her relationship with your father." Eve gulps in a large breath of air before carrying on. "I had warned your mother about *The Protectors*, but she was deeply in love with your father, and he felt the same.

"Yet a warning had already been sent, and I had pleaded with your parents to separate. They refused. I told them I wouldn't help them, hoping they would go their separate ways if they thought there was no one to help, but they left and I never saw them again.

"They wrote to me when you were born, and your mother wrote to me when your father was murdered, and that was the last time I heard from your mum. If I had been more supportive, if I..."

"They would still be dead and so would you, Grandma," I interrupt. My grandmother's grip on my hands tightens as if she can prevent me from leaving unlike my mother.

"Mum and Dad talked about you often, and I grew up with knowledge of you and a picture of you by my bedside, and one of you and Mum on the mantel piece. They loved you and told me often how much they missed you. I once asked Mum why I'd never met you, and she told me it wasn't safe. For us to go back would endanger you. She wrote you letters every week, and after she signed them she would burn them."

"Why did she never post them?"

I watch as a look of puzzlement flickers across her face, before my grandmother focuses her attention back on me. I see regret and confusion swirling in her gray eyes, as well as sadness and grief.

"Because she was terrified they wouldn't reach you and someone would find us. The letter Mum sent you after Dad was murdered was sent because we were moving. They knew where we were. Sending the letter wouldn't matter for we'd gone by then," I explain.

"Why did you think you had driven me away?" I gently ask turning my hand so I held my grandmother's back.

"Because you were gone. I haven't heard from you since you left me at lunch. That was two days ago," sighs Eve, with a note of reproof in her voice.

"Oh my God, oh no, it's just so much has happened," I exclaim. "I found a body in the woods."

A shocked gasp escapes with her questions, "What? When?"

"After I left you at lunch." My grip on her hand tightens as I prepare to tell her the final part. "He was mortal and was murdered by *The Protectors*."

"No, you can't be right." She shakes her head in shocked denial. "Humans are safe…" Trailing off, Eve stares at the ceiling as if it holds the answers she's looking for.

Changing the subject before I tell more than I should, I tell Grandma Eve my news about the house and my hope that I would be able to move in by the weekend. After discussing furniture and what work needs to be done to the house, we eventually call it a night.

Wishing my gran a good night, I quickly look in on

Jasmine and find her fast asleep. I climb the stairs and prepare for bed. I'm so exhausted I'm surprised I don't fall asleep while getting undressed. With a jaw breaking yawn, I finally crawl into bed.

Chapter 6

On waking up, I feel rejuvenated and relieved at having spoken to my grandmother. I hadn't realized how upset I felt, not at the argument itself, but by the lack of communication between us. I hadn't realized Grandma Eve blamed herself for the deaths of my parents. I feel relieved I'd put her mind at ease, and so I decide I will do something nice for her.

I quickly get myself washed and dressed and head downstairs for breakfast before heading out for my morning run. Zipping up my lightweight jacket, I call Jasmine, lock up, and pocket my keys. By silent agreement, we head toward the woods, but away from where the murder happened.

We run in silence.

The only sound the pounding of my footsteps and the lighter padding of her paws in rhythm with mine. There is the occasional snap of a twig underneath our feet and the wind rustling the leaves of the surrounding trees like a parent would fondly ruffle the hair of their children.

Squirrels run back and forth as they gather nuts for their families. The birds gather worms to feed their young. The further we run the lighter I feel.

I know we made the right choice keeping secret that Jasmine is a shapeshifter. With a crazy unknown man out there, it's safer this way; otherwise I'd fear he'd come after my grandmother. Of the three of us, she's the one most easily found on her own. Also, with us moving out in less than a week, safety is the key.

****

After a couple of miles, I become aware the gentle rustling of the wind had changed to a more distinct whipping of a storm brewing quick and fast. As one we turn around, pick up our speed, and head back the way we'd just come.

A rumble of thunder growls overhead, and the sky opens up crying out her anger and frustration. Another rumble races across the sky, followed by a flash of lightning, and the rain beats down harder and faster drenching us in seconds.

Speeding up, we run even faster, just as another rumble of furious thunder grumbles and growls, followed by a blazing fork of lightning striking farther into the woods, as the crash of thunder roars overhead.

I can feel the heat from the lightning bolt as it zings over my head, and in that split second I know where it has landed. The trees and earth are being cleansed from the act of violence that had taken place and with a gut wrenching instinct, I know something has happened to the only drop of blood from the killer. Gritting my teeth, I run faster and finally break out of the woods and race toward the house.

I quickly phone the fire brigade and then the number Detective Kheda gave me.

"What happened to the blood sample?" I demand when he answers the phone.

"How did you know something happened to it?" enquires Kheda, surprise and frustration layering his voice in equal measures.

"Mother Nature just cleansed the area, and she is very pissed off," I reply. "Now what happened?"

"Someone broke in and destroyed all the blood samples and results. I can't be sure if our sample was the one they were after or if it's just an unlucky coincidence."

"Fuck. Okay I have to go." I hang up in frustration. I can't or won't believe this happened by chance. The lab was broken into, and all blood samples destroyed on the night we find and hand in the killer's blood. I grow more determined to find the killer, and the answers about how *The Protectors* came about, and why.

****

I tell Jasmine what Detective Kheda said as we head upstairs to get showered and changed. I let her shower first and when she exits the bathroom, she is in dog form but smelling of my shampoo and shower gel.

After I have showered and dressed, we head back downstairs and I prepare some brunch for us. I stare out the window, without seeing anything. My thoughts chasing around my head, I feel unsettled and restless.

Thinking about the destroyed blood, I decide to send Victor a text message to keep him updated. I know I would be seriously pissed off if no one had informed me. Thinking of Victor sleeping, I wonder if he sleeps naked, as an image of his gloriously muscled body lying naked beneath cotton sheets flashes across my mind. I release an involuntary moan.

Needing a distraction from my wayward thoughts, I decide to cook dinner for my gran. Writing out a shopping list, I quickly put on my shoes, grab my purse and keys, and collect my phone, and leave through the front door, lock up and climb into my car before driving

65

to the locale supermarket.

I arrive at the store and realize I've forgotten the shopping list. With a grumble of annoyance, I stalk into the supermarket and snag a basket, pausing to decide what I need to buy for dinner. With a huff of annoyance, I go to the fruit and veg aisle, collect some potatoes, carrots, and leeks, and then I move on to the meat counter and pick up some pork chops.

I look at the spices and collect some garlic, chives, and paprika, all I now need is a bottle of wine and some dessert. I pick up a fresh cream cake and ice cream and a bottle of white wine before heading to the checkout to pay for my purchases. As I near the cashier, conversations cease around me. Hmmm, I wonder what they were saying?

"Please don't stop gossiping on my account." I cheekily smile.

Someone gives a gasp of shock, and from behind me comes a rich deep laugh, like melted chocolate running over rich velvet, dark and deeply sensual.

Turning around I look into Victor's face, with a sigh of appreciation.

"Hello, Victor, how are you?" I politely ask as I mentally strip him of all of his clothes and an image of him naked in bed flashes before my eyes, but this time I'm curled up beside him just as naked. *Bad girl, do try to behave,* I mentally tell myself off as I suppress a lascivious grin spreading across my face.

"I'm very well, thank you, and I must say you're looking quite delectable," replies Victor with a wicked glint in his eyes, and a knowing smirk on his face.

Damn, can he read minds, or was I being a little obvious when I was checking him out?

A snigger behind me snaps me out of my mental debate. With an embarrassed flush, I turn around toward the lady at the tills and empty my shopping basket. I pack my items as soon as they are scanned, pay for them, and wish everyone a nice day. I say goodbye to Victor and calmly leave the shop.

In reality, I want to smack the sniggering woman. I had noticed the spiteful look in her eyes when I'd turned away from Victor, but thoughts of harm happening to my gran, kept me from doing anything stupid.

Chapter 7

Something bugged me on the journey home from the supermarket. I don't mean the idiocy of being glared at or talked about either. Or the way thinking of Victor makes me want see him naked. When I finally realize what it is, I slap the heel of my hand several times on my steering wheel, calling myself "Stupid, stupid, stupid."

Looking exasperatedly at a worried-looking Jasmine, I tell her, "I can't believe I have been so stupid. How could I not have thought of this earlier? I mean it is so obvious, sometimes I really need to get my head out of my own ass."

At my last comment, she starts snuffling away.

"It's not funny," I scold gently trying not to laugh as well, as I get an image of myself walking around with my head stuck where the sun doesn't shine and trying to remove it.

"Okay, maybe it is a little funny, but we must speak to Kheda as soon as possible. Surely the doctor or technician or whoever was in the lab can describe the person who destroyed all the blood samples. Why didn't I think of this earlier?" I demand as I carry in the groceries.

****

Once inside I quickly put away the shopping and phone Kheda from my mobile. After the fifth time of his phone going to voice mail and my not leaving any message, I decide to leave it for a while before trying to ring him again. Instead, I phone Victor and tell him what I thought about the doctor being able to give a description. I let him know I will call him back when I hear from Kheda.

"Please do and thank you for keeping me updated as well, Candi. Take care of yourself, and I'll speak to you soon."

After I hang up, I stare at my phone for a couple of minutes, before putting it down with a mental shake. Catching Jasmine giving me a curious look, I laugh.

"His voice does things to me I haven't felt in a long, long time, and that's only his voice. Can you imagine if I actually had sex with him? Oh, I say, it would be quite amazing." I answer my own question on a breathless sigh, as I feel my body react to the thought of him touching, kissing, licking, and finally…

My phone rings, snapping me out of my fantasy. It's Kheda ringing me back.

"Hello, Detective, thank you for ringing me back. The doctor or technician who was doing the DNA tests, did they describe who destroyed them? Even if he didn't see the vandal's face, they might be able to describe other things like weight, height..."

"He can't describe anything." With a growl of pure frustration and grief, Kheda continues, "He's in a coma, and even if or when he comes out of it, the likelihood of him being able to describe anything is... His eyes and tongue were removed as well as his ears," Kheda finally spat out. "So no, he won't be able to describe anything he saw."

"Oh, I am so sorry." I gasp in shock. "See no evil,

speak no evil, and hear no evil," I whisper.

"What did you say?" demands Kheda.

"Nothing…well…have you ever seen the no-evil dolls? There are three of them, each one covers their eyes, ears, or mouth so they cannot speak, see, or listen to evil actions. In this case the doctor has been prevented from hearing any questions, speaking about what happened, or seeing who did this to him." I feel sick to my stomach at the implications.

"I have to go, Candi. I'll talk to you soon."

****

I stare at my phone, all I can see in my head are the no-evil dolls, with a shake of my head, I hang up, explain what Kheda said, and then phone Victor and relate everything to him. Hanging up my phone again, I decide to start making dinner, just to keep myself busy if for no other reason.

After preparing dinner, I put it in the oven and return to the sitting room, light a fire, and plop onto the sofa to watch something to take my mind off the murder.

As it turns out, *The Phantom of the Opera* is just starting. Jasmine curls up on the floor beside me and rests her head on my feet to watch the film. Soon I become enthralled in the story. Personally, I would jump his bones in a second. Who needs a pipsqueak like Raoul if you had the Phantom? Grandma Eve arrives home halfway through the film and quietly joins us on the sofa to watch the rest.

During the next break, I serve dinner for all of us. Grandma gives me a raised eyebrow, but says nothing when I give Jasmine her share of the meal, excluding the wine of course. There is no way in hell I would be able to explain giving a dog alcohol. It would be more likely to get me in some serious trouble with the RSPCA.

I sob my heart out at the end of the film. Feeling devastated for the Phantom as he is once again left on his own. His heart broken as Christine and Raoul leave him to start their new lives together. If I could climb into the TV, I would have taken the Phantom into my arms and taken him far away. What can I say? The bad guys are normally gorgeous. Thinking of the killer on the loose, and with a shudder I change that to film bad guys are normally gorgeous.

****

"Thank you, dear, for a wonderful dinner. I didn't think you cooked, but you have proven quite wonderful at it," states Eve with a contented smile.

"I can cook. I just don't enjoy doing it and so prefer not to." Smiling at my gran's expression, I collect the dirty dishes and head into the kitchen so I can tidy up.

"Since you cooked I'll wash up."

With a shake of my head, I ignore my grandmother. I place the dirty dishes on the counter, rinse them, and fill the sink up with hot sudsy water.

I very efficiently even if I do say so myself wash, dry, and put them away, clean down the counters and cooker, before snagging the bottle of wine and returning to the sitting room where I find Grandma Eve snoring on the sofa.

I top up my glass and channel flick until I find an old film to watch. A western about four fallen women, who go on the run, hunted by a posse, and tracked by Pinkerton detectives. With a sideways look at Jasmine,

I notice she has sat up straighter and her tongues hanging out in pure delight at the prospect of watching it again.

"A blast from the past, huh?" I laugh delighted as I curl up comfortably on the sofa again to relax and watch an old favorite.

We manage to watch the whole film before Eve wakes up. When she does, I'm surprised when she invites me along to the local pub, The Witches' Brew.

"If you're back to stay, Candi, you must begin socializing, and The Witches' Brew is a good place to start. Now go and get yourself ready. It will do you a world of good and you never know, you might meet a nice man. You're too nice to not be married, never mind single," Eve informs me with a serious expression.

Hearing a snuffling sound behind me, I turn toward my laughing best friend and glare at her, too shocked to say anything to my grandma. I head upstairs for a shower and to drag some clean clothes on. I slap a little makeup on and return downstairs to wait.

Seeing Jasmine I give a quick spin and ask, "Do I look OK?"

To be honest it has been a very long time since I've gone out, and I'm not sure if I'm under-dressed or not. I'm wearing my favorite pair of black skinny jeans that hug my long legs. I've teamed it with a simple black lace top and my favorite stiletto ankle boots.

For jewelry, I've put on feathered earrings in black and emerald green and a silver watch. I also wear a simple silver belt, with silver and black eye-shadow on to give my eyes a wonderful smoky look, teal eyeliner to make them pop and apricot glamour lipstick.

A simple look, especially with my hair slicked back into a ponytail held up with silver scrunchy. A huge doggy grin and a large paw, as if to high five me, answers my question.

Returning her smile, I grab my coat, phone, and a small purse I plan to carry. Hearing my grandma descend the stairs, I go to meet her, and gasp with delight at her elegant transformation.

"Grandma, you look wonderful," I exclaim in pleasure.

She's wearing elegant, low-heeled red shoes with a simple strap, teamed with a black dress with poppies scattered across the bottom half. The top half is black with little capped sleeves and a red belt cinches her rather tiny waist.

She also has a simple red clutch bag secured under her armpit, red lipstick, and peachy eye shadow. Her hair is done up in an elegant twist secured with a red clip.

"You look beautiful as well, dear," Eve replies as she looks at me in pleasure. "We shall have a lovely evening," she declares as she collects a black wrap from the coat stand and heads outside. "Don't forget your keys, dear."

On this reminder, I quickly grab my keys, give Jasmine a quick hug, close the front door, and lock it behind us. We walk to the pub, which is a good twenty minutes' walk away.

Upon reaching the pub, I notice people being scanned as they enter, their species flashing on a sign above them for everyone to see. This shocks and horrifies me. Especially when the witch in front of us enters. and the sign flashes her known association with other species.

I'd heard of these scanners, but never seen one. They are illegal, but since *The Protectors* own them and people fear them, they are able to get away with it. Some of the patrons avoid the witch, as if by distancing themselves from her they can save themselves.

I stop my grandmother from entering, gather some energy, and with a final prayer to my Goddess, I throw a magickal diffuser at the door, capturing the ward and dragging it screaming from the door. With a flick of my wrist, it explodes like beautiful fireworks. I enter the pub to shocked silence.

"How did you do it?" Eve asks me so quietly, I almost don't hear her.

"I asked for help from our Goddess, Grandma Eve," I reply as if it's the most natural thing in the world. Thinking it should have been obvious.

"You must talk to her a lot for her to grant you so easily."

"I talk to our Goddess almost every day, Grandma. Mainly to say hello and ask how she is," I reply as I head toward the bar to get a drink. "What are you drinking?"

"A glass of Chardonnay, please, dear. I'll grab us a table. I need to sit down."

I'm surprised and concerned by Eve's reaction to my speaking to Hecate. Did she not speak to her often? Looking at my grandmother, I become more concerned. Something is not right with her. Something has changed in the twelve years I have been gone. Hopefully nothing too drastic.

"What did you do to my wards, witch?" demands a small pale squidgy creature with slimy-looking skin. I notice he said "witch" as others might say "bitch."

"Do you own this bar?" I ask as I try to figure out exactly what he is. Or at least I am guessing it's male, but only because the voice seems slightly masculine. The body looks like a squat, blobby mass with stumps sticking out for arms and legs with a head on top. It's wearing trousers and a jumper, so not helpful at all.

His skin tone is gray, and he has muddy brown watery eyes and no hair, eyebrows, or eyelashes. His nose is more like two slits for nostrils, yet his lips are large and puffy. He is the strangest thing I've ever seen.

"No, I don't, but them be my wards, witch, and you, you..."

"Removed them," I helpfully supply since he/she appeared at a loss for words.

"How? No one can remove my wards. They're the best."

"Well, if you say so, but you should know they are against the law, so I was only doing my civic duty by removing them. No need to thank me. I don't mind helping, for obviously, a law-abiding citizen like your good self was about to take them down, weren't you?" I innocently enquire, turning toward the barmaid I smile, and order my grandmother's Chardonnay and my drink.

****

As the creature slithers away, I ask underneath my breath, of the barmaid, "What was that?"

"Mr. Vesper. He works for *The Protectors*. How did you destroy the ward?" she replies, looking slightly frazzled and a lot relieved.

"Why was it allowed to be put up? I'm Candi by the way."

"I'm Nici, nice to meet you, and it wasn't

75

'allowed,' it was just put up. No choice in the matter." With a shake of her head, she passes over my drinks.

"How much do I owe you?"

"They are on the house, with major thanks."

"No problem at all. Those kinds of wards shouldn't be allowed, they're too dangerous, also illegal. Thanks for the drinks, Nici." I grab them and weave my way over toward my grandmother. Sitting down, I pass her a glass of wine.

After a rather large gulp, she seems much more herself, and I'm pleased to see some color returning to her pale cheeks. Taking a sip of my own drink, I savor the taste before swallowing, glancing around at the still speechless patrons.

"Is it always this quiet? I feel like I'm in a library."

And then as if a spell is broken, everyone starts talking at once, conversation returns, and I notice the witch who had been avoided previously, is now being talked to. Fear is a terrible, crazy thing, but fear with reason is so much worse.

****

Everyone starts looking lighter, happier, and freer. Once again enjoying their evening in their favorite pub, talking to whom they wish, without the possibility of being murdered for associating with someone who interacted with another species. I sit back to enjoy a quiet drink with my grandma, which results in a few more, as drinks appear with quiet nods of thanks from different people.

After the sixth drink arrives, we decide we'd best leave or we would be severely intoxicated by the end of the evening. As we stand up to leave, someone appears at our sides to drive us safely home, courtesy of Nici.

With a smile of thanks to Nici and the young man, we say goodnight and thank the customers who bought us drinks. As I leave I place my hand on the building, and a crackle of power flickers across and through the building. Dark corners become bright and warmth and peace re-enter the pub.

Seeing Nici hurrying to me, I stop to explain, "After a ward like Mr. Vesper's, it takes a while before a protection spell can replace it. As people become happier, this will spread to enclose the land. No harmful spells will work here anymore. Will you make sure the witch who entered before we did receives a safe lift home please, unless she can stay here for the night? Mr. Vesper won't be pleased, and sadly, she will be an easy target tonight."

"I'll keep her here tonight. Thank you so much for what you did. I don't know how you did it, but thank you."

"My Goddess helped me. Take care as well please, and thanks for the lift home and the drinks. Goodnight." I hurry to catch up with my grandmother following her out of the building and into the waiting car.

Five minutes later, we pull up at my grandmother's house, say goodnight and thanks to our driver.

Unlocking the door, we enter the house, and re-lock it before saying goodnight and heading off to bed. I am exhausted. I go to the bathroom and quickly wash off my make-up, and get ready for bed.

After leaving the bathroom, I thank Hecate for her help, feel a warm embrace, and hear Hecate answer, *"Helping my children, help others, is a pleasure, child. Be safe, daughter of mine. You have much to do."*

I happily climb into bed and am about to fall asleep

when I hear my phone ringing. Groggily reaching for it, I mumble a hello and come wide awake as Victor's voice rolls over me like liquid fire, heating every part of my bloodstream with desire.

"Good evening, Candi, I hope I haven't woken you."

"No, no, I was just about to go to sleep. What's happened?" I demand hoping like crazy it's not another murder.

"I want to see you and was wondering if you could meet me?"

"When?" I reply in a whisper before clearing my throat and trying again, "Sure when?"

"Now. Meet me at the bridge in five minutes, please."

Before I can say anything else, I hear a click in my ear. The cheeky sod had hung up on me. Climbing out of bed, I get dressed and stuff my wallet, keys, and phone into my pockets, before silently descending the stairs. I exit the house and lock up behind me, hurry to the bridge where I spot Victor leaning against the railing on the other side.

"You're late," he murmurs as he extends his hand toward me.

Crossing the bridge, I allow him to take my hand, which he tucks into the crook of his arm, before leading me down the road. I don't ask him where we're going, and to be honest, I don't really care.

We end up at The Blue Lagoon Bar. The darkness inside is only relieved by neon blue lights randomly placed about the pub. The pub's furnishings are blue velvet curtains and dark blue leather booths. The only contrast is the redwood tables and bar counter. Seedy is the word that comes to mind when I look around. Glancing at Victor I'm pleased to see the grimace of distaste flashing across his face, yet he still pulls me inside the bar. Leading me to a booth tucked into the furthest corner, Victor leaves me so he can order us some drinks. In a few minutes, he returns with two pints of lager and places one before me.

"It's the only thing safe to drink in this place," Victor apologizes.

"Okay, so why have you dragged me out of my bed, to take me here?" I enquire as I wave my arm around, indicating the bar.

Grasping my waving hand, Victor clasps it in his larger one, and with a shake of his head smiles at me. "I brought you here, so I can get to know you better. I did tell you yesterday I'd see you today."

"Yessssss, but why here?"

"Because, no one will disturb us or interrupt us here. I want some time alone with you, somewhere where you'll feel safe, and will know I don't mean you any harm. I can't go to the witches bar, and I own Vlad's Bar across the street. This place is…"

"Disgusting, yes, I agree," I interrupt, hiding a smirk behind my pint before taking a sip.

"Actually, I was going to say neutral ground," Victor chides me with a rumble of delicious laughter that ripples over my skin like decadent chocolate.

"Okay, I'll play, for a while. Since you dragged me here from my nice warm bed, I get to ask you a question first."

"Deal. But if you want a nice warm bed, mine is available and very nearby." Victor smiles. Tracing a circular pattern on my hand, as he leans forward to entice me with his words.

Taking a fortifying gulp of my drink, I feel the blush heighten on my cheekbones. Lust shoots through my body, as the image of Victor and I entwined flashes in my head. His golden body splayed across his sheets, cradling me in his embrace as he makes mad passionate love to me. Is it wrong I want to say yes and have my fantasy come true? Biting my lip, I stifle a moan as it tries to escape. I notice Victor's eyes dilate and wonder again, can he read my thoughts?

"When were you born? And how can you walk about in sunlight?" I just barely manage to ask, too afraid to ask if he can read my mind as there's no way I can control my lust-filled thoughts when I'm around him.

"Two questions are cheating, but I'll answer them, just this once. I was born in the year 1823, right here in County Cork. I was turned in the year 1848. I'm able to walk in daylight because the sun doesn't affect vampires.

"To protect us from hunters, the original vampires spread rumors of creatures unable to face sunlight and mirrors. All falsehoods, but necessary ones. Think how the witches have fared during persecutions. Vampires were also ruthlessly hunted, and with our healing abilities, the torture was…beyond unbearable.

"My sire's brother died during their experiments," With a shake of his head as if to remove dark thoughts, Victor smiles at me as if he wants to devour me, flashing just a little fang. "My turn, ah, ah, you had your turn, Candi." Victor laughs as I try interrupting him. "Are you attracted to me?"

"Uh, yes. I thought it was obvious," I scoff then try

and back track. "I mean…"

"No, don't be embarrassed. I'm very attracted to you, too. In fact, I don't remember ever wanting someone as much as I want you. I think, like you, I'm not sure of how it makes me feel. I'm just glad I'm not the only one feeling like this." Victor admits, though the tightening of his jaw as he practically spits out the words is far from flattering. I do agree with it, completely.

We chat for another hour about nothing in particular, just getting to know one another. I desperately want to find out more about the myths of vampires and what the truths are.

We keep away from personal questions, shying away from anything to do with family or romantic history, as if by asking a question will make our fragile self-control snap and one of us will leap at the other, ripping each other's clothes off in our need and haste.

I sneak another wanton look at his mouth and catch him looking at mine like a man dying of thirst, realizing my mouth is the reservoir he's been looking for, and all he has to do, is take it.

Chapter 8

When I arrive back at my grandmother's, I sneak in like a thief in the night or a teenager breaking curfew. I quietly lock up and climb the stairs. Quickly I remove my clothes and put on my pajamas and that's all I remember. I must have passed out from exhaustion before my head even touched my pillow.

I'm woken up by Jasmine in the bathroom; poor thing must have been bursting for a pee since I'd forgotten to take her out last night when I got back, both times.

"Good morning; how are you today?" I call out to her as I clamber out of bed. My eyes are so bleary I can hardly see through them, and I feel exhausted, but strangely refreshed at the same time.

As the bathroom door opens and no one comes into my room I decide to enter, obviously she needs to speak to me and the bathroom is the safest place, there are no windows so no one can spy on us if she is in human form. Walking in, I spot her sitting on the edge of the bath in the farther corner, so she won't be glimpsed by anyone in the bedroom. Calmly I close the door, cross the room, and give her a quick hug.

"So how was last night? I'm guessing something happened; so tell me everything, and don't leave anything out," Jasmine demands.

Quickly I update her on what had happened last

night, including Grandma Eve's surprise at how Hecate had helped destroy the ward. To be honest it still puzzled me. I tell her about my phone call from Victor and meeting up with him.

"I can't understand why she was so surprised. I mean her reaction was as if she has never seen Hecate give help, or I don't know..." I shake my head in puzzlement.

"Maybe she hasn't, Candi. You have to remember not everyone speaks to the Goddesses of old, let alone regularly and mainly to say hi. Most people if they speak at all, just ask for something and never to say thanks. It makes a difference and it shows. You obviously surprised and maybe made your gran look at her relationship with Hecate."

Thinking about the first time Jasmine realized I had such a special relationship with the Goddess, I remembered it was quite an eye opener for her. Ever since she made an effort to say hello and ask how Hecate was, until it became no effort, that's when she finally heard a reply. I still remember the awe on her face the first time Hecate spoke to her. "What about you? Did anything happen here or was it all quiet?"

"No, it wasn't all quiet. Someone came poking around, but I don't think they were expecting a dog, because I heard them scuttle back when I started barking and soon after they left."

Giving a deep sigh, she runs her fingers through her long black hair, before continuing, "Look I think they were snooping around because of you. Especially with how you so easily destroyed a ward, it wouldn't go in your favor. When are you signing the papers for the old Winters' house again?"

"Today at two p.m. You're probably right, the sooner we move out, the better and safer my gran will be."

It's sad, but I think she's right. Whoever was trying to snoop around is most likely trying to find something to use against me. But I decide I will tell my grandma about the snooper, then realize I can't because it was Jasmine who was here on her own, and as a dog would have no way of telling me about the unwanted caller.

"Damn," I mutter in frustration.

"Hey, maybe we can look for footprints in the mud, and if we find any, we can give your gran a heads-up, just in case it's not you causing unwanted attention."

Giving her a grateful look, I make her turn around, so her back's to me, so I can pee. My bladder at this stage is about ready to explode.

"Now, for the juicy news. You went out on a date with Victor. I want details."

"I don't think you can call it a date, to be honest, I'm not sure what you would call it. We met up, went to The Blue Lagoon Bar, which sells great lager, but is a complete dive. We admitted we're attracted to each other, and neither of us is majorly happy about it, or knows how to deal with the fact we have never felt so strongly about anyone else. And since Victor is one hundred and ninety-one years old, it's quite scary," I admit.

"Wow, one hundred and ninety-one years old? Really?"

"Well, he's been a vampire for, ummm, one hundred and sixty-six years."

"Oh my God, talk about mind blowing, and he's never felt…"

84

"Wanted, someone as much as he wants me." I leave out what he confided about his sire's brother. His trusting me and sharing such information gives me a warm fuzzy feeling, and I like the fact he trusted me enough to tell me. Though I do wonder what exactly happened to his sire's brother and why he wasn't rescued.

Not knowing what to say, she changes back into dog form, so I jump into the shower. Once I've finished we leave the bathroom to billowing steam. Dragging on underwear and a ratty T-shirt, tracksuit bottoms, and my trainers, I pull a brush through my hair before tying it up in a loose ponytail, slap on some moisturizer, and jog downstairs for some breakfast, with Jasmine at my heels.

I quickly get her some fresh water and her breakfast. Once she's eating, I pop the kettle on and sort out my own breakfast. With a sense of contentment, I cradle my mug and wish my Goddess a happy morning.

Finishing my coffee, I take my dishes to the sink, where I quickly wash, dry, and put them away. We head out for our morning run, and a sneaky look around for any sign of footprints in the mud.

To say our search is uneventful is an understatement. Whoever visited the house last night had left no sign. They had cleaned up after themselves too well, and I mean every print was gone; there should have been paw prints and my footprints.

Whoever had been nosing around last night had wiped our prints with theirs, maybe they hadn't realized we were there, maybe this was someone trying to spy on my grandmother.

Making up my mind, I decide I will tell her

Jasmine had seemed upset this morning, and I had noticed all prints had been wiped. That way I can let her know as much as we do about the unknown caller. With my decision made, we go back inside to get ready to see the solicitors. Finally, it's Friday and I'm signing for my home today.

Quickly I change into black trousers, heeled black boots, and a black shirt. I tie my hair into a single plait down my back, apply eyeliner, and lipstick. I grab my coat and head downstairs. I lock up, and Jasmine and I climb into my car to head to the old Winters' house for a final look around before signing for the house.

****

As we arrive I sense the house being happy to see us again, so I climb out of the car and head toward the front door. With a happy feeling, I place my hand on the door and say hello to the house and to my shock, I feel a wave of power and see a series of images.

Men had arrived, after I agreed to buy the house. They had tried to take the bath and some other items, but the house hadn't let them. They had tried to dump rubbish, and the house and surrounding lands threw it back at them.

"The agreements had been set, and they tried to break them. I will not allow wrongdoing to occur to those who shall live here," whispered the house in a fog-like voice, gently surrounding me.

"Thank you, now we must go and sign the papers. We will come afterwards and start the renovations. I hope you will like the plans I have."

Going back to the car, I drive straight to the bank to collect the money, and then to the solicitors to sign and pay for the house. With a feeling of excitement, I enter the office of Jameson and Smyth Solicitors and inform the secretary I'm there for my two o'clock appointment with Thomas Smyth.

Five minutes later, I'm in his office reading the paperwork. After assuring myself everything is as it should be, Mrs. White, old Mrs. Winters' daughter signs and I sign as well. I take out the money and once counted out to everyone's satisfaction, I pay my solicitor's fees, stamp duty fees, land registry fees, and finally the engineer's report fees for the survey he'd done.

With a sigh of relief and all the keys to the house and photocopies of all documents, I finally leave the solicitor's office feeling exhausted, but very happy, as I'm now the proud owner of the old Winters' house.

****

I'd already arranged for my furniture to arrive later that day. Everything is finally coming together smoothly. With a feeling of immense relief, I climb into my car and head for the off license. Today deserves a celebration bottle of champagne.

I decide I'll give Victor and Kheda a ring, to see if they would like to help celebrate the signing of the deeds to my new home. I realize to do so will cause great problems. How can I explain to my gran I am associating with a vampire and werewolf? I know the dangers, and yes, I am willing to be around them, but I cannot jeopardize my gran's life by having a party that might put her life in danger.

I will have them over later after dinner for a celebration. I will tell my grandmother I will be having Victor and Kheda over, and she is welcome to stay. But most importantly of all, I will tell her the truth about

Jasmine. Well, once I have permission and when we are all at the old Winters' house just in case the person snooping around Gran's house left any magical or technical listening devise.

As I climb back into my car, I tell her my plan for the party, and about telling my grandmother about her. After all Jasmine can now stay human if she wants, especially when safely on the property of the old Winters' house.

With a sigh of understanding and a bark to confirm her agreement, she gives me the permission I need to tell my grandmother the truth. I hope she will understand about her, but also about Victor and Kheda as well.

Chapter 9

"A shapeshifter! You willingly brought a shifter into my house?" Eve demands, as she angrily paces the sitting room in my new home.

I watch in alarm as Gran wrings her hands together, as if wringing my neck. More worryingly, I notice how she makes great effort to relax her hands. Finally taking three deep breaths and releasing them, she turns toward me.

"What were you thinking?" she screams in frustration and fear. Obviously, she has not calmed down or got herself under any form of control.

"I'm sorry I didn't tell you the truth, Gran, but, until a couple of days ago, she was stuck in her dog form. We didn't even know if she was going to be able to come out of it," I explain as calmly as I can, though to be honest I'm getting annoyed by my grandmother's extreme reaction. What the hell would her reaction be concerning my association with Victor and Kheda? If she can't handle them, how the hell will she react to the girls from the army, who became my sisters in arms as well as life? All of us are a supernatural of some sort or another.

"In my army unit, I became friends, and then chosen sisters, with the women in my unit. We depended on each other for our survival and our abilities. Our *supernatural* abilities, especially, brought us closer and saved our lives on more than one occasion. Each one of us is from one type or another supernatural heritage. Grandma, if you can't accept her, you can't accept me either. I never restrict myself to being friends with just witches and humans. I'm surprised you do." I bluntly finish my statement with a frown, as I shake my head in regret.

I watch Eve staring at me, as if she is finally seeing the woman I have become, and realizes she doesn't know me at all.

A witch who speaks to the Goddess and who the Goddess speaks back to, as if to an equal. A woman, who is friends with not only shifters, but also other supernaturals. One who views them as family. Finally I see the distrust, and with a shake of her head, Eve takes a large step back. Numerous emotions flicker across her face: regret, confusion, fear, anger, and finally repulsion.

"I'm sorry, Candi, I have to think. I also think it will be best if you moved in here as quickly as possible," Eve mutters, anger and confusion lacing her voice, before she turns and flees my new home.

I watch in stunned silence as she leaves, heading toward her car. I can't believe I had allowed my grandmother to run away. I notice the moment she stumbles, her head bent, a hand reaching up to swipe at her face. It looks like she's crying.

"Oh Goddess, I made my grandmother cry. There probably is a special place in hell for people like me," I mutter in disgust at myself.

Hearing Jasmine laugh, I turn toward her and give her a wry grimace. "It's not funny," I chide her.

"It is, Candi; you can't seriously believe you have

done anything wrong. Being friends without discrimination is not bad, far from it, in fact. Okay, maybe it is dangerous, but definitely not bad. Candi, you are family, and so I will tell you something, your grandmother has a problem. It has nothing to do with you. You are not at fault. Let her have her space, she knows where to find you. She loves you; she will be in touch as soon as she is ready."

With a great big groan of dissatisfaction, I plop down on the sofa with a thud and put my head in my hands.

"I know life is not easy, but does it have to be so hard?" I moan in frustration. I don't expect a reply to my complaint.

"No, it doesn't have to be so hard, Candi. If you want, I'll leave," she replies quietly, but seriously.

"Don't you dare! That's not an option. I meant what I said to my grandmother, if she can't accept you or the rest of my friends including Victor and Kheda, she can't accept me.

"I am not losing you, or giving anyone up, to make life easier for others, because it would be miserable for me," I calmly state. Looking at her, it's obvious she hates the thought of the trouble she might cause me by staying.

Taking a deep breath, I decide to head over to my gran's house, collect what I can fit in my car, and see if she's up to talking yet. At least if she isn't, she will know I'm not mad at her. With my decision made, I turn toward Jasmine.

"I'm going to go and get our stuff from my grandmother's house. Please stay here, I invited Kheda and Victor over," I hastily carry on before she interrupts.

Grabbing my car keys, phone, and jacket, I pause on my way out the door. "Jasmine, you're my sister, never, ever, think by leaving, you would be helping, because you wouldn't, far from it.

"Also, outside of discriminations and fears, we have far bigger things to be solving. We need to stick together, now, more than ever." I give her a quick hug, before turning and leaving my new home.

****

I quickly cross to my car, unlock it, climb in and drive to my grandmother's house. When I arrive, I notice her car isn't there. Letting myself in, I collect Jasmine's things first and load them into my car. Then I go upstairs to my room, and pack my clothes and toiletries. Once they're packed I bring them downstairs and load them into my car.

Returning upstairs to my room, I cross to my writing desk and quickly write my grandmother a note. I'm getting a really bad feeling about her absence.

Hey Grandma,

I collected my things and was surprised you weren't here. I'll see you for lunch tomorrow, but can we meet at twelve o'clock instead of one please? Give me a ring if this doesn't suit you. Thanks for coming over tonight. I'll see you tomorrow.

Love, Candi

My grandmother and I have no lunch plans for tomorrow, but if something has happened to her, they wouldn't know it. I cross my fingers that I'll get a phone call from my grandmother, asking me what the hell I'm talking about. Picking up my note, I bring it down to the kitchen, leaving it on the counter with a mug containing a tea bag on top of it. A simple guarantee it'll be noticed, as the mug will have to be moved to read the complete note. Also, if anyone other than my gran picks up the note, we can get fingerprints off it.

Hopefully it won't come to it, I think giving a slight grimace, before going back to my room to collect my desk. I give it a thorough going over to make sure no bugs have been planted on it. Finding none, I bring it downstairs and load it into my car, then finally, go back upstairs for my chair.

I go over it carefully, but this time I find a tiny device on one leg. Leaving it there, I carry it downstairs, and once I cross the threshold of the house I stumble, reposition my grip on the chair with a peeved *Fuck's sake*. Sadly, I manage to knock off the device, and whoops, stand on it. I load the chair into my car, return to the house, and lock up. Climbing into my car, I drive off.

On returning home, I quickly get out of my car and grab my desk chair, and walk into my home.

Jasmine is just coming to help. I quickly shake my head. As I move into the sitting room, I check the chair again. Finding nothing, I tell her to stay in the sitting room and check everything I bring into the house for devices.

Going back to my car, I collect my desk next, and slowly I unload and "check" to make sure I haven't dropped anything while unloading

I crawl out of my car, after collecting a scarf. I knock a small listening device onto the ground, and with great satisfaction, I stand on it and crush it.

Locking up, I return to my home with my scarf held loosely in my hand, in case anyone was watching.

When I arrive in the sitting room, it's Jasmine's turn to put a finger to her lips. She has found three more devices.

I decide to flush them down the toilet; wrapping them in tissue, I drop them into the loo and flush. I stare into the toilet until I'm sure they're gone. Quickly I wash my hands and return to Jasmine.

"I flushed them," I explain to her raised eyebrow.

Between us, we tidy everything up and put the lot upstairs into our rooms. Once everything is put away, we meet in the sitting room, where I update her on what has happened at my grandmother's.

"To be honest, I think something has happened to her," I finish with a frustrated sigh. "I hope I'm wrong, but finding these listening devices is not helping." Getting up from the sofa, I start pacing. Back and forth, back and forth before finally with a growl of annoyance I run upstairs and pull on sweats.

I'm going for a run and check out her house to see if she's back yet. When I exit my room, it's to find Jasmine in dog form, wagging her tail with her tongue lolling out the side of her mouth.

"Thank you my sister," I whisper in gratitude.

As we descend the stairs, there is a knock on the back door. Quickly we head toward the kitchen and open the door to find Victor and Kheda. I let them in and explain the situation.

"I have to go and make sure she's okay. I'm so sorry, but I have to cancel tonight," I apologize.

"I'm going with you," Victor answers, looking me in the eye.

"I'm sure Kheda is, as well as Jasmine, so shall we go look for her? I gather we're going through the woods. Would you like me to flit you there? Kheda and Jasmine can run over."

"Are you sure? Thanks, yes, if it's okay," I stammer in shock at the offer of so much help.

In the next instant I'm in Victor's arms as if I weigh nothing, then we're speeding through the woods with Jasmine and Kheda running behind us in the distance.

Chapter 10

We arrive at the outskirts of my gran's property, in the woods to keep us invisible, her car is still missing, but we notice someone skulking in the bushes further ahead. As Victor releases me from his arms, I slide down his body and carefully place my feet on the ground. No way in hell do I want the skulking bastard to hear us because of me stepping on a twig!

Besides, Victor's body is rock hard. And wow, a girl has to enjoy herself, even under extreme circumstances. Like trying to figure out if my gran has just gone out and about, and all this is a major coincidence.

"Damn, there really is a special place in hell for bad grandchildren, or if there isn't, there should be," I mutter under my breath.

"What's the matter, Candi? Did you enjoy being in my arms a little too much?" Victor enquires with a wicked smile and gleam in his eyes. "If it helps, I enjoyed you being in my arms, and especially, you sliding slowly down my body."

"Hem, ahhhh, you, yeah," I stammer, flushing a bright beetroot color. Sadly I do not do flushing prettily.

"It's all right. I'm not going to take you right here, right now, however much I would like to," Victor interrupts my stammering with a slight rumble of laughter flowing up his body to mix delightfully with his rich sinful voice.

"My God, phone sex with you would be amazing," I blurt out, before clapping a hand over my mouth. My eyes have widened so much I can feel the delicate skin around them stretching. *Holy shit, I had spoken out loud!*

"We are definitely going to have a very private talk later Candi Reynolds, but sadly our two furry friends are just arriving, and we must decide what to do with him," gestures Victor, pointing toward the man hiding in the bushes.

****

Jasmine and Kheda trot up at that moment. Kheda huge in his wolf form, with inky black fur and glowing green eyes. Jasmine shifts back into her human form and raises an elegant eyebrow at me when she notices my bright red face. Before she can say anything, I quietly point out the hiding man, so no one will make any noise.

"What's the plan? Are you going to avoid him or question him?" she quietly asks.

"Question him, but not here, in case it gets noisy," I whisper. "We need to take him somewhere private where no one will think to look for him. I'm positive there are more of them involved in this spying, if not outright kidnapping and murder."

Noticing Victor looking at me, as if only just seeing me properly for the first time, I give him a puzzled look in return.

"You object?"

"No."

"So why are you looking at me so"—waving my

hand back and forth as if it was going to supply the rest of my statement—"weirdly," I finish still not satisfied with my phrasing.

"You've surprised me, that's all. I had assumed you wouldn't want to...take him somewhere private to question him."

"Well, if he screams, I can't have anyone running to his rescue," I bluntly reply.

"I have a warehouse that is soundproof," Victor supplies with a blink of his beautiful eyes. His only indication of surprise. "But I must insist our good friend here"—Victor waves his hand at Kheda, letting everyone know which good friend he's talking about— "Does not come with us. I'm sorry, Kheda, but at the end of the day you're a detective, and we can't have you there."

"It's best you go now, Kheda, because he is going to tell me everything I need to know, and to be honest, if he has hurt my gran, well let's just say it's not going to be pretty," I state, with vehemence dripping from my words.

Feeling the surprised look of Victor and Kheda, I give a gentle snort. "What, you expect me to ask politely and hope he gives me an honest answer? No, he will tell me everything I need to know, and everything he knows. I'll need music; do you have a CD player, Victor?"

"Yes, why do you ne..."

"Jasmine, will you run back to our house and collect my CD bag please," I politely instruct, as I interrupt Victor.

"Where shall I meet you?" enquires Jasmine before transforming back into a dog.

I notice Victor staring at us with an expression of dawning comprehension, as he realizes it will be me, not him, extracting the information from the man.

Finally, Victor looks back at Jasmine and answers her question. "Where you and Candi were when you first saw me, before we met."

In the next instant, she stealthily runs back the way she'd come, with Kheda by her side.

****

In a blink of an eye, I crouch down, and silently head toward my target. So quietly not even a leaf rustles beneath me, I move through the woods. A silent, deadly predator, stalking my prey, until finally I'm in position and pounce with accuracy and deadly precision onto the man's back.

"Where is my grandmother?" I growl low and threatening in his ear.

With a shudder and a gasp of surprise, as all air whooshes from his body at the sudden and brutal attack, the man underneath me wheezes out, "I'll tell you nothing, witch!"

"Ah, but you will tell me everything you know by the time I'm done with you, that I promise," I croon, as I give a quick hand chop to the side of the man's neck rendering him unconscious.

I squat and pick him up, sling him over my shoulder. Standing up slowly to keep my balance, I turn toward Victor who's staring at me with his jaw hanging open. Raising an eyebrow at Victor, with a slight smile of amusement, I wonder if he's been turned into a statue.

"Are you all right, Victor? You seem to be gaping in rather an unbecoming fashion, or you're trying to catch flies." I snicker at him.

Snapping out of his stupor, Victor quickly crosses to me and relieves me of the unconscious man. Turning my back to him, I once again crouch down. Grabbing a fallen twig with some leaves on it, I quickly brush over the ground to remove any trace of the disturbance caused in capturing the unknown man. Returning to Victor, once I have completed my task, I give him an expectant look.

"Where to next? You're the only one who knows where we're going?" I ask as I throw the twig far into the trees. Victor grabs me, one arm around my waist pulling me flush against his side, and with a wicked grin whispers, "Hold on tight."

****

Wrapping my arms around his neck, I cling to him, as he shoots up into the air, holding the unconscious man and me. I wrap my arms tightly around his neck. Good thing he's already dead or he would have passed out through lack of oxygen.

Tangling my legs around his, I'm half-tempted to wrap them around his waist, but it would have caused the man dangling over Victor's shoulders to fall, and I wanted to question him, not have him free falling from the sky.

We land beside a warehouse in the middle of the woods. In one smooth motion, Victor releases me, punches in a security number by the door, and opens it, before I have my balance back. I follow him into the warehouse as he flips switches.

I'm surprised how spacious and non-warehouse-like it is inside. There's a kitchen and dining table big enough to seat twelve to the left. On my right a sitting room with two three-seater sofas and two single chairs, a coffee table, and a TV.

We walk pass these and head toward the back of the warehouse where some rooms have been constructed. A spacious bathroom is on the right with a bedroom next to it. On the left, another bedroom and next to it…a room with a cage. Its contents hold a metal bed frame and chair, both bolted to the floor. I turn to Victor with a raised eyebrow.

"It's a holding cell for vampires, both new born and those awaiting sentencing. Reinforced steel, so no need to worry about him escaping," Victor informs me as he dumps the man on the bed. Victor locks him in, then locks the bedroom door, and punches in a code. Placing a hand on my shoulder Victor stops my retreat as he turns me to face him.

"You're an unusual woman, Candi. I've never met anyone like you, and to be honest, I like it." Victor leans into me but remains just out of reach. His eyes tangle with mine and search for…Whatever it is, I think he finds it, for with a nod and a slight smile on his delicious mouth he turns away and walks toward the door.

"I'll go and get Jasmine now. Once we get back we can start questioning him."

Chapter 11

Thankfully she'd found my CD collection and arrived at the designated area the same time Victor did.

"Thanks, Jasmine," I say, taking my CD wallet from her. Turning to Victor, I ask rather sheepishly, "Umm, can I borrow your CD player please?"

"Yes, I'll get it for you now." With curiosity lacing his voice, Victor asks, "Why do you need music?"

"Strangely enough, it helps me concentrate and extract information quicker."

I don't follow Victor when he goes to retrieve his CD player. Instead, I head back to the holding cell, flicking through my music.

"No, no, no, maybe, definitely not." The last one I snort at. I'd forgotten I had it, but there was no way I was listening to pop music while interrogating someone. Now don't get me wrong, I like pop music, but cheerful bouncy music with a happy vibe is definitely not appropriate for an interrogation. Granted, most people wouldn't find any music suitable, or maybe it's the interrogating most people would find inappropriate?

"Ah, yes, now we're talking," I crow in delight, drag out a mixed rock soundtrack from a vampire film I love, just to stop as Victor comes back and gives me a rather queer look.

Quickly taking the CD player from him, I insert my

selected CD of choice. I go to open the door, but just in time remember it's locked. Turning toward Victor, I look at him.

"Do you want me to interrogate him?"

"No, but I do need you to unlock the door," I reply shaking my head in denial. "Victor, I'm going to assume you have cameras in there. I hope what you see doesn't change what you think of me. I like you."

Taking a deep breath at the look of growing puzzlement on Victor's face, I continue, "I like you a lot, but what you might see me doing—" How can I explain the unexplainable? With a grimace of annoyance, I shake my head again. "Can you unlock the door please?"

****

Moving quickly Victor reaches the door and unlocks it. But blocks my way by stretching a muscled arm across it. He still wears his puzzled look, but his voice is calm.

"We'll talk when you're finished. This is not the first interrogation I have seen, and I've participated in many during my lifetime. There is nothing you will do that could possibly shock me. I've seen too much. Oh, and I like you, too," Victor finishes his statement, stroking his fingers down the side of my face.

He opens the door and unlocks the cage. "Will you be all right in there on your own? I'll have to lock both doors behind me for security measures, if you want me to stay, I will."

"I'll be fine, thank you, Victor. Lock me in." I have to admit, I like his concern for me, but like it even more that he doesn't insist he be the one to extract information, or even be in the room with me.

"We'll be watching and listening. Be safe."

****

Stepping into the cell, I sense Victor swing the door closed behind me and with a clang of finality he locks it. Next, he closes the outer door but doesn't lock it. I place the CD player on the floor by the door.

"Now, I know you're awake so you can stop pretending," I inform the prisoner just before he springs off the bed and tries to jump me. Turning swiftly, I punch him in the solar plexus. "That was not nice," I growl before grabbing him and dragging him to the chair.

I heft him up and plop him down on the chair as he struggles to catch his breath. I stroll back to the CD player and hit play. The opening chords start playing, and I notice a hitch in the wheezing coming from behind me.

"Now the first question I'm going to ask you is simple. What's your name?"

"I'm not telling you, witch. You can't make me," he laughs.

"No? Okay, when you're ready to tell me, let me know," I reply with a friendly smile, just before I punch him in the face and break his nose.

"Ahhh, you broke my nose, you fucking bitch," he garbles, as blood runs down his face.

"You will have lots more broken if you don't tell me what I want to know," I reply and kick him in the calf.

A scream of pure agony rips from his throat as his fibula bone gives a sickening crack. "Benny, my name's Benny O'Brien, you crazy fucking cow."

"Now, that wasn't so hard, was it, Benny?

Especially, since that was the easiest question. Why were you watching my grandmother's house?"

"I was to wait for you to come back and take you in," Benny mutters, before spitting at me.

"Take me where, Benny?" I ask with venom lacing my words.

Benny starts to shake and snivel. "I'm only doing what I'm told." And then he tries to throw a punch at me.

I quickly deflect his punch, grab his wrist, and break his arm in one quick brutal maneuver. "Now Benny, just answer my questions and I'll stop hurting you. Stop the screaming Benny, and answer my questions, then I'll get you some help. Where were you going to take me?" I enquire, as I walk in a circle around him.

"I can't believe you broke my arm," sobs Benny, his voice laced with pain and shock. His chin trembles uncontrollably, and his pasty complexion looks even paler. He watches me circle him, not knowing when the next blow will come. I slam my fist into his cheekbone, breaking the bone.

With a scream of terror, Benny finally answers my question. "I was to take you to George Seabast the Fourth's house," he moans.

"What? Does he have my grandmother?" I demand, but to be honest I'm confused by this turn of events.

"Your grandmother? I don't think so," Benny sobs, sounding just as confused.

"Why were you hiding in the bushes staking out my grandmother's house?" I growl.

"Ah...yeah, you, I was paid to take you, but I know

nothing about your grandmother. I promise," whines Benny. "Please, don't hurt me anymore."

"What does he want me for," I snarl, looming over Benny with such savageness he starts to scream in terror.

With a disgusted look, I turn my back on him and walk toward the cell door. Benny lunges at me, and I turn just in time to see the manic look in his face turn to shock, as my fingers elongate into razor sharp claws. I slash my claws across his stomach.

"Oh Benny, you shouldn't have done that," I murmur, as I push him back into the chair and drive my claws through his thigh pinning him to the seat.

"Tell me what I need to know, and leave nothing out." With my free hand, I call forth a flame, and cauterize his stomach wound.

"Now, let's start again, and this time, I won't be so easy on you." I growl the final part, before swiping my hand out of his leg to push it through his side. I turn my claws into flames, and burn his wounds from the inside out, catheterizing the bleeding as his howls of pain echo through the cell.

"Stop, stop, please I'll tell you," Benny begs, as blood, snot and tears wash down his face mingling with his saliva.

"He wants to punish you for embarrassing him."

"That's not all Benny, or you would have told me straight away. You wouldn't have been stalking my grandmother's house, if that was all. You know more than you're telling me," I inform him so quietly he has to strain to hear me.

I know the instant my words register, for his pasty face blanches even more until it's turned a grayish green color.

"You knew!"

"Of course I knew." I transform my fingers back into claws, and lash them across his stomach.

"Now before I spill your guts across this floor, tell me where my grandmother is. Trust me, Benny; this is your last chance."

"George-Seabast-the-Fourth-has-her-at-his-place-in-a-shed-around-the-back." Benny pants as he rushes the sentence out in one long word. "Please, don't hurt me anymore. I've told you the truth, honest," he begs before bursting into even louder sobs.

"Don't worry, Benny, I won't hurt you any more unless I find out you have left anything out or lied to me. Then, I won't go easy on you at all." Before he can say anything else, I whisper a healing spell.

His wounds start to knit back together. I turn my back on him as he screams in pain, his bones mending and wounds closing. I walk toward the cell door again, this time I look up toward the ceiling, letting Jasmine know I was ready to leave. When I reach the door, Victor unlocks it, letting me out.

"Oh, and Benny, if anything has happened to even a hair on my grandmother's head, what happened here will look like a party to what I will do to you." I collect the CD player and leave, leaving Victor to lock up behind me, and Benny whimpering and screaming in pain and terror.

Chapter 12

Jasmine greets me with a cold bottle of water, and silently she points me to a bedroom I can use to shower and change into clean clothes. I hate the extra time I have to take to get clean, when anything could be happening to my grandmother, but supernaturals have a great sense of smell, and we can't take the chance of being found because I reek of Benny's blood. It could get us all killed.

Closing the bedroom door, I drop the CD player onto the nearest chair. It's still playing on the loop I'd put it on.

I strip off my blood-splattered clothes, and as I walk past the bed, I spot my favorite hunting clothes. Jasmine must have put them there.

A plain black sports bra, black knickers, black socks, black vest top, black cargo pants, black leather jacket, and black knee high boots. There is nothing worse than having a spot of color give away my position.

In satisfaction, I walk into the bathroom and step into the shower. Turning the water onto hot I wash my hair and body in unscented soap and shampoo. Once finished I switch off the shower, wring my hair out, and towel dry myself before wrapping the towel around my body, and return to the bedroom to get dressed.

****

The first thing I notice is the silence. Someone had turned off the music. The second thing I notice is Victor, lounging on the bed. He looks dangerous, like a great big panther, who's finished a snack and is looking for the main course.

"Victor can you leave please, I need to get dressed?" I grip my towel tighter around my body.

"We need to talk about what happened in the cell." Victor's voice ripples over my skin and soothes my nerves.

"We can do it later. I need to get dressed and rescue my grandmother," I mutter, as I reach the bed and reach out to scoop up my clothes.

Fast as lightning, Victor's hand wraps around my wrist. I hadn't even seen him move.

"We'll talk now. You can dress while you talk, can't you?" He rubs the leaping pulse on the inside of my wrist.

"Okay, fine, we'll talk now. Let me go and turn around," I huff in frustration.

With a twist of his lips Victor releases me but doesn't turn around, instead he just raises an eyebrow. With a snort of derision, I grab my clothes and head back toward the bathroom and walk straight into what feels like a brick wall. To make things worse, I would have landed on my butt except for Victor grasping me by the elbows to keep me upright.

"What the hell is wrong with you?" I demand in annoyance, as a scowl furrows my brow.

"You have nothing I haven't seen before, and as you put it, we are in a rush to rescue your grandmother. Now get dressed and tell me, what happened in the cell."

Dragging myself out of his grasp, I storm back to the bed and sit down to put on my knickers. I drag them up my legs under the towel. Victor watches, his eyes dilating the further up my legs they go.

Ha, he might have seen plenty of naked women. but he isn't going to see me naked unless I want him to. Lifting my hips off the bed, I slide my knickers in place. Next, I put on my socks and combat trousers; at this stage, it is more than obvious Victor is very aroused.

"Well, as you saw I'm more than just a witch," I answer, as I pick up my sports bra next.

Victor's eyes snap up to meet mine, and I raise a sardonic eyebrow at him. I put my arms through my straps and hook it behind my back. Next, I pull on my vestie top and adjust my sports bra properly. Hey, gotta make the girls comfy, and with Victor looking hot and bothered, all the better in my opinion. Finally, when completely covered I remove the towel and let it drop to the floor.

I grab my boots, slide the first one on, and lace it up to my knees, the other one following a second later. With a wicked look directed at Victor, I can't help asking, "Did you enjoy the show?"

Next thing I know my back is pressed against the wall, and every hard muscled inch of Victor is pressed against me, his manhood throbbing against my pelvis.

"Later, I'll enjoy the show in reverse," Victor rumbles his promise, as desire drips from each word he speaks.

"Yeah, umm, shall we go and rescue my grandmother now?" I tentatively ask. Blimey, I shouldn't have said anything, but I didn't think my little teasing would cause such a reaction.

Slowly Victor peels himself off me. His hands release my hands, which he had restrained above my head, making my breasts thrust against his rock hard chest. He leans backward, his chest rising off mine, which pushes his hips further into me, making me gasp and my eyes dilate.

He steps backward, releasing me altogether. By this time, my breathing has hitched, and I have to physically shake myself, before I'm able to step away from the wall. It is the only thing supporting me. I stumble on shaky legs to the bed and grab up my jacket, making a quick exit out the bedroom door, without looking back.

****

Jasmine is waiting for me in the kitchen. When she spies my flushed face, she looks like she's about to ask me something. Until she sees Victor coming out of the bedroom after me, then her jaw drops open in surprise... I give my head the barest of shakes, to say nothing had happened.

"Okay, Candi, I've got your stuff." She tries to hide her smile and distract me by indicating my knives, phone, gun with silencer and extra ammunition (silver), and finally plasters. It's never good to leave your blood behind. Too many spells require blood, and when your blood is different like mine is, it's even more dangerous. I can heal myself, but it's not always practical to think I will be able to.

I strap on my belt which fits snugly around my hips, put my bowie knives into their sheathes and my gun into its holster at the back of my belt. I have two extra knives in a pouch inside each of my boots and everything else except my phone gets distributed between my pockets. I put my phone in my jacket pocket with my keys and wallet.

Once again I catch Victor staring as I load my weapons. This time, I just shake my head at him, in a silent denial, of what I have no idea. To which I get a dirty smile back and he mouths "chicken" at me.

I give a snort, and remember something really obvious.

"Does anyone know where he lives?" as I realize I have no idea of where we're going.

"Yes, I printed off a map of his lands, and the surrounding land as well. I also noted who lives where," replies Jasmine with her usual efficiency as she puts the map out on the counter so we can all study it.

"Huh, he lives near the college campus," I murmur. Something is niggling at the back of my head, I just can't work out what the importance is.

After studying the layout a bit longer, I fold up the map and put it in my jacket pocket. Finally, we leave to rescue my grandmother.

Chapter 13

The moon rises high into the sky, and in an otherwise pitch-black night, it is our only illumination. Silently we move out of the college campus and cross into the border area of George Seabast the Fourth's land.

Jasmine had transformed back into her dog form at the warehouse, Victor and I move with silent stealth beside her. We move as one through the night and hunt my grandmother's kidnapper, and the man who'd sent someone to kidnap me. As we near the house, we silently separate to surround it.

"Where are they?" a shrill voice hollers from inside the house.

I can't tell if it's a male or female speaking, so I flatten myself against the wall and peer into the window. To my surprise, it's the old woman from my grandmother's shop. What has she got to do with all this? There are other people in the room, but I don't recognize any of them, which isn't surprising, as I hardly know anyone in town. I do notice George is missing. I duck down and slide under the window, so no one can see me. I carry on around the house.

I don't see anyone else until I bump into Jasmine, who has finished her search, and Victor who silently drops from the roof, scaring the shit out of me.

Quickly he clamps a large hand over my mouth to

stop me screaming. I yank his hand off my face, and signal toward the room that I had noticed everyone in. In a blink, Victor is at the window and then back to us. Damn, he's fast.

****

The three of us head away from the house and farther into the gardens. I tell Jasmine what I'd seen, finishing with the fact George is missing from the group.

"If we find him, we'll probably find my grandmother," I finish, my voice so quiet it barely travels to Jasmine and Victor.

"Salasen was in the room," Victor adds. When he sees our blank expressions, he adds, "He's a vampire high lord. I've never trusted him, and if I'm correct, this means he could be one of *The Protectors*." Victor finishes on a grim note.

"Are you saying they're all a part of *The Protectors*? We could get them in one go..."

"No. Look, they are definitely not the ones in charge, but what we can do is document who is here and put names to their faces. There has to be a chain and to be honest I'd say they are at the bottom of it." Victor shakes his head in obvious frustration.

Silently I head back toward the house, retrieving my phone from my jacket pocket I turn off the flash, zoom in on the window, and take a picture of everyone inside, then hurry back to a grinning Victor.

"Clever woman," Victor murmurs in appreciation, "I knew I liked you for more than your beauty."

Jasmine and I share a quick glance at his comment, and I quietly move off to find the shed as I suppress a smile. Once again, we carefully split up to search the area, this time keeping each other in viewing distance.

Our search of the outhouses and stables turn up nothing. We broaden our search farther into the land heading toward the woods and the property adjoining George Seabast's. A scream of anger helps us find the shed hidden amongst the forest on the far outskirts of the property. As one, we head toward the shed, and slowly search for a window.

"Where is Benny?" Someone screeches in anger from inside. A different voice murmurs a reply that is too quiet to hear.

"Ahhh, do I have to do everything myself? Why do I hire you imbeciles? Find them and bring them here," the first voice demands.

We retreat into the woods to wait and see who comes out. With quick hand signals, and a nod of silent agreement, we decide to take care of each person who comes out if, and only if, we can do so quietly.

A minute later, two big burly men walk out of the shed. We share surprised glances; they're werewolves. I track them with my eyes and once they retreat into the woods, we stalk them.

Victor leaps into the air, grabs one of the men, and in a smooth motion snaps his neck, dropping him quietly to the ground.

I simply shoot the other in the head, the sound of the gun muffled by the silencer. Victor catches the second werewolf and puts him next to the first. We return to the shed, as silently as ghosts wandering through the night.

****

Standing in front of the shed, I raise my hands. A wave of energy erupts from them, hitting the door and flinging it open. With a *crack,* it crumbles into splinters and dust. I walk forward with Jasmine at my heels.

Victor stands rooted to the spot, his mouth hanging open, as he stares in astonishment. I will have a lot to explain later. Upon entering the dirty shed, the smell of feces and unwashed body odor assails my nose making me gag. Looking about, I am surprised it's still standing.

I spot my grandmother gagged and tied to a chair. She's been beaten. Her poor swollen face is black and blue from bruising. Her hands are strapped to the arms of the chair preventing her from casting spells and her legs have been broken. With a quick look around, I spot George, cowering in the corner.

"Come here," I instruct with thunder reverberating in my voice and lightning crackling from my fingers.

My gran's eyes grow wide, as she watches the power swirling around me. Victor goes to my grandmother's side and quickly removes her gag and bindings. He's just about to rip his teeth into his wrist to help heal her, when Jasmine stops him with a quick growl forcing her body between them.

"I'm only trying to heal her nothing else," Victor soothingly replies before trying to step around her.

"There's no need, Victor, I'll heal her. Thank you," I interrupt.

One of my hands turns into warm bright light and shoots toward my grandmother's body, seeping into her skin. A cry of pain turns to a moan and finally a gasp of surprise, as her broken legs heal and the bruising and swelling disappear from her face.

"How?" she asks in shock.

"Come here, George," I instruct again, ignoring my

grandmother's question. George's appearance shocks and puzzles me when he finally leaves the corner he'd been cowering in. Well, as far as the chains that bind him allow him to come. A glance at Victor and Jasmine show they are just as shocked as I am. The only person who isn't is my grandmother.

"Okay, what the hell is going on?" I demand in frustration.

"We were both held captive," my grandmother answers as if it should be obvious.

"Who held you captive? The last I flipping well know, someone called Benny tried to kidnap me, on the orders of George," I snap. A scowl of annoyance furrows the skin of my forehead, as I gesture toward the chained man.

I do a double take and look more closely at him. Upon closer inspection, I realize the emaciated man in front of me, though he looks like the George Seabast the Fourth, could no way in hell be him.

You didn't go from healthy to bones in a couple of weeks, well not naturally any way. Also, from the smell of feces and body odor oozing from him, he had been there for quite a while.

"Who the fuck are you?" I demand, as I drag my hands over my face in exasperation. This situation was getting seriously complicated.

"This is George," my grandmother explained before George can say anything. "He's been fed upon, and drained of his magic." Regret and sadness laced her voice. "I couldn't help him."

"Are you telling me this happened in only a couple of hours?"

Thankfully, Victor decides to do something other

117

than ask questions. He goes over to George to help him sit down, breaking the chains with a quick snap. George curls into a ball and starts crying pitifully. I go over and gently lay my hands on his shoulders causing him to panic and scuttle back with a cry of fear.

Making soothing noises, I again move toward him grasping his shoulders, so he can't move away.

Once he calms down a bit, I start to transfer healing energy into him, enough to heal any injuries and give him enough energy to move. Once I've finished, Victor gives him a tiny bit of blood, and to my shock and surprise, I see George's body start to fill out. Until, once again, he's in perfect health.

He looks as if nothing had happened to him at all. The smell coming off him is the only testimony to what he's been through.

"Okay, we need to get you both somewhere safe. Someplace no one will think to look for you," I inform them.

I don't trust George. I know we just found him in a bad way, but, well...the thing is...there are way too many unanswered questions and I prefer answers. Also, I have a feeling not everything is as it seems. I just can't put my finger on what.

"I'm hungry, we should go somewhere where we can eat, and you can tell us exactly what happened here tonight."

Everyone gives me a look, and my stomach gives a loud growl in answer, as if to prove my statement. I notice George relaxing as he hears my stomach growl. Maybe I'm looking too closely. Maybe he's hungry as well. Okay, I say he's definitely hungry as I remember his emaciated body with a shudder. Still, I don't trust him as far as I can throw him, and something is definitely off and not just his smell.

In silence, we move out of the shed. I stop once outside to look back. There is something niggling at me.

"Where are the guards? I know we took care of two of them, but we heard someone give them orders," I demand.

Victor and Jasmine still at my question, and George gives my grandma a wary look, as if she is about to sprout horns. I take out my phone and send Victor a text, then switch my phone to navigation and key in restaurants.

"Okay, there's a place called Spuds near the college. We can go there and get something to eat. It's not far away, which is good and bad. Good because it's close, and bad for the same reason, it'll be easy to find us. Victor, why don't you scout around and see if you can find any guards about the place, and meet us there when you're done."

"No problem, I'll see you soon." Glancing around, he moves swiftly off.

The rest of us slip away in the opposite direction. Well Jasmine and I slip away, George and my grandmother, not so much slipping, as stomping. At least that's how it sounds to me anyway, and by the doggy grimace I see her give, I'm not the only one thinking it.

Because of the noise they're making, I take them the long way around, using my phone to guide me. At last we reach Spuds, and as we enter, the smell of hot food assails my nose making my mouth water and my stomach growl in appreciation.

We find a booth at the back of the diner and walk toward it. Thankfully, the diner isn't busy at this time of the evening, though we do get plenty of stares, and quite a few lip curls of distaste. I sit facing the door to see anyone entering.

****

My grandmother sits next to me, but I make her slide over to sit by the wall. George sitting opposite me automatically slides into the inside of the booth, and Jasmine jumps up next to him giving him a big doggy grin. I'm surprised when he grins back at her.

"Hey girl. Good doggy. Sorry about the smell," he whispers in mortification. "Do you mind if I go and clean up?"

I give him an understanding smile, and Jasmine jumps down to let him out.

As he moves out of the booth he turns to me. "Can I take your dog with me, please? I don't feel safe," he rushes, darting a scared look at my grandmother.

"Of course you can, George. We'll be here when you get back."

A couple of minutes later the waitress arrives and hands me three menus.

"Can I have a fourth, please. One of our party hasn't arrived yet," I explain.

With a smile, she hands me another menu before walking away. Ten minutes later Jasmine and George finally return.

Though George still looks a mess, he smells better and by the looks of his soaking wet clothes, had tried to clean them as well. I send heat toward him, and his clothes dry. He gives me such a look of gratitude I feel like crying.

Thankfully my phone vibrates in my pocket distracting me. I excuse myself with a simple, "I'm going to the toilet. I'll be back in a sec." I calmly walk in the direction that Jasmine and George had gone when they went to the toilet. Slipping out the back door, I meet Victor.

"Your grandmother's at home. I don't know who's in there, but it's not her," Victor informs me.

"Clever, I was wondering where the other person we heard in the shed had gone," I answer as things start clicking into place.

"Look, come in the front door to join us, as you were meant to, but give me a sec to get back to the table," I say to Victor as a slight plan starts to formulate in my mind.

"Okay, I'll see you in a sec," then Victor vanishes.

****

I go back into the diner and straight to the bathroom, flush a toilet in one of the stalls, wash and dry my hands, open the door and bump into my "grandmother" as I exit.

"Oh, sorry. Grandma, is everything okay, are you okay?" I ask with concern in my voice and my expression. *Ha, my acting is definitely getting better!*

"Yes, dear, I'm fine; I was just making sure you're okay. You were gone a long time."

"Well, I'm heading back to the table now. Has a waitress come to take our orders yet?" I enquire pleasantly as if being hunted down and questioned about what you're doing in a toilet and why it takes so long is normal.

"No, not yet. I'll go back with you."

I stand to the side of the booth so my

"grandmother" can slide back into the inside seat, then I sit down. Looking up I notice Victor "arriving." I wave at him, so he will know where we are.

"Ah, Victor has arrived," I unnecessarily inform everyone.

A second later Victor is standing beside the booth. Jasmine hops down allowing Victor to slide into the seat beside George, and then she hops back up into the booth. If anything happens, Victor can escape with them.

****

The waitress arrives, and we order our food and drinks. I order water and a steak for Jasmine, a double decker burger with chips and a soda for myself. Victor orders a rare steak for himself and a soda. My "grandmother" orders a salad for herself and tea. If I hadn't gotten confirmation this was not my grandmother, her food order would have confirmed it.

George orders steak, a double decker burger, a portion of chips, mashed potatoes, bread, apple pie, and cream, and a large soda. The waitress's eyebrows rise in surprise at the large order. I wonder exactly how long he had been chained up for.

"I'm sorry," George mumbles as he flushes bright red in embarrassment. "I'm just so hungry."

"No need to be sorry you're safe now," Victor replies.

In silence, we wait for our food. George's stomach starts making noises, as if it finally realizes it's going to get fed, and now can't shut up. At last our food arrives. George attacks his, and everyone else digs hungrily into theirs as well.

Once we finish eating and everything has been

cleared from the table, I calmly turn toward the woman impersonating my grandmother and asked her, "So who the hell are you?"

Everything goes quiet. If a pin dropped, you could have heard it and tracked its path. Then my grandma's impersonator stabs me.

Chapter 14

I quickly knock her out and curse at the knife sticking out of my leg.

"God dammit, where did she hide that?" I exclaim in exasperation.

I quickly pull out the knife and heal myself, and then wipe the knife clean and pocket it. I cannot take the risk of leaving blood behind. The waitress had rushed over the moment the commotion at our table started. She looks at us not sure what she'd seen.

"Hi, can we have the check please?" I ask politely my arm wrapped around my grandmother as she rests her head on my shoulder. "My grandma doesn't feel well," I explain.

She quickly gives us our bill, and Victor pays. We hustle out with me "helping" my grandmother.

"Okay, we need a safe place to go. Somewhere where we can find out who this really is," I say giving the woman I'm supporting a shake. "And to keep you safe, too," I add looking at George.

"There's a Bed and Breakfast in the next town. We need to get George someplace safe, preferably out of Paradise Falls," Victor supplies.

"Okay, we'll need my car. Can umm, you get it for me please, as you'll be a lot quicker?" And then on a quick thought, "Can you drive?"

"Yes, I can drive. Give me your keys. I'll be back

soon."

I fish my keys out of my pocket and hand them over. Victor quickly disappears. We carry on walking. After a couple of minutes, George helps me drag the unconscious woman.

****

"How long were you...?"

"Chained up," George supplies.

"Yeah."

"A week, well I think it was a week. I don't know how it even happened. I mean one minute I was talking to you, and being an ass, the next minute I arrive home and wake hours later, chained up and feeling weak. The worst was feeling helpless." His chin trembles making him looking like he's going to cry again.

With effort, he pulls himself together and gives me a shaky smile. "I don't know who she is, or why this happened. What I do know is she, if she *is* a woman, gave the orders.

"There were two werewolves with her, and they were huge. But they did what she told them to do and when she told them to smash her face and break her legs, they looked terrified, as if they could already imagine the punishment they would get for doing it, even though she told them to do it!" continued George in a terrified whisper.

"I've never been so terrified in all my life," he finishes on barely a whisper.

In sympathy Jasmine goes to him and presses her side against his leg. I awkwardly pat his arm from where I can reach it while holding up the woman between us.

I'm thinking she's been unconscious a long time

when she tries to make a break for it. Jasmine must have been thinking the same, as she runs in front of her and trips the woman up. With a high-pitched curse, the woman falls flat on her face, and I jump on her back knocking her out again. Poor George almost passes out from fright. He's been through a lot, and I don't think he can handle much more.

"George, do you know someone called Benny?" I suddenly ask as I sit on the unconscious woman.

"Benny? Yes, he's my butler. Why?" Surprise flickers across his face at the sudden change in subject.

"He tried to get me to come to you this evening. He said you had sent him to my grandmother's to retrieve me," I reply trying to figure out how to phrase my answers.

"Why would he do that? I never told him to. Mind you I haven't told anyone to do anything since being abducted," George replies remorsefully.

A couple of minutes later, we hear a car speeding toward us. Quickly I jump off the woman and drag her into the bushes. Jasmine herds George into them, and I gesture for them to get down. Following my own instructions, I crouch down too, keeping my ears tuned toward the oncoming vehicle.

As it comes closer, I realize I definitely don't recognize the car, so we all flatten ourselves down even farther and listen to it speed by. A couple of seconds later we hear it screech to a stop and reverse. It drives into the trees where there is no road.

I share a look with Jasmine, and I hear George's gasp of shock. Guess none of us knew about that particular entrance.

"Fucking hell." I gasp in sudden realization and

punch the unconscious woman in the head. At George's squeal of terror, I give him a look. "It's where she tried to make a break for it," I all but growl in anger.

A couple more minutes pass before we hear another car coming at a regular speed. This one I recognize as mine, and I quickly hop up to wave Victor down. As he pulls over to the side of the road, I gesture for the others to get into the back seat. Once they're safely inside with George buckled, I close the door and collect the woman from the bushes.

Hefting her up over my shoulder, I run to the boot and dump her inside. This time I search her and remove her phone, switchblade, and keys. I quietly close the boot and run to the passenger door, climb in, and close the door as Victor drives off.

****

We reach the next town just before dawn, but Victor carries on driving through it. We pass through Bandon without stopping, and turn off at the next exit on the left by Innishannon where we finally stop. George is snoring happily in the back, and Jasmine's resting. Every now and again, she'll shift ever so gently, or lift her head up to see where we are. At a nod from me she stretches and gives George a gentle nudge to wake him up. He wakes with a start and looks like he's about to pee himself and throw up.

"It's okay, George, you're safe," I murmur quietly, so as not to frighten him any further.

"We're letting you out here," Victor informs George in a matter-of-fact voice.

"I don't understand. Where am I, and why can't I stay with you guys?" whines George in a petulant voice.

"We're in Innishannon. You'll be safe here, and you can go wherever you want to. I can't take you where we're going, and I would advise you not go back to Paradise Falls any time soon, as it's apparently not safe for you there," replies Victor. He hands George a wad of money.

"There's a hotel a bit farther down the street, and a bus stop in front of it. I have to take care of the demon, and I don't fancy the police wanting to know what's in the boot if she starts banging on it again. George, you'll be fine, you're safe."

After five more minutes, George finally gets out of the car, slamming the door closed. He glares at us, with his arms crossed as if to change our minds about leaving him behind. Victor puts the car in gear and drives off.

I see him glance at me out of the corner of his eye, as if wondering if I will say anything about leaving George behind. Victor's right, we can't get caught with a demon who looks like an old lady in the boot. As for taking George with us, I don't even know where we're going, but, I agree, George isn't safe in Paradise Falls, our ultimate destination. In answer to his silent question, I give him a slight smile of understanding and close my eyes to rest.

As dawn approaches, the sky pales and starts to brighten with shades of gold and red mingling with blue. The birds wake and start their morning chorus, and my jaw cracks with an enormous yawn. It has been a long twenty-four hours, and I'm knackered. Victor gives me a smile as he glances in my direction.

"We're almost there," he whispers.

I don't know where almost there is, but I'm

surprised at how much it doesn't bother me. I trust Victor, end of story, so the details don't matter.

****

Ten minutes later, we arrive at our destination. Where it is I still have no idea, but it is beautiful. Trees, with cherry blossoms surround us, and give off a wonderful scent. We drive through an orchard and pass some ash trees, and then all hell breaks loose in the boot. Screaming and banging, you'd swear my grandmother's impersonator was being tortured.

"What the hell is going on?" I demand in shock.

"Ash trees." At my question mark of an expression he elaborates further. "She's a demon, and their weakness is ash trees. Not sure why, but they can't travel through them, so this is the most secure place to keep her," Victor finishes with a shrug.

I glance wearily at my boot, wondering if the demon woman is going to break out of it.

During the start of the commotion, Jasmine had crawled off the back seat and onto the floor of the car, keeping as far as possible from the boot. If I had been driving, we would have landed in a hedge the moment the ruckus had started.

With a wary eye on the boot, both Jasmine and I sit stiffly for the rest of the short journey down the lane and toward a garage. Victor reverses into it, so the boot of my car is at the back. Finally, Victor turns off the engine. I fling open my door and scramble out of the car as if it has turned into some bizarre terrifying creature that is about to attack me. Jasmine, I notice squeezes through the gap between the front seats and follows me out of the car.

"We won't be staying long," Victor gently

reassures us as we move further away.

"Thank God," I mutter in relief, as I give the boot another wary look as the ruckus increases.

****

I have just taken a look around and am surprised at how large it actually is. It's a double garage with a huge workbench at the back, with a bright red toolbox sitting neatly on the right hand side of the bench, and an old red toolbox on the left hand side. What surprises me the most is the height of the ceiling. It's at least 14 feet high, and so are the doors. Why hadn't I spotted that earlier?

Suddenly, a very large man appears beside Victor between one breath and the next, making me jump. Seriously, he is huge, at least seven feet tall and built like a brick shit house, with hands like sledgehammers. I would not want to mess with him!

A voice like gravel erupts from him in a language I don't understand, until my brain realizes he's speaking English, but with his words together. What he said was, "What did you bring them here for?" but what I heard was "Whatdidyoubringthemherefor?" And with a low gravel rumble, I thank my lucky stars I managed to decipher his words at all.

"They're friends, Little Michael. They're okay; it's the demon in the boot that's the problem. Is your father here to give us a hand?" Victor smiles as if to sooth a frightened child and let him know all is all right in the world, as the demon in the trunk screams bloody murder and hammers on my boot.

I give him a weary look at hearing his name. Is this some kind of joke?

"He'scomingnow," rumbles Little Michael.

I'd just managed to break up the words, "He's coming now," when it feels like a mini earthquake is shaking gently under our feet.

"It's okay, ladies. It's just Big Michael, Little Michael's dad coming," soothes Victor with a reassuring smile.

Jasmine and I take a superstitious step backwards toward the back of the garage, and at the same time a step closer to each other, just as Big Michael enters.

At thirteen feet, Big Michael is humongous. His body is half his height, but packed with bulging muscles, and his arms look like tree trunks. He swings his round bald head around to take in the situation. As his eyes land on Jasmine, he acknowledges her with a polite "Shifter." When his round silver eyes land on me, he pauses, his big eyes grow larger, and the silver of them grows much brighter, until they look like quicksilver swirling in his eye sockets.

"We've waited a long time for you, Double Magick Woman," Big Michael rumbles at me with a slight smile. "Have you read the prophecy yet?" Big Michael enquires curiously.

"Um, no, we don't know where it is," I reply, wondering how he knows I have two different kinds of magick in me.

"The old ones took it somewhere safe. I'm not sure where though, but you do need to read it." Big Michael nods before turning toward Victor who is gaping at me in surprise.

"Close your mouth, Victor. You're not trying to catch flies," Big Michael rumbles with a gentle laugh, before turning toward my car boot and the demon inside who at last has gone silent.

****

I watch as Big Michael and Little Michael move swiftly toward the rear of my car. As Big Michael towers over Little Michael, I realize Little Michael is a teenager. Flipping hell, where was the mother? And how big is she?

Looking at Little Michael, I can't help wincing a little at the idea of giving birth to such a large child. I soon stop wondering as Little Michael releases my boot, swinging it open, and all hell breaks out as the demon erupts from it.

Big Michael grabs hold of a leg and drags the screaming demon back toward him, with an impatient growl, and one of his sledgehammer fists knocks her on the top of the head.

"Be quiet, demon, you'll wake the baby, and my misses will be pissed." At these seemingly innocent words, a shudder rolls through the demon and she slumps to the ground, her ankle grasped firmly in the paw of Big Michael's fist, as he hoists her up off the ground and wraps his arm around her waist. With a nod to me, he exits the garage, hostage firmly secured in his crushing embrace.

Little Michael pauses in front of me and with a shy smile gives me a similar nod and glides after his father and hostage. Victor turns to look at me, about to say something, but shakes his head, before closing the car boot, and silently indicating we should get in.

I open the back door for Jasmine who hops in and sprawls across the back seat. Closing the door behind her, I open the front passenger door, climb in, and buckle up.

Silently we drive off, back through the wooded

drive and head back the way we'd come, until we come to the turning to Innishannon where we bypass it and instead go straight. I gather this is so we won't run into George again, which is fair enough. I'm exhausted and Jasmine is already fast asleep.

I glance toward Victor and am surprised at how tired he looks. With a guilty start, I remember he had been awake the whole night driving.

"Victor, do you want me to drive for a while?" Turning to look at him, I patiently wait for his answer.

With a startled look, Victor gives me a grateful smile.

"If you would, I would appreciate it. I'm exhausted," Victor admits.

****

We pull over and swap seats. Once we're both belted up, I indicate I'm pulling out and drive off. I keep to the back roads the whole way home, and finally we pass through Courtmacsherry. A couple of minutes later I drive into Paradise Falls. I head for my house even though I want to go straight to my grandmother's. Once home I wake up Jasmine and then Victor.

"Where am I?" Victor enquires groggily.

"You're at my house. Come in and sleep," I reply before getting out and opening the door for Jasmine. With an enormous stretch, she leaps from my car, gives me a happy tail wag, and trots off in the direction of my grandmother's.

"Where's she going?"

"To my grandmother's to make sure she's okay." Locking up my car, I head up the steps to my house with Victor walking beside me.

Unlocking my door, I brush my hand along the

wall as I enter my new home in greeting to the house. A feeling of warmth surrounds me and Victor as well, from his gasp of surprise.

Chapter 15

"Welcome to my home, the old Winters' house." I wave a hand about to indicate my home, turning to Victor with a smile.

"Do you want anything to eat or drink, before going to sleep?" I mumble suddenly feeling shy.

"No. I'm fine thanks, just exhausted." Victor smiles at me in a reassuring way, as if to sooth my nerves.

I lead him upstairs to the spare bedroom (my office has a small bed). With a look at Victor, I admit to myself I don't want for him to sleep down the hall from me. I'd rather he sleep with me.

I want the fantasies I've been having about him to come true, but I'm unsure of myself, and we're both exhausted. But...taking a fortifying breath, I turn to Victor. "This is the spare room. You can sleep here, or you can sleep in my room." On this bold statement, I walk out of the spare room and into my own bedroom.

As I open my bedroom door, Victor suddenly grasps me by the hips and pulls me hard against his lean body. His manhood pulses through his jeans straining to reach me.

"I want to stay with you, Candi, but if I do, we won't get much sleeping done, that I promise you." His rich dark velvet voice lowers to a pulsing growl, making every nerve in my body scream in anticipation.

My stomach muscles quiver, and my womanhood moistens in readiness to the promise in Victor's voice and body.

I step out of his grasp and turn toward him with a wicked smile curving my mouth. "Promises, promises. Why don't you show me how you're going to keep me awake." My voice sounds like a wanton purr with my demand, surprising me.

Without another word, Victor pushes me gently away from him and into my bedroom, crosses the threshold, and closes the door behind him. Silently he grasps hold of my wrist and pulls me against his rock hard body. Gently, he runs his hand up my arm, and over my shoulder and neck to cup the back of my head. His other hand, snakes around my back to hold me in his embrace. Placing my hands on his muscular chest, I explore the contours of his torso through his top. I reach up and drag his head down to my waiting mouth.

With the gentlest of caresses, we explore each other's mouths. In silent agreement we open up and deepen our kiss. His tongue brushes mine and twines with it, before retreating into his mouth, where mine chases after.

With a groan coming from deep inside me, I deepen our kiss and rub my body against his, making me feel like a cat in heat, as my arms circle his waist, grasping his firm ass and hauling him even closer to my body.

With a low growl, Victor grasps me by the ass and hauls me up his body so I have to wrap my legs around his waist. I move my arms quickly around his neck, one hand delving into his thick ebony black hair. Damn his hair is soft! With a muffled purr of acceptance, I thrust my hips into his as Victor walks us to my bed, gently lowering me on it. He reaches around his back and loosens the laces of my boots, before pulling off first one and then the other.

Quickly I yank off his T-shirt and stop kissing him long enough to pull it over his head and toss it away, and for the first time I see his naked chest.

"Oh my," I murmur in awe and reverence at the sculpted beauty of his body. I realize my imagination was sadly lacking as it did him no justice at all. Leaning forward I lick his chest and gently bite him.

With a growl from deep inside, Victor grasps my jacket and removes it, pulls off my vestie top and sports bra with quick efficiency, then with such gentleness, he runs his fingers along the sides of my torso before spreading his hands over my ribs to cradle my breasts.

He gently massages them before bending his head to suckle at my left breast causing my nipple to tighten and stand at attention. Removing his mouth, he gives my nipple a last lick, before moving onto my other breast to continue his ministrations.

My busy hands have been exploring all I can reach of his chest and back, now my fingers trail down his velvet skin, to meet the waistband of his jeans. I grasp his buckle and pull it undone after a slight fumble.

I tackle the button of his jeans, and finally, with a cry of satisfaction, the button comes undone, and I slide the zip down and reach inside to release his pulsing manhood. It springs out to meet me with eager expectation, pulsing with a life of its own. Grasping the long thick velvet phallus, I experimentally squeeze it before stroking him swiftly, and giving another gentle squeeze.

Victor releases my breasts and stands up to shuck off his jeans, shoes, and socks. He bends over and removes the belt with my knives and gun, unbuttons my trousers, and pulls them and my knickers off in one smooth motion. Lifting my left foot, he pulls off my sock and kisses my instep before releasing it, repeating his actions with my right foot.

Instead of lying down beside me, he spreads my legs and kneels between them. Reaching for my hips, he drags me forward so his head nestles between the V of my thighs and places my legs over his shoulders.

Keeping one hand splayed across my stomach, with his other he opens the lips of my labia and inserts a finger into the moist welcoming entrance of my body. He gently stretches me before pushing in two fingers as he watches me, thrusting his fingers in and out while rubbing my clitoris.

****

With a gasp and moan, I try to push away from his knowing talented fingers. Panting heavily I demand, "I want you now, Victor, please." I'm begging by this stage, and my voice breaks on a sob of need.

Removing his fingers, I reach for him, but his mouth replaces his fingers, and his tongue infiltrates my vagina and mimics his fingers' earlier actions until I come with a gasping shout of release.

Victor finally stands and climbs onto the bed. He lifts me farther back onto the bed before penetrating me with his long, hard, thick, pulsing penis, gently at first, allowing me to adjust to the largeness of him.

With small thrusts and retreats, Victor inches his way inside me, until at last he's fully sheathed within. He pauses for a second to give me a gentle kiss of reassurance, before thrusting harder into me. I wrap my legs more firmly about his shoulders and reach down and cup his balls with one hand, and stroke them as he thrusts harder and faster.

His eyes normally a beautiful silvery green now glow with a blue fire, just like they had the first time I had seen him. A second later, I can feel my second orgasm rise inside of me, and Victor gives me a very satisfied smile, as he senses it growing, his fangs protrude from his full bottom lip as he thrust harder and faster with a sensual twist of his hips.

I thrust my hips to meet his, and clench my muscles to tighten around his manhood every time he withdraws, just to push back inside harder and faster.

Finally with a scream of pleasure my orgasm ripples through my body bringing on a third one, as Victor gives a final thrust into me and roars his completion, before collapsing on top of me. Wrapping his arms around me, he rolls onto his back, and I lay sprawled on top of him.

****

"I'm sorry, I meant to take my time," Victor apologizes, as he caresses my back and buttocks with gentle circular motions, arousing me once again.

"No need to apologize." I laugh with a slight pant as I recover my breath, before kissing him.

A second later his penis lengthens and thickens inside me once again, and with a startled look, I meet his beautiful silver green eyes, just as blue fire bleeds into them and his fangs elongate.

"You're eyes and fangs," I murmur as I trace his lips, and prod a fang with my index finger.

Victor gives my finger a gentle nip and a lick. "I'll

never hurt you, and my eyes change color with intense emotions," Victor explains, as he stares intently into my eyes, as if begging me to believe him, but unsure if I do.

I lean down and kiss him again, letting him know I trust him. For answer he thrusts up into me, and we start our dance once again, this time with me on top. I sit up and meet his thrusts, lifting my hips off him, only to thrust back down to meet his rising hips. Victor sits up, and I wrap my long legs around his waist still rising and falling onto his penis.

"Do you trust me not to hurt you?" His voice sounds rougher than his usual velvet tones.

I give him a startled look, and gasp yes, just before Victor suckles my nipple and pierces it with one of his fangs.

Pleasure shoots through me almost making me come. With a wide-eyed look, I grind my hips into Victor's, and tighten my muscles around him in a tight velvet grasp, before releasing him. Victor releases my breast to move onto its twin, suckling and piercing it, before continuing his delightful suckling.

With pleasure shooting through my breasts, I speed up the tempo our bodies are dancing to, until I feel a ripple shudder through me as the beginnings of another orgasm lifts its head inside me.

The magick inside me starts dancing, and I let it seep between us, making Victor gasp as heat enters his belly. As he lifts his head in shock and pleasure, I give him a sultry smile and grind myself into him again, before lifting off and thrusting down harder.

Victor twists, so I'm on my back with my legs still securely wrapped around his waist, and starts thrusting deep into me. I unwrap my legs and lift them onto his shoulders, making every thrust penetrate that much farther. My hands grasp his ass, and I dig my nails in forcing his hips back to mine, until our bodies speed up to our final climax. This time when we collapse and untangle our sweat-slicked bodies, I notice the pink tinged fluid of Victor's ejaculation.

Seeing my look Victor explains, "A vampire's body fluids, sweat, tears, and ejaculation, are always blood tinged as we are just blood and water. Though I'm sure you know already we can't procreate, or carry disease, hence no need for condoms. Though, I normally do use them," Victor admits going slightly red.

"Oh my God, are you blushing, Victor?" I laugh in shock. "Actually I didn't know for sure, you're the first vampire I've met, so anything I know about vampires is from books, and I have no idea how much of it is real. So dhampirs aren't real?"

"No. Though I have heard rumors…I don't see how they can be, as that would mean we can procreate, if extremely rarely."

"As for protection, I use magical means," I reply with a laugh, feeling puzzled at Victor's uncertainty.

At Victor's curious expression I release my magical condom. A cone-like wisp slides from my body bringing with it the last of Victor's sperm.

"Obviously, this is something I would normally do in the bathroom," I add with a grimace. With a wave of my hand, the mess disappears and clean sheets are left behind.

"Where did it go?" Victor stares blankly at the spot that a minute ago held a magical condom and sperm.

"In the toilet where it belongs." I grin as I get up. "I'll be back in a sec." I hurry out of the bedroom and into the bathroom. Quickly I check to make sure the magical condom had arrived in my toilet, sometimes magick can go awry, and thankfully this is not one of those times. I tidy myself up and prepare for bed before returning to the bedroom. As I re-enter I let out a huge yawn almost making my jaw crack.

"Come here." Victor's voice holds a note of demand yet is soothing. He extends a hand to me.

Crossing to him, I take his offered hand and allow him to pull me onto the bed. I willingly curl into his embrace, the blankets tucked up around us.

"Go to sleep, Candi," Victor whispers as he gives the top of my head a gentle but fleeting kiss. "It's been a long and exhausting day, and we need our strength for what's to come. Rest now, Candi, sleep well."

Those gentle words are the last I hear before I fall into a deep exhausted sleep, safe in the warmth of Victor's embrace.

****

The next morning I wake up still anchored to Victor's side, which is nice, but weird. Nice because it has been a very long time since I had taken a lover. Okay, more than nice. I can get used to it, which I'm not sure is a good thing.

The weird part of it is, well, I'm technically in the embrace of a dead man. Granted a drop dead gorgeous dead man, but a dead man nonetheless. On such a strange and slightly creepy thought, I untangle myself gently so as not to disturb him, and leave my bedroom to go to the toilet and have a shower.

To my surprise, I feel sore, as if my muscles

haven't been used so completely in years. With a shake of my head and a secret smile on my lips, I catch a look of myself in the mirror, and pause to take a really good look. My skin glows a wonderful peaches and cream with a rose blush about it. My eyes sparkle like emeralds with a secret, and my mouth is plumped and rosy from Victor's kisses. Looking further down my naked body, I realize all my skin is flushed, as if it has come alive during the night, especially around my erect nipples, which are still throbbing from the piercing of Victor's fangs.

Surprise filters through my mind as I realize they haven't healed, and drawing my magic toward the happy points of my breasts I heal them. Almost instantly, the rosy flush dissipates and my body turns back to its normal shade of peach. Quickly I go through my morning routine. Once washed and dried, I return to my bedroom to dress for my morning run.

I notice Victor is still sleeping and decide to leave him where he is. Grabbing my jacket and throwing it over my tank top I head downstairs, collect my keys, and leave heading toward the woods and my grandmother's house.

****

It'd rained at some point during the hours we'd slept. The damp smell of the grass and smell of rot from leaves and animals are quite potent this morning. Underneath the smell is a trace of burnt hair and sulfur.

With a sinking feeling I investigate. As I duck under low-hanging branches and squeeze between fallen trees and rocks, I am thankful to find the corpse of a deer.

With the way my luck was going, I had been half

expecting another murder by *The Protectors*. It's still an unnatural death, but one caused by a supernatural creature, most likely a witch going by the smell. But the killing would have been for black magick purposes.

So not good. I groan in annoyance, as I rub my hands over my face in sudden exhaustion.

I fish my camera out of my pocket, and take photos of the surrounding area and the deer's corpse. I return to the trail I'd left, and carry on to my grandmother's, this time at a faster pace.

The sooner I can get to her house, the sooner I can find out if she knows anyone who uses black magick, the better, and maybe safer, we all will be. Black magick is not something to mess around with, and practitioners of the dark arts are not to be trifled with.

With my feet pounding along the uneven track, prickles of warning, shiver up my skin, letting me know the witch who'd killed the deer was still there. With a grunt of effort, I lean forward and run faster, my calves beginning to burn with the strenuous effort I'm putting them through. With a sob of relief, I spot the roof of my grandmother's house. Pounding out of the woods, I peg it across the grass and hit the drive with a skid of my trainers.

Losing my footing, I go down hard smashing my knee into the gravel, and scraping the shit out of my hands. With a grimace of pain, I scramble awkwardly to my feet, and carry on at a limping run until my injuries have healed completely. Once again I speed up, and at last hit the porch steps of my grandmother's house.

Grandma Eve, with Jasmine at her side in dog form, opens the door before I can knock. I fling myself through the door, pushing both of them inside before slamming it behind me as I lean panting against it. I slide down it to land in a heap, trying to catch my breath. Grandma Eve disappears only to come back a moment later with a glass of cold water in her hands, which she promptly passes to me. Taking the glass from her, I take a grateful gulp, and then climb unsteadily to my feet.

"Thank you, Grandma," I say, with a wave of the glass in my hand, almost spilling it.

"What's happened?"

"Someone killed a deer in the woods." My voice comes out in a breathless wheeze, so I take another fortifying sip.

"I know it's not nice to kill them, but sadly people do." With exasperation lacing her voice, she gives me a condescending look.

"Yes, but, do they normally use black magic to do it?" I exclaim in annoyance. "I wouldn't have come running here as if the hounds of hell were at my heels, unless it was important, Grandma." A scowl of annoyance wrinkles my brow as I glare at my grandmother.

I glance at Jasmine, thinking she's awfully quite when I notice her staring unrelentingly at the door her ears pricked to attention. With a start, I remember when I'd fallen, I'd cut myself and some of my blood must have dropped onto the stones. Flinging open the door, I rush outside.

I hear a cry of alarm coming from my grandmother, and Jasmine barking, but I ignore them both, and call with power for my fallen blood to come to me.

"Blood of mine, fallen this day

Come to me, leave none behind
Danger comes, to do away with me
Blood, fallen of mine, return to me."

With a *crackle*, power leaps from me like lightning in a whirlwind, heading straight for the area where I had fallen, and farther back toward the woods. Suddenly, we hear a shout of surprise and a curse, the lightning wind returns to me. I hold out my hands, and the wind gently deposits the gravel with my blood on it, into my palms.

"Thank you. Blessed Be." I release my spell.

****

Turning, I walk back into the house, past Jasmine who keeps an eye on the woods, and past my gaping grandmother, straight into the bathroom where I wash the blood off the gravel, and deposit it in the bin. I storm out of the bathroom and round on my grandmother.

"You know more about what's going on here than you've told us," I fume, my eyes narrowing to slits, as I feel the truth of my statement shimmer through me.

My grandmother gives me a cold, calculated look, before responding.

"Everyone knows more than what you've been told. Oh come off it, don't look so hurt." Eve laughs at the look of betrayal flashing across my face.

"Surely you honestly can't believe no one was aware of the killing of humans and the black arts? You're not stupid, Candi," Eve cruelly lashes out.

"I really don't know you, do I?" I quietly ask, even though I don't expect an answer.

"How could you? You left me years ago, to what— make a family out of the likes of her?" Eve's scream of

146

rage is unexpected, and I think it shocks her, too.

"What became of you, Grandma, for you to change so much, you would willingly sacrifice the life of an innocent and take part in black magick?" Shaking my head in disappointment, I look at my grandmother properly and see a layer of darkness surrounding her aura.

"The darkness is attaching itself to your aura, Grandma," I tell her with sadness lacing my words. I turn away as I feel tears pool in my eyes. I will not cry in front of her, I will not. "Let's go, and Grandma, if you change your mind about the path you're following, you know where I am." Breaking into sobs, I open the door and leave with Jasmine by my side, my grandmother staring after us, with darkness attached to her and bleeding into her eyes.

"Not everyone has the power you have; some of us need to take it." Eve's shout of frustration follows me.

As we hurry away, I wonder, what could have possibly happened to make my grandmother power mad. Doesn't she know how dangerous too much power is? As we enter the woods, I'm not sure if I hear my grandma crying in anguish and heartbreak.

****

Peering out of the woods, he watches with cruel eyes, as Eve Allhallows crumples in her doorway, sobbing, as her granddaughter and that dog of hers walk into the woods. He notices with a disgusted snort, how some of the darkness leaves Eve, as she acknowledges her wrong choices in her loneliness and greed for power. With a final glare at the weak pathetic woman, he thoughtfully looks in the direction he'd seen the granddaughter disappear and decides to follow.

Chapter 16

Slowly, retracing my way through the woods, I mull over what I have found out. What had changed for this to happen? It had to be something big surely, but…

"I don't understand, but how can I, when the only person who can give me the answers is my grandmother." I fling my hands up in the air, as if this act will give me the coveted answers I need to understand what was happening, and why.

"I just don't understand." Silent tears trail down my cheeks, and I brush them away in frustration. Crying will not get me answers.

Leaning her furry body into the side of my leg, Jasmine gives an understanding and sympathetic whine.

"This is so much bigger, we need the others." With a nod of resolution, and pleasure that I can take some form of positive action, I hurry home.

****

Letting ourselves in through the back door, I'm puzzled to hear the sound of men talking. Quickly we cross through the kitchen, down the hall, and into the sitting room. Victor and Kheda, who a moment ago were chatting like old friends, look at Jasmine and me in concern.

"Are you two okay, you look like…has something happened to your grandmother?" Concern flashes across Victor's face, and he crosses over to me. He gently rubs my arms, as if the simple action can erase all my hurts. I realize with a start of surprise, that he genuinely does care what happens to me. How is it possible he can care for me after such a short time?

"My grandmother...my grandmother is practicing black magick, and so are...I have no idea how many others." I try not to cry, even though my voice is thick with emotion.

Kheda appears shocked, grinding his teeth he jumps up from his seat and starts to pace. "Are you sure?" His voice is demanding, as he swings around to look at me.

I give him a withering glare that could peel his skin from his bones.

"Okay, obviously you're sure, but how do you know? I mean, your grandmother? Black magick, are you really sure? Because if you are, this is bad." Kheda trails off, as he sits down heavily in the nearest chair, and puts his head in his hands. Rubbing his face roughly, he looks up and with a big sigh nods. "What do we do?"

Taking a deep breath, I let it out, look at Jasmine, give a nod of my head I come to a decision.

"Jasmine, go upstairs and put some clothes on. There is no need for you to stay in dog form anymore. Kheda, we need all the information on what happened at the hospital, without anyone else knowing. Someone knows something, and they're hiding it pretty damn well. Victor, have we let Benny go?"

"Is it safe for her to be in human form?" Kheda's voice changes to concern, as he watches Jasmine leave the room and trot up the stairs, fear and apprehension flicker over his expressive face.

"We need her in human form, and to be honest, it won't make any difference anymore. If no one knew she was a shapeshifter beforehand, they will now." A tired sound escapes from me as I watch her climbing the stairs. I hope I'm doing the right thing by insisting she transform back and hope it isn't just to fulfill my own need to have my friend back.

****

A few minutes later, Jasmine comes skipping down the stairs, wearing tight soft jeans that hug her lean body and worship her long legs, a black vestie top and trainers. Her long black hair is pulled back into a ponytail swishing happily from side to side.

"Okay, how about we all go out for lunch?" she demands, grinning at everyone in pleasure at finally being able to stay in human form.

"Sure, but where?" I look around at the others. Seriously, where would it be safe for a shifter, werewolf, vampire, and witch to go grab a bite, without having *The Protectors* ready to kill us?

"We could go to my bar, if you want. We do sell food, and the chef is pretty talented."

"Yeah, sounds good to me," Kheda agrees, in obvious relief. "No one would look twice at different species being together in a vampire bar, though we will still have to be careful."

"Okay, let's go." I look at myself. "Umm, I'll meet you there; I need to shower and change clothes." I quickly head upstairs to strip off what I'm wearing and set out some fresh clothes.

I decide to wear my trainers, just in case I need to move quickly. Heading to the bathroom, I turn on the water, climb in, and have the quickest shower on record. I dry off, dress and slap on moisturizer, before running my brush through my hair and tie it up. It will dry in its own good time.

I hurry downstairs and am about to leave when I decide to cast a quick protection spell on my house and land. I have no interest in black magick being done here. Negativity on that level, I do not want or need. I light a white candle for purification, and cast my spell.

"Let no unwanted guest be allowed
To enter or harm my home or land.
Let all be safe, be you animal or human.
If upon my place, I protect thee.
Allow my guests safe passage
To come and go.
As I wish it
As I have said it
So mote it be."

Blowing out the candle, I collect my wallet, and stuff it into my jacket pocket on my way out, locking my front door behind me. It is so quiet, for a second I feel afraid. Everything is going to shit around me, and I don't know what to do about it.

Shaking my head, I cross toward my car and decide at the last moment to walk instead. After all, apart from a psycho killer running around, it was a nice day out. Walking at a brisk pace away from my car, I begin to wonder what kind of food a vampire's bar supplies, when I feel a tingle of awareness shiver up my spine.

Someone is here who shouldn't be. I pick up my pace a bit more, but not enough for anyone to realize I know I'm being watched. I think about tracking them, but decide against it. I don't feel any threat just curiosity.

****

After a couple of minutes, I exit my property and arrive on the main road, feeling a bit safer but still rattled. I keep up my pace and finally reach East Bridge and hurry across to the other side. Once my feet touch down on the other side, every bone in my body relaxes. Heading to the free car park, I enter the woods, crouch, and look back toward the bridge.

I spot my grandmother, standing in the middle of the bridge looking around. Shaking her head, she crosses back over and walks toward her shop. Was she following me? Was it my grandmother I'd sensed earlier trying to enter my land? No, it definitely wasn't her. Could it be a coincidence she'd spotted me?

"Ahhh, enough already," I mutter in annoyance. I can't try second-guessing what I just don't know. It will drive me crazy.

Shaking my head, I stand with a grimace. If anyone had spotted me muttering to myself in the woods, they would definitely think I'm crazy! With a snort of derision, I scurry along to Vlad's Bar, but keep to the woods.

I feel a strange sense of safety in them; actually, it's probably a stupid sense of safety, due to the fact I have found three bodies in the woods. With this thought I speed up. With a feeling of relief, I finally arrive at the bar. With a final glance around, I step through the door and straight into darkness.

Chapter 17

The darkness is complete. I can't even see my hand in front of my face. I know because I wave it in front of me just to make sure. Just as suddenly as the enveloping darkness surrounds me, it's gone, and I'm in a beautiful bar with an oak counter and tables and red cushioned stools and chairs. Simple tapestries adorn the walls and a great fireplace covers one wall near the bathrooms, with a peculiar old wooden chart listing species eye color:

VAMPIRES = BLUE EYES
WEREWOLVES = GREEN EYES
SHAPESHIFTERS = SILVER EYES
WITCHES = GOLD EYES
DEMONS = ORANGE EYES
ZOMBIES = YELLOW EYES
FEY = PINK EYES
HUMANS = NO LUMINOUS COLOR CHANGE

I take all this in and the gaping faces. Why is everyone staring at me? Have I stood in something? With a discreet sniff, I rule out that scenario thankfully.

"Okay, why are you all staring at me, and what's with the weird chart?" I inquire, pointing to the eye color chart above the fireplace.

Clearing his throat Victor stares intently at me. "It's a species eye color chart."

"So my eyes changed to gold, weird, but okay,

what's the problem?" I demand. Seriously, why are they all staring at me unless…?

"Your eyes went violet, not gold. I've never heard of anyone having violet eyes…what exactly are you, Candi? I mean, I know you're a witch, but are you more? But how can it be? I mean, it's not possible right? But Big Michael did call you Double Magick Woman…"

Victor, who has been steadily pacing stops in front of me, stares into my eyes for what feels like an eternity. With a spreading smile, and a slight shake of his head, Victor seems to come to a realization that causes him great pleasure.

"We have got to find the book of prophecies."

"Okay, actually we have to stop a murderer." Looking at Victor I wonder if he's okay. "What is the big deal about this prophecy book anyway?" I finally demand in frustration. "I mean seriously, I never heard of it until a couple of days ago.

"Was it really only a couple of days? Flipping hell! Anyway, never mind about how long it's been. What was I saying…?" I trail off, going slightly red at how quickly I fell into bed with Victor, flushing even redder when I realize I can't wait to repeat such a fantastic experience again, or…I put the brakes on my mental thought. I don't want or know how to finish it.

"Look, let's get you something to eat." Gently taking hold of my hands, Victor leads me to the counter so I can order. The bar is thankfully empty, except for our small group and the barman, who appears to be in shock.

"Okay, well, that was different," laughs Jasmine breaking the ice.

"Certainly one way of putting it. Here's the menu, Candi, and…yeah." Kheda trails off, for once looking at a loss for words. Rubbing his left hand over his mouth, he seems to shake his surprise off. Looking at Jasmine, he finally relaxes.

"Thanks. I could murder a mug of coffee, if you have any please," I ask the barman who still hasn't moved. Opening the menu, I peruse it, giving me time to gather my thoughts. "Okay, can I have the hot chicken salad, a jug of water with lemon in it, and my mug of coffee please?" I politely ask the staring barman. I look at the others with a raised eyebrow.

"We've already ordered, but asked Simon not to send our orders up until you've given yours," Victor supplies. "Simon, can I have a quick word with you, please?" Excusing himself, Victor goes around the counter and out a door with Simon following him.

"So, what's with the strange sign anyway?" I ask, as I wonder what Victor is saying to Simon.

"It's so anyone who enters can tell what paranormal species has walked in. When you walked in everything went black for you, but we all saw your eyes light up with their supernatural color. Though, what yours is I have absolutely no idea…" Kheda trails off looking at the sign above the fireplace.

Crossing over to inspect the strange sign, I notice above Vampires there is a space, as if something else could fit. Seeing Victor come back, I call him over and point it out. With a look of surprise on his face, he lifts it down from the wall, gently runs his long talented fingers above Vampires = Blue Eyes.

With a look of resignation he goes to put it back, I reach for it spreading the tips of my fingers evenly across the area where something else could be written, before pressing firmly down into the old wood.

A quiet click is the only sound it makes, before the section I'd pressed smoothly lifts up to reveal a hidden compartment containing an old scroll. I reach in and remove the scroll passing it to Victor. I close the now empty compartment and attempt to put the plaque back.

Kheda moves quickly and takes it from me, hurriedly putting it back on the wall. He drags Victor and me back to the bar with a hiss of "Hide it," directed at Victor, nodding at the scroll in his hands.

****

I watch Victor quickly stuff the scroll in his pocket, and with great effort shake the surprise from himself, just before Simon arrives carrying a jug of lemon water with four glasses, a pot of coffee, and a mug which he puts in front of me.

"Thank you, Simon. Shall we sit at a table?" Picking up the tray, I march to a table big enough to hold all of our food and us comfortably, which thankfully happens to be in the farthest corner away from the bar. Imagine that!

I quickly unload my tray and pour myself a glass of water and a mug of coffee. I guzzle my first glass of water, and then happily sip my coffee. Jasmine, Victor, and Kheda grab their drinks and follow me. Once we're all seated, I turn to Victor expectantly. When he doesn't move, I blurt out, "Are you going to open it or what? Come on, I'm going to explode from curiosity if you don't." I encourage him, as I practically jump up and down in my seat.

Looking at me, Victor bursts out laughing, extracts the scroll from his pocket, carefully unrolls it, reads it to himself, pauses and rereads it again before looking at us with a baffled expression. Finally he hands it to me to read.

Victor,

Time's gone by with no hope of the Pharaoh's book of prophecies being realized. I've kept it by me these many years, but now I will put it somewhere safe.

Follow the clues I leave behind to find it. I only hope I'm doing the right thing, and it is you who finds the two magicks one. Be careful on the quest I am sending you on, and only share this with those you trust with your life, and mine as well. The Protectors *have many who would stop you from finding the book of prophecies.*

Remember, to find what is missing you must retrace your steps to where you saw it last. Be safe, find the two magicks one, and destroy The Protectors *once and for all. I hope to see you again, but I fear it is a wish not to be realized. In this life and the next, I wish you happiness.*

V

"V is your sire?" I ask for lack of anything else sensible to say.

"Yes. It seems we need to...ah, here's our food." Victor smiles as he quickly takes the scroll from me re-rolls it and puts it in his pocket in a blink of an eye.

"Tattoo Parlor is very good, and I definitely recommend going there," I hastily say.

"Thank you, I was wondering if it was any good because of its name more than anything," Jasmine replies as she scrunches up her face prettily. "Oh yummy, our food has arrived and I am starving." she beams at Simon, making him smile back at her.

"Rib burger and chips?"

"Yay, that's mine," states Jasmine, licking her lips in anticipation.

With a smile, Simon places her dinner in front of her.

"Mashed potatoes, sausages, and peas?"

"Mine thanks," Kheda scowls, obviously not impressed with this pup of a boy looking at Jasmine in such a way.

Seeing Kheda's expression, I stifle a laugh, which turns into a cough. Catching Victor's eye, I realize I'm not the only one trying not to laugh at Kheda.

"So the warm chicken salad is yours." Simon smiles as he passes me my dinner.

"Thank you." Smiling back at Simon, I take my plate from him, only to notice this has caused Victor to glower at the poor man. My salad looks divine, crispy lettuce, hot chicken, peppers, carrots, croutons, hot baby mushrooms, coleslaw, and grated cheese with a Caesar dressing drizzled over it. Hmm, yummy. I can feel my mouth watering in anticipation.

"Ah, and your steak, Victor," flushes Simon, as he quickly passes Victor his dinner before scuttling away.

"Poor boy, you two are terrible," I murmur, with a nod of my head toward Victor and Kheda, so they know whom I'm talking about. I fill my fork up with delicious crispy salad, chicken, carrot, and coleslaw before popping it into my mouth and munching away on it happily.

Stifling a laugh at their expressions, Jasmine

hastily bites into her rib burger and moans in delight.

****

Silence descends on our table, as we all dig into our food, until with a happy sigh we all finish. Leaning back in my chair, I drink my coffee and pour myself another mug topped off with loads of milk. A comfortable silence descends on us, broken eventually by Jasmine inquiring about the scroll.

"What did it say?"

Victor quickly informs them, and we all sit in brooding silence for a while longer, until Simon arrives to remove the plates.

"That was lovely, thank you. Can you give my compliments to the chef please?" I beam.

"And mine as well," Jasmine pipes up. "Man it was divine."

"No problem, ladies. I'll pass on your compliments." Simon smiles before hurrying away with the plates.

"So what happened earlier to upset you so much," Kheda inquires curiously.

I quickly update Victor and Kheda on the morning's events. Surprisingly it doesn't take long to do so. I tell them what happened on my way to the pub.

"I think we should all stick together as much as possible. I mean, if they're using black magick, we can't take any chances. Also carry plasters with you. If you cut yourself, you need to make sure you don't leave any trace of your blood behind. Blood magick is the most powerful, and trust me, you don't want to mess with a witch pumped up on blood magick," I finish with a grimace of distaste.

We fall into contemplative silence for a while, each

of us digesting all we've found out, until Kheda's phone rings. Standing up, he walks away from the table before answering it. All of us have exceptional hearing and by the looks of it, everyone is trying not to listen to the one-sided conversation.

Until we see the blood drain from his face. Now he has our full attention. A second later Kheda hangs up and runs a shaky hand through his hair, returns to us. A shadow flits across his face, and in that second he arrives at a decision.

****

"*The Protector's* have struck again, three werewolves, two vampires, and a witch. Apparently they were killed at different times over the last couple of weeks. It could be the same killer who killed the human you found in the witch's woods. I want all of you to come with me. I know I'm asking a lot…"

Without giving Kheda time to finish his sentence, we all stand and put on our coats. "I'll have to go to the bathroom quickly before I go, and then I'm ready," I interrupt before hurrying off to the bathroom. A second later Jasmine joins me, and as quick as we can, we do our business and hurry back to where we find Victor waiting.

"Kheda had to go to the toilet as well," he explains with a smile.

"Victor, do you think the two vampires could be the missing ones?" I ask quietly.

Exhaling noisily Victor looks at me. "Probably, the time is about right, but we'll never know as it will be ashes we find," Victor replies in frustration.

Kheda exits the bathroom, and we leave. We all realize at the same time we have no cars with us.

"How far is it?"

"Hunters Park, inside the caves," answers Kheda with a grimace.

"Okay, let's go," I grumble as I start off at a run. A minute later the other three join me, and as if in one body we speed up.

As we pass people, we receive some weird looks. Someone else curses us, but since we're running on the road, I don't get what their problem is. Then again, it's not often you get such a weird bunch of supernaturals together, let alone running as if the hounds of hell are chasing after them.

Ten minutes later we arrive at Hunters Park and turn left toward the caves, located at the far left corner. Within a couple of minutes, we notice the yellow tape cornering off the crime scene, and a crowd of people surrounding it. A couple of harassed-looking officers try to keep everyone back. The scent of fear is intense and makes my nose itch, but there is another scent underlying the fear, not as strong, but there. It takes me a second to realize it's glee.

Someone in the crowd is enjoying themselves. I come to a sudden stop, and Victor runs straight into me. I would have fallen on my face, but he grabs me and steadies me. Kheda and Jasmine stop beside me with puzzled expressions.

"Do you not smell it?" I demand trying to find the source.

"Smell what?"

"Glee. Someone is enjoying themselves, immensely. The scent is just under the fear, but it's there," I answer as I sniff the air.

With a perplexed look at me, Kheda and Victor

start sniffing to catch the scent. I know the instant they do, because their eyes widen in surprise. Jasmine had started sniffing the air the moment I had mentioned the scent, so she caught it first.

We try scanning the people to see if we can spot someone who looks happy, or have an emotion on their face screaming I did it, but wherever he or she is I can't find them.

****

Gleefully he watches the commotion at the cave. Serves them right for taking trophies. Soon they will be arrested, and their idiotic behavior will be stopped. The Protectors *are not for pleasure of ownership, but prevention of cross bloodlines. His extra killings will go toward framing the imbeciles, especially the female werewolf.*

A grin of pure pleasure at his cleverness spreads across his face. Quickly controlling his smile before anyone else notices, he looks around in time to see the detective arrive with Eve's granddaughter, a vampire, and a female shapeshifter. Noticing them stop and sniff the air he decides it's a good time to leave. Eve's granddaughter had sensed him following her earlier. He did not wish for her to catch his scent again. With a final smug look, he disappears into the shadows.

****

We move toward the taped-off area where an officer is trying to convince people there is nothing to see. Strangely enough, no one seems to believe or listen to him. As we move toward him, he lets out an annoyed huff, until he spots Kheda.

"These three are with me, Foster," Kheda informs the officer, indicating the three of us.

"You might not want to take civilians in with you," Foster replies with a look of distaste on his face, as he looks at us before he moves the tape aside to allow us through.

I share a look with Jasmine, and going by her expression, she can't tell if his dislike is at the crime scene, Kheda, or us. With a slight shrug off my shoulders, I cross over into the crime scene and follow Kheda to the caves. As we near them, the scent of evil surrounds us. The smell of death hits us in an overpowering stench. I stop and glance around.

"Is there a stream around here?" I look around while trying to breathe through my mouth.

"Yes, there's an underground one inside the cave. Probably explains why they're inside instead of out."

"What I would like to know is, why was the human killed elsewhere when the rest of them are here? I mean, if most of the victims were killed around the same time as the man in the woods, why wasn't he murdered here as well? Why was it so important he be found first?"

A second later, a young officer rushes out of the cave and throws up in the nearest bush.

"You okay?" Kheda offers the shivering officer a tissue, while looking at him in concern.

"No, I'm bloody well not all right. Fuck, how someone can do something like that I have no idea!" The young officer wipes his mouth with the tissue, his hands shaking badly, his face pasty and sweaty.

"Stay out here, and make sure no one else comes in," Kheda instructs the officer. Turning toward the three of us he nods, then heads into the yawning mouth of the cave.

Chapter 18

The cave's musty damp smell blends with the scent of coppery blood and death. Someone had set up sconces to light the way. I'm surprised, until I notice the stiffness in Kheda's shoulders and the tightening of his mouth as he glares at the sconces, and guess it wasn't the police who had done this. We're met by a burly detective who glares at us, before pulling Kheda to the side to have a word with him. Seriously, does he not realize we can hear him?

"Detective McKnight, I want to know, why in all that is holy have you brought civilians with you to a bloody crime scene?" The detective growls his question at Kheda, displeasure dripping from his voice.

"Detective Callahan, these civilians are here to help identify the victims. Also they're helping me on this case. Now is there anything else?"

I notice the respectful tone Kheda uses with the zombie detective. Even though they wouldn't be able to socialize due to different species regulations preventing interracial socializing, it's obvious Kheda respects him, but it's also obvious he is annoyed. The detective is dismissive toward the three of us, even though if the circumstances were different, I believe Kheda probably would react the same way. After all, civilians are normally not brought to crime scenes. Kheda must have been having the same thought process, as suddenly he lets out a disgusted sound and shakes his head in exasperation.

"No, I've nothing to tell you, except I've never seen anything like this, so be careful, detective, you and your helpers," Callahan replies curling his lip in disgust, before exiting the cave.

****

The first body is that of an old woman. She'd been propped up against a plank of wood, against the wall of the cave. Apparently wood plays an important factor in the killings. Like the previous victims, the old woman's mouth is smiling a gruesome smile, with her intestines displayed around her. But unlike the other victims, the old woman's hand is beckoning us further into the cave. Taking a closer look at the woman, I recognize her as the rude witch from my grandmother's shop, the one who had wanted a revenge spell. What was her name again?

"I recognize her from Magick of Old."

"You know her? What's her name?" demands Kheda glad to have a lead.

"No, I don't know her. I served her once in my grandmother's shop," I correct as I try to remember her name. "She was after a revenge spell, but I wouldn't give her one, and her name was Mrs…Mrs. Hayes, I think."

"Sounds about right," agrees Jasmine, studying the corpse of the old woman. "It's the smile that made me not recognize her at first."

At this, Kheda and Victor stare at her, as if she has two heads.

"It's why it took me a moment to recognize her, too," I admit.

"Bloody hell, what an unflattering way to be remembered," Kheda states with a disgusted snort.

"Look, at least we remember her, and we only met her once so give us a break," I growl in annoyance. "But we did see her last night, at George Seabast the Fourth's house," I add in surprise. "Unless it was someone impersonating her, or she was killed straight afterwards." I stare in befuddlement at the dead woman. We were gaining more questions than answers.

Ignoring me, Kheda withdraws a notebook from his pocket and writes in:

FIRST CORPSE: WITCH.

NAME: MRS. HAYES.

Peering over his shoulder I watch what he writes. With a snort I mutter, "Yes, so much more flattering."

With a huff, he puts his notebook away and proceeds toward the next body. Once he has a clear view, he comes to an abrupt stop.

"Fucking hells bells, he was supposed to be away on a camping trip."

"I gather you know him?" Jasmine quietly asks as she rests her hand on his shoulder.

"Yeah, yeah, I know him. He's my cousin."

In shock, we stare at the dead werewolf. I see the pain in his blue eyes and realize just how young the victim is, eighteen at most. His shaggy brown hair is artfully messed up. He must have taken ages each morning to get it just right. His young face was just beginning to show the promise of adulthood.

He was a handsome kid and would have broken a lot of hearts if he had lived long enough. His hand is also beckoning us deeper into the cave. A chill skitters its fingers down my back, as I take one last look at the young werewolf.

Slowly we leave Kheda's cousin behind, as we proceed to the next corpse. Just around the bend we find a female werewolf. She looks about twenty-five, with big brown eyes and shoulder-length blond hair. Her face and breasts have been mutilated.

"I think the killer could be a woman." I move closer to the dead woman and realize she was beautiful.

"Why do you say that?" A puzzled frown pulls across Victor's forehead.

Turning to look at Victor I point to the dead woman, and in a calm voice reply, "Jealousy. What was done to this woman was done because the killer was jealous. She was beautiful, but the killer couldn't leave it at taking this poor woman's life. She had to destroy her beauty."

Looking at the young woman, I shake my head. "Up until now I was assuming the killer was a man, but now I'm positive it's a woman." Going by the look of comprehension dawning on the others' faces, they had been assuming the same thing.

Leaving the woman behind us, we carry on to the next corpse. What we find has us all staring in horror.

Bile rises in my mouth, which I force down with considerable effort. Before us, the two vampires and the last werewolf were laid out in lurid positions. All three have been stripped of every inch of clothing.

The female vampire lay on her back on top of a wooden board, her jaw forced wide open, her full lips pulled back over her elongated fangs. Her eyelids removed, so even in death she couldn't block what was before her.

The male vampire knelt with his head between the

female's legs, his arms locked in a position to support his weight, his palms holding the female vampire's hips. His eyelids had also been removed.

The male werewolf stood behind the male vampire. His eyelids had been removed, his hands secured onto the vampire's hips. A strap around his waist is securing him to the vampire. All three of them share the same wooden board.

****

"Oh my God, this is really, really sick," I whisper putting a shaking hand over my mouth. "How the hell did…Have they been…?" I gasp in shock as I notice bruises on the werewolf.

"What the fuck are you on about?" Kheda angrily demands. "Oh." Realization dawns as Kheda follows my glance, and his face pales in shock.

I kneel down so I can have a better look at the male vampire and spot similar bruising on him, too.

Feeling even sicker than I had when I first saw them, I look for a source of water. A little further, I find the stream. I take a couple of minutes just to breath and get my heart rate under control, before I head back to the others.

I find them exactly where I had left them, all of them, looking pale and grim.

"Do any of you know them?" I quietly ask.

"No."

"Do you want me to take pictures?" I finally ask, feeling sick at the thought.

Kheda closes his eyes and turns toward me with a disgusted look on his face until he realizes it is a job I would prefer not to do.

"Please, we need the pictures. This way we can

study them away from the precinct, if necessary."

Taking a minute to compose myself, I remove my camera from my pocket and start to take pictures. I systematically walk through the whole cave, starting at the stream and finishing at the mouth of the cave.

Once I develop the photos, I will be able to do a complete reconstruction of every wall, floor, and ceiling, as well as every angle of the corpses. If there is anything to find, we will find it. Once I've finished, I put away my camera, and we leave in complete silence.

****

"I need a shower, badly," I murmur. The smell of fear and death cling to me in a slimy coating, with a horrible scent of glee, floating underneath it. I scan the crowd again this time looking for a female. I spot the nervous young woman from my grandmother's shop, and she still looks nervous to my eyes. I continue scanning and spot some people from The Witches' Brew and from random meetings in town. None of them stand out as a stark raving mad killer.

We leave quickly the way we'd come, I notice people regarding us curiously as we pass through the crime scene tape. Ignoring them, I hurry past and away from the caves as fast as I can, without bringing any further attention to myself.

Soon we leave the stench of death behind. Instead of going home, we walk farther into the park. Beautiful lush green grass rolls over the landscape, which is dotted with flowers and trees of all types. Ash, birch, and oak abound with a lot of rowan scattered among them.

Looking at all the rowan trees, I begin to have an idea of how the killer is preserving the dead vampires who should have disintegrated. Moving farther into the park, I head over to a more wooded area and find a group of about thirty rowan trees near a stream. I plod over to the stream and find a family of toads. With a sinking feeling in my stomach, I go back to the rowan trees and search the branches.

"What are you looking for?" a frustrated Kheda demands as he watches me search the trees.

"Did you know the rowan tree is a magical tree?" I ask, as I carry on with my search.

"Umm, I'm not sure. I think I might have heard fairy tales about the tree when I was a kid." A frown of concentration furrows Kheda's brow as he tries to remember what he'd heard.

Jasmine and Victor move closer so they won't miss any of what is being said.

"Several of these trees have either branches or bark removed from them. The rowan tree is a very powerful magical tree. Wands are made from it, and it can be used to prevent bodies disintegrating, like the vampires we found. They must have drunk something with rowan bark in it, probably blood, or they have a part of the tree inside them somehow. There is a family of toads by the stream; they have toxins, dangerous toxins that cause muscle paralysis."

At the three blank expressions, I spell out what I think happened to the victims. "The vampires most likely drank from the killer, who is using rowan in her food or drink, which would have prevented their bodies from disintegrating when she killed them. She would have used the tetrodotoxin from the toads to paralyze them, so they couldn't move while she murdered them. They would have been aware of everything she did to them."

"What kind of person could do such a thing?" Victor demands as he practically spits out his question. Angrily he starts pacing in the short space between the trees before coming to a stop in front of me. "Who could have done this? Who would have the knowledge to do this?"

Looking into his tormented eyes, I notice the anguished face of Kheda, who is most likely thinking of his young cousin, and finally Jasmine who looks just as pissed off as Victor. "I'm thinking a witch. Well, the knowledge is from a witch at the very least," I amend.

"The thing is *The Protectors* would have the information on file. They've been killing for God knows how long, so the first witch would have given this information when they joined. But with the black magick ritual from earlier and the fact the human man was found in the witch's woods, I still think it's a witch doing these murders."

I plop down on the wooded grass and lean my back against the rowan tree nearest me. I feel exhausted suddenly, physically and emotionally drained.

"There is one thing I don't understand though," I add feeling completely puzzled. "If they are paralyzed how is the male werewolf standing? Everyone else has always been leaning against something to keep them upright or in the male vampire's case kneeling. I know he's strapped to the vampire, but how are his legs able to support him?

"Kheda, can you get someone to find out if the werewolf has braces inside his legs. I don't remember seeing any stitches, but if it's a witch doing these killings, she could have easily healed his wounds so no one would notice."

Removing his phone, Kheda phones in the question, while a distinctly green color tinges his face. With a gruff "Thanks, keep me posted," he hangs up.

"I think you should all stay at my house until this case is solved. I've put wards up for protection, and the house itself protects and lets us know if anyone enters the land's boundaries. Why don't you get some clothing and anything else you might need and meet us back there?" I quietly ask Victor and Kheda.

Victor crouches in front of me, so he can make direct eye contact with me. I guess he doesn't want to miss any reaction to his question. "Are you sure it's wise? All of us being seen together could cause *The Protectors* to come after us next."

"That's just it; whoever killed them has seen us all together today at the crime scene. By rights the only one of us who should have been there was Kheda, but we went with him as part of his group. We are now all most likely on the killing list if we weren't already," I finish bluntly, making Kheda blanch white in shock, as he realizes the ramifications of his actions.

"Fucking hell, I'm sorry. I didn't think of the killer being there when I asked you to come with me, though I should have, as murderers are known for revisiting the scene," he stammers in mortification.

Placing a gentle hand on Kheda's face, Jasmine smiles at him. "There's no need to apologize, Kheda, we needed to go, and sooner or later, we all would be on the list." With that statement she kisses Kheda, wrapping her arms around his neck until with a groan he pulls her closer and eagerly responds by plundering her mouth.

"So we stay at yours. What then?" Victor asks ignoring Jasmine and Kheda.

"I think...I don't know, Victor." Shaking my head as if to confirm my lack of knowledge. "But I do believe we need to stick together. Whoever the killer is they're not who you would expect.

"She possibly managed to trick two vampires into drinking from her, but at the very least she managed to take them together somehow and talk three werewolves into going with her or meeting her somewhere she wouldn't be disturbed. Paralyzed them and moved them to the cave. But she would have to have been someone the old witch knew and trusted.

"She was looking for a revenge spell, and she was mean, not someone who would trust easily, I don't think. Though, mind you, she could have been easily caught unawares and just taken, more of an opportunity killing than a planned one."

I feel I'm on the right track with this line of thinking. But who the hell is the killer, and how did they find the time to do all of the murders?

****

Kheda's phone rings, interrupting my swirling thoughts. His silence speaks volumes, his face flushed a moment ago from kissing, drains away to a grayish color. In silence he hangs up, dragging a shaking hand through his hair. He looks at us with wide, shocked eyes. Shaking his head, he collects himself before telling us what the officer on the other end of the phone had told him.

"The werewolf had braces inserted in his legs to keep him standing. The female vampire had a wooden stake inside her with the end sticking out. The end was in the male vampire's mouth." Rubbing his face vigorously as if to wipe away the knowledge he had just received, Kheda looks at our shocked faces and shudders.

"When the male vampire was moved, he disintegrated. We have got to find the bitch who killed them," he growls as anger rumbles up inside him, changing his face into a savage expression. "I'll go get my stuff, and meet you all back at your house." Grabbing Jasmine, he gives her a fierce kiss before stalking off.

"I'll walk you out of the park, and then I'll go and get my stuff."

"No, get your stuff, there are two of us, so we'll be the safest out of all of us," I object.

With a stiff nod of acceptance, Victor kisses me then flits away.

"Why didn't he fly off?"

"I don't know, but I think we should hurry up and get home," Jasmine replies giving me a gentle shove out of the trees.

In silent agreement, we instinctively take the long way around to try and avoid anyone who might be lurking about. Twenty minutes later, we exit the park and head to West Bridge and cross it. We hurry past the college campus and diner we ate in yesterday. Was it really only yesterday we rescued George and my grandmother's demon impersonator? Blimey, time is either going slowly, or I needed a holiday! "I need a holiday," I decide.

"Yeah, me, too," Jasmine agrees with a disheartened sigh. "Or a drink. Actually, I'd settle for a drink right now until this mess is over, and then we can go on a sun holiday."

On that thought, we stop at the supermarket, buy a bottle of whisky, a bottle of rum, a two-liter bottle of cola, a six-pack of lager, three pizzas, and a bag of chips. With our arms loaded, we get in line to wait our turn to pay.

"I'm serious, they were allowed into the cave," a woman whispers loudly to the checkout assistant as she eyes us. "Why do you think that was, hmm?"

"I think you should stop your gossiping, Susan, is what I think," the checkout assistant hisses back. With a huff, Susan pays for her shopping and storms off, but not before sending us another pointed glance.

With a shake of her head, the till operative serves the next couple of customers as quickly as she can, and finally it's our turn.

"Don't mind Susan. She don't mean no harm, but she is a terrible gossip," Mary the till operative informs us as she puts our shopping through. "Just be careful, and try not to go out alone. You protected my aunt the other night in The Witches' Brew, which is why I'm giving you a heads-up."

"Thank you." I pay for our shopping and a couple of bags, pack, and hurry home. Thankfully, we don't meet anyone else. But the feeling of being watched is unmistakable.

Twenty minutes later, with a sense of relief I unlock the door, and we put away the shopping and bags.

Feeling contaminated from the twisted killings at the cave, as if some of their horror has seeped into me, I head upstairs to scrub myself clean. Once finished I switch off the shower, dry myself, and wrap the towel around me sarong style before exiting the bathroom.

I quickly dress, grab the airbed out of the cupboard, and go to my office where I already have a single bed made up for unexpected guests to sleep. I plug it in and collect my dirty clothes while it's blowing up.

With a grimace, I bring my washing downstairs. Remembering to empty my pockets, I put the washing machine on a long wash. Collecting my wallet, phone, keys, and camera I put my keys away in the drawer in the hallway, go back upstairs, and load the photos onto my laptop. Once done I save them and head to my room. I do not want to look at those pictures tonight.

I make room on my dressing table so I have space for my laptop and printer. Once this is done, I collect them from my office and set them up. I quickly make the airbed. Once finished I slowly go downstairs and straight into the sitting room. Feeling exhausted, I sit down on the sofa and curl my legs up beneath me. A minute later, Jasmine, looking tired but refreshed after her shower, enters carrying two glasses of rum and soda. With a moan of satisfaction, I gratefully accept one from her, and take a large slurp from mine.

"Thank you so much," I exclaim gratefully.

"You're welcome. Shouldn't they have arrived by now?" she anxiously asks. "I mean, it's been almost two hours since we last saw them." Nervously she stared out the window, tension straining every muscle in her body.

I get up and pad over to stand by her. Fishing out my phone, I check to see if I have any missed calls or messages, but no one has tried to contact me. As we stare out the window, we see a car coming up the drive. The tension leaves our bodies when we recognize

Kheda's car, which he parks beside mine.

A further feeling of relief washes over me as I notice Victor in the passenger seat. By the time they climb out of the car, we have the front door open. The guys quickly grab their stuff from the boot, and Kheda locks it behind him. A minute later I close and lock the front door behind them. We are all safe. The house seems to let out a pent-up breath as if it had been worried about us, too, startling Victor and Kheda.

With a smile of greeting, I inquire if they would like a drink first or to see the room they will be staying in.

"If it's okay with you, I would like to put my things away, then I'll happily accept the offer of a drink." Kheda offers me a grateful smile.

With the decision made, I lead them upstairs to my office. As we pass the bathroom, I point it out, so Kheda will know where it is. I take them straight to my office and apologize that they have to share. I might have slept with Victor once, but I'm not jumping to any sort of conclusions. Anyway, how do you ask in front of others, do you want to sleep with me? If Victor ends up sleeping with me, the sleeping arrangements will change accordingly.

"I'll leave you guys to unpack. I have to go and sort out my washing."

I scamper downstairs, and put my washing into the dryer, and let Jasmine know the washing machine is free. Personally, I'm beginning to get hungry so I put the oven on. Turning around, I smack into Victor's powerful chest with a little squeal of surprise.

"Bloody hell, Victor, make some noise in future. You frightened the shit out of me!" I growl, my poor heart pounding in fright, and maybe, a bit of lust as well to be honest.

"So you want me to sleep with Kheda?" Victor looks at me with a raised eyebrow.

"Well, umm, I'm not quite sure how to answer that, to be honest," I stammer flushing red in embarrassment.

"You see, personally, I would prefer to be sleeping in your room, with you!" Victor smiles as he gently massages my shoulders.

"You would? I didn't want to presume. You still can, if you like?" I shyly answer as I reach up to pull his head down to mine. Before our lips meet, I remember I'd forgotten to pay for my lunch.

"Oh my God, I haven't paid for my lunch," I blurt out in mortification. "I'm so sorry…"

"Don't worry about it. We all got rather distracted by a murder," soothes Victor. "Anyway, lunch was on me, so you wouldn't have been paying. Now, where were we before you interrupted us, hmm?" Victor gently grasps my chin to hold me still, so he can slant his mouth across mine, in a gentle but sensual kiss.

Chapter 19

I hear Jasmine whistling to let me know she's coming out of the utility room, so I quickly pull away from Victor as she enters, and Kheda comes in from the hallway.

"Would anyone like something to drink?" she asks, giving me a wink.

"Yes, please. What do you have?" Kheda replies as he eyes Victor and me.

Victor keeps massaging my shoulders, as if unable to lose complete contact with me, while I lean into his embrace, reveling in the feel of his touch. I know Jasmine is pleased I'm not running as fast as I can from whatever is happening between us, like I normally do.

I finally understand I'm ready to be happy and live life instead of putting romance on hold, no matter how short, or long it will be.

"We have whiskey, rum, cola, lager, or a mix if you want," Jasmine answers, giving Victor and me a big grin and wink of approval.

"I'll have a whiskey and soda please," Kheda replies, looks at Victor and me, gives a shrug of his powerful shoulders before looking back at Jasmine with a look of raw longing.

I hope he will take a chance. I understand his fear of losing her to *The Protectors*; I know the fear well, as if it's an old friend. But now, the fear has outstayed its welcome, and I'm taking a chance at happiness. I hope Kheda will too as Jasmine really likes him, and they would make each other happy.

"Sometimes you have to take a chance. Fear can't rule your life, or you'll never be happy." Jasmine quietly tells him, before turning her back on him to prepare his drink.

"I'll have the same please, if you don't mind?" requests Victor breaking the silence.

Disentangling myself from his wonderful ministrations, I take the pizzas and pop them into the oven. Casually, I turn to Victor. "You can put your things in my room, if you want to stay with me." Feeling the fiery red blush burning my cheeks, I know my bold statement has been ruined. Hastily I go in search for my drink. Where did I last have it?

I find it on the hallway table. I must have put it there when I'd locked the door. Picking it up, I take a fortifying gulp, move into the sitting room to stare out the window. Darkness has crept in at some point, I realize in surprise.

The world seems so quiet, and yet a twisted killer is out there somewhere, searching for her next kill. With a shiver, the image of the victims in the caves flashes before my eyes.

"They didn't drink from her."

"What did you say?" Kheda asks, entering the sitting room.

"They didn't drink from her. Sorry, the vampires, they didn't drink from the killer. The stake was keeping them both whole. It's why the male vampire turned to ash when he was moved. They didn't drink from her," I repeat in growing excitement.

"And this is important why?"

"It means, they didn't trust, or know her well," I reply as if it was obvious. "Look, if I'm right, Mrs. Hayes the witch was an opportunity killing; maybe she was on the list. But probably more a personal list, than anything else. The werewolves and vampires I believe were targets, but they didn't know the killer intimately. So we're probably looking for a witch who works in a public place. Someone who comes into contact with and is able to observe all supernatural species. Sees who they're associating with, to create her list. But it has to be someone the victims would be comfortable to go with, maybe even meet."

"Okay, I get where you're coming from, but it describes a lot of people, Candi. I don't see how it helps to be honest."

"Okay, how about this then. You're looking for a female witch, about thirty years old, give or take. She's plain to look at, but is physically fit, though she would disguise her athleticism by wearing ill-fitting clothes. She's also used to talking to people, but will come off as non-threatening.

"Someone who is easy to talk to and trust. But someone who is easily forgotten. Someone who could ask for help and because she is recognized for always being nice and friendly, no one would hesitate to offer their services.

"She would drive something with a large enough boot to comfortably hold a large werewolf, maybe even two bodies as she would have to have taken the two vampires together.

"And finally, she lives alone or at the very least, if she lives with someone, they would be a family member she controls. At home she will have her own gym, probably a treadmill, weights, and a punching bag.

"So Kheda, does that description help?" I take a sip of my drink, still staring out the window. The silence in the room is deafening, so I turn around to look at Kheda, to see why he's so quiet. At some point Victor and Jasmine had joined us. Jasmine gives me a thoughtful look, while Victor and Kheda just gape at me in surprise.

"I think you're right," she agrees as she thinks of my description. "She would have to work either part-time in the morning, or a split-shift, to serve the college kids and the morning commuters. But she needs to be finished at lunch time; or she works the evenings, maybe both."

"Yes, she would have to work near the college campus either side of the bridge. Definitely not the witch village, except maybe the supermarket, but I doubt it," I add excitedly.

"She would need a convincing ruse, to be able to send one vampire away to collect something for her while keeping the other with her. No way in hell would she be able to take care of two vampires, without one escaping or attacking her in defense. Not unless she had help…" I trail off in thought.

"How the hell did you come up with such a detailed description?" A look of wonder and bewilderment flashes across Kheda's face as he looks at me and Jasmine.

"When we were in the army, we were in a special assignments unit. We would profile a suspect, before going after them," I quietly reply thinking back to those days.

In one sense they were the happiest times of my life. I'd made wonderful friendships and developed my magical abilities in unbelievable ways.

When I left Paradise Falls, I had no idea how powerful my magick could be, and I had no idea how freely developing my abilities and embracing them fully could enrich my life. But some terrible things happened while in the army, and before we all left, we essentially became a supernatural hit squad for the government.

Granted they hadn't realized what exactly we were, but they did know we could hunt down and find anyone. All we needed was a profile, or enough information to figure out a profile to hunt and track our suspect. Once we had information, there was no stopping us.

Taking a deep breath, I look at Jasmine and ask a silent question. With a nod, she looks at Kheda and Victor and lets out a large sigh.

"Ask them first if they agree, then summon them," she replies.

"Ask us what?" Kheda demands, as he looks at us in puzzlement.

"When we were in the army, we were part of a specialized team that could hunt down anyone once we had a profile. What we're asking is, if you would like us to summon the rest of our old team.

"If we summon them, they will come, and we will find the witch. The thing is...well, the thing is"...Taking a deep breath, I let it out in a great rush. "The thing is, the last time we were together changed us all. Our last mission we were on was a rescue mission, and we took revenge on the captor who had kidnapped a member of our team. We haven't seen each other since, so I'm not sure how it will go down…" I trail off.

There was no way in hell I was saying any more. That night we'd lost so much of ourselves, in fact we had almost lost our humanity. It was why we separated afterwards. I had thought we had lost Jasmine completely after rescuing her, when she couldn't change back.

I still don't know all that had happened to her, but when I remember how we found her, her poor body broken and bloody still causes a rush of red hot anger to burn and erupt inside of me. When we rescued her, she was in human form, and to help speed up her healing we encouraged her to transform, but fear kept her stuck, and we thought we had lost her.

Slowly but surely she healed, but only since meeting Kheda. She seemed determined to regain her human form, and now I was sending us into a dangerous mission once again.

The thing was, if we didn't go after the witch, eventually she would come for us. I glance toward her, and when she catches my eye, I see fierce determination staring back at me.

Clearing his throat to get our attention, Kheda finally says, "Make your calls. We need to solve this case and stop the killer."

"Actually, it's not quite so simple. We don't know where they are, so we have to summon them instead, but it can only be done on the night of the full moon. In other words, in three nights time," I say with a shrug of apology.

Victor is watching me with a quizzical expression.

I can almost hear the gears in his brain working overtime, as he figures out what I'm not saying, what he knows already, and putting the rest of the pieces together. I wonder if the pieces are in the right order.

****

We manage to rescue the pizzas just before they burn. I look at Victor and call him aside. I know he can eat food, as I've seen him do so earlier, but surely it's not what he actually needs to survive. I mean, don't vampires drink blood?

"Victor, don't you need blood to survive?" I ask looking him in the eye, even though I want to look anywhere else. I mean, what if all the stories are wrong and I'm making a complete fool of myself?

"Yes, I do, but I ate earlier, and brought some plasma bags with me. I put them in the back of your fridge. I hope you don't mind?"

"No, of course I don't. I just wasn't sure if the stories were true, as you were eating earlier at the pub."

"We can eat food, it just doesn't do anything for us, though the steak I had was rare, so the little bit of blood is better for me than other food. Sadly though, it's fresh human or supernatural, not vampire blood I need to survive."

"So the blood in the fridge…?"

"Won't sustain me for long. Even though it's human, it's not fresh anymore, so I won't be at my full strength in case of an emergency," Victor adds in obvious frustration.

I feel like laughing. Does he think I'm going to start looking at him as if he's a monster now that I know he needs blood for subsistence? Looking at his expression, I realize he probably does.

"In that case, take a little blood from me tonight, I will have time to recover from any blood loss, and you will be at full strength," I quietly tell Victor so no one else can hear. Gently I kiss him, tracing the contours of his handsome face with my fingers, as if imprinting his features into my memory for good.

The look of surprised pleasure on his face as he realizes I accept him completely makes me want to cry. His wonderfully strong arms wrap around me, pulling me flush against his powerful body. As he rests his chin on the top of my head, a hum of contentment escapes me. I feel at peace.

"You make me feel human again," Victor whispers before kissing me so gently, all his emotions coming to the surface, until a cough interrupts us.

"Sorry, guys, but pizza's getting cold," Jasmine informs us with a big smile on her face.

I extract myself from Victor's embrace, take his hand, lead him into the kitchen to get some pizza, and top up my drink. I look to Victor to see if he wants food or drink and receive a smile and a shake of his head in the negative. We join the others in the sitting room to munch our food in silence. I notice Jasmine and Kheda sitting so close, you wouldn't be able to stick a ruler between them.

A warm glow of happiness spills out of me, as I realize they are growing closer, like Victor and I. Did we have a relationship, and if so what kind? I ponder. As if in answer Victor drapes his arm around my shoulders and pulls me closer to his side. He keeps his arm there as if it belongs. I continue munching my pizza, but lean into him in welcome acceptance.

****

Once we finish eating, Kheda turns to me and asked about the photos. "Have you had time to print them yet?"

"No, I've downloaded them to my computer, but I haven't done anything else to them."

"Well, can you do so now, please?" Kheda demands in frustration. "We need those photos to help solve this case, so why haven't you printed them off already?"

"I'll get on it right away. Look, I know we need to solve this case A.S.A.P, but let me tell you something. I didn't want to look at those photos again today. Sometimes, you just need to have a break, so you can look with fresh eyes." I stand and take my plate and glass, dump them in the kitchen to sort out later, then storm upstairs to sort out the blasted pictures.

As I pass the sitting room I hear Kheda ask, "What did I say to upset her?" As if he honestly couldn't understand why I would be upset.

"Kheda, you're a good detective, but at times you're such an ass," Victor informs him in disgust. "Candi had to take the photos. We were repulsed at what we saw, never mind having to take pictures of all the different angles. Use your head, why wouldn't she be upset?" Victor walks out of the sitting room, where he finds me halfway up the stairs, where I had paused to listen.

Giving him a wry smile, I carry on up the stairs and into my room. I'm delighted he understands why I don't want to do the photos tonight, but Kheda has a point. The killer isn't going anywhere, and we need to solve this case, sooner rather than later. In other words, I had to suck it up and get on with it.

I boot up my laptop. Once done I pull up the photos and systematically crop and fix each one to my satisfaction, before printing them.

"What the hell is it?" Victor asks in surprise, staring at the printer on wheels, printing a photo of the back cave with the stream. "These are amazing," he marvels, just as a stunning photo of the werewolf and the two vampires is printed.

"You definitely have talent. I mean if you didn't know they were dead, it is an amazing photo…"

"Yes, but we do know, so it's gross beyond words, and depressing as hell," I say with a grimace of distaste, as I glance at the picture coming out of the printer in large exquisite detail.

Eventually all the photos are printed. Victor and I collect them and bring them downstairs, where Kheda and Jasmine sit talking on the sofa. I feel strangely peeved with them. I realize it's because I'm about to see the photos for the third time since taking them, and they're about to see them for the first.

Why is it okay for me to be put through this so often? With a grumble of annoyance, I give myself a mental shake. I have to get off this self-pity crap, and it's annoying the shit out of me. After all, there was no way in hell I would let anyone else go near my equipment!

"Okay, here are the prints." Crouching down I lay out as many as possible. But due to their sheer size, only the entrance and witch are shown in amazing detail.

Hearing a gasp from behind me, I turn to look at the shocked expressions on Victor, Jasmine, and Kheda's faces. Even though Victor had seen the photos coming out of the printer, and Jasmine knows how precise I am in my photography, it hadn't given them a heads-up to what I now displayed. They literally had a bird's-eye view of the crime scene, but from different angles.

"My god, these are amazing," whispers Kheda in awe and shock. "I'm sorry, I wasn't expecting this. I can almost smell the damp and decay just by looking at them." Kheda apologizes as the horror of the cave stares back at him, in stunning precise detail.

"Okay, this is what I'm thinking, if everyone helps move the boxes and furniture out of the room, we'll have enough space in here for at least two full sections at a time." Rubbing my forehead, I feel the beginning of a headache throb in the centre of my forehead, feeling like a distant banging drum.

We carefully collect the photos and bring them into the kitchen, depositing them on the kitchen table. We rearrange the kitchen and move the sitting room furniture and boxes in. By the time we're finished we're all exhausted and call it a night. Personally, I'm happy not to look at the photos again tonight, and I think everyone else is too.

"I think it would be wise for no one to go out alone. A minimum of two people out together, but no one left alone either," Kheda informs us as we troop upstairs to our rooms.

"Okay, but I go running every morning. Who wants to come with me?"

"I will," Jasmine answers in understanding. The moons pull is a powerful thing and has to be answered, even though there are still a couple of days before the night of the full moon.

"I need to go running as well. The full moon is almost here," Kheda echoes as if he'd heard my thoughts.

"If you go a bit later, Kheda, I'll go with you," Victor says coming to my rescue without even knowing it.

"Yeah, okay. I suppose all four of us running around the woods would be noticeable." Kheda laughs. It's the first time any of us have heard him laugh and the rich deep baritone sounds wonderful. Hearing a sigh behind me, I smother a smile as I realize Jasmine finds it very pleasing.

"Okay, good night, everyone. I'll see you at six a.m." I smile in gratification before heading into my bedroom with Victor on my heels. Closing the door behind him, I watch Victor lean back against it, watching me with sudden intensity. I feel my desire rise swiftly.

"At last we're alone," purrs Victor, as he pushes away from the door and stalks toward me, giving a wonderful impression of a great big panther. Grasping a hold of my hands, he reels me into his embrace, bringing me flush against his body. His arms wrap around me, as he bends his head to give me a thorough kissing. His velvet tongue delves into my mouth to explore every inch of it, before massaging my tongue with his.

Our tongues start a wiry dance as they twine around each other and withdraw, before plunging back into each other's mouths once again. I wrench my mouth from his, so I can breathe in some oxygen; once I've gulped in enough, I latch my mouth against his again, as if coming home. My arms circling his back pull him to me as one hand reaches for his hair and delves into the silky mass bringing his head closer, until our teeth smack. With a panting laugh, I withdraw myself from our embrace. Crossing the room, I close the curtains.

I notice the doubt in Victor's eyes when I pull away from him. Does he honestly think I don't want him? Crossing my arms in front of me, I grasp the ends of my T-shirt slowly pulling it up my torso, over my head before letting it slide to the floor. I reach for the clasp of my jeans slowly undoing them, pushing them down my long legs till they meet my trainers, which I toe off. I finished removing my jeans and socks, leaving me in my matching red lace bra and panties.

Most of my underwear doesn't match, but I'd hoped Victor would stay with me, so I made a special effort. Going by Victor's slack-jawed, wide-eyed appreciation, my effort met his approval. With confidence, I walk toward him, a sultry smile curving my mouth. I extend my right hand to him and then I'm in his arms again. I don't even see him move!

****

As his strong arms plaster my body to his, I feel his rock hard penis pulsing through his jeans, straining to reach me. My desire brings a flush to my skin, and my scent rises in anticipation of what is to come. I watch Victor through half closed eyes breath me in, so I surround him, inside and out. Blue fire bleeds into his eyes, his fangs elongate. He gently kisses me, before pulling away.

I watch at first in puzzlement, then in raw fascination, as he slowly removes his clothes until finally, he's wearing only his boxer shorts. His engorged penis pushes against the material, as if trying to reach me. With a gulp, I tear my eyes away from the fascinating sight, to lock eyes with Victor. Once we make eye contact, he pushes his boxers down, freeing his member from the confines of his clothing. My eyes widen in appreciation at the beauty of him.

Even though we'd made love the night before, I hadn't seen all of him. And what a glorious vision he is. Slowly so as not to frighten me, he pulls me flush against him once more. Wrapping his arms around me he lifts me up, and I wrap my legs around his waist, his penis nudges against my vagina trying to gain entry, my lacy panties preventing the joining we so desperately want. Reaching down I move them to the side allowing his hot shaft to slide into my waiting, moist cave.

Slowly, oh so slowly, I slide down onto his throbbing shaft. My heat surrounds him as I impale myself, holding him, squeezing him in my velvet grip, before withdrawing only to deepen my glide, as I stretch to accommodate his girth. Slowly we make love, gently exploring one another as I rise and fall on his phallus. We kiss, deep exploratory kisses, learning every contour of each other's mouths, until our climaxes ripple through our bodies, and we scream our releases into each other's waiting, open mouths.

"Drink from me, Victor. You will need your strength for tomorrow, if not tonight." My voice, husky and low, sounds more like a purr from a tiger than words.

"Next time," promises Victor as his penis thickens and he begins thrusting into me again. As the tempo of our bodies increase, he gently kisses the side of my neck, his tongue licking deliciously against me. Gently his fangs slide into me, and he drinks my blood. With every sip he takes from me, my body winds tighter, light and power rising up inside me. Just when I feel as if I'm about to explode in fiery ecstasy, he withdraws his fangs, a flick of his tongue to catch any stray drop, and my wounds close.

"What are you?" he gasps as he thrusts harder into my welcoming body, as my blood spreads its way through him.

"I'm me, I just have more magick than others," I gasp my reply, as I feel a second orgasm crashing through my body like a freight train out of control. I smother my scream of satisfaction by sinking my teeth into Victor's shoulder, breaking his skin and drinking the few escaping drops of blood, bringing him to completion.

"You bit me?" gasps Victor in shock, lying on his back panting, placing fleeting kisses along the side of my face he strokes my back.

"I'm so sorry; I've never done that before." My face blushing scarlet, I try to wiggle off Victor's powerful body.

"Shhhhh, there's nothing to be ashamed of, and to be honest, I liked it," Victor sooths as he holds me still. "If you keep wiggling, you're going to get more than you bargain for," he bluntly adds, with a deep chuckle rumbling seductively through his body, and vibrating beneath my ear.

"You can't be serious?" I gasp, giving a tentative wiggle, and yep, he is standing to attention again. I can't help feeling rather satisfied I can bring on such a reaction so easily.

We start our dance all over again, until finally I

collapse sweaty on top of him, my body so relaxed and my muscles feeling like jelly. I shakily withdraw from him, stagger off the bed, where I land on the floor in a heap. "Fucking hell, my legs won't support me," I exclaim in wonder.

"Where are you trying to go?" laughs Victor in delight.

Giving him a wry look, I blush bright red and admit I'm trying to make it to the bathroom. Valiantly, Victor climbs off my bed, kneels in front of me giving me a wonderful eyeful, picks me up and carries me into the bathroom, kisses me, and places me gently on the toilet before leaving and closing the door securely behind him.

I sit staring at the closed door for a couple of minutes, my fingers tracing my lips where I can still feel our final kiss. A goofy smile spreads over my mouth. Would I ever have enough of him? In shock I realize no, I wouldn't, as long as he wants me I'll stay and embrace our time together. I release my magical wisp of a condom and pee, wash my hands, hurry back into my bedroom, and straight into Victor's waiting embrace.

"I was just coming to get you. I wasn't sure if you would need assistance in returning to me," Victor says so quietly I have to strain to catch his words, as he strokes my body and leads me back to bed, where we climb in and I curl my body around his.

I just close my eyes to go to sleep when I feel Victor wrap his arms around me, anchoring me to his side, and to my shock he admits, "I've never wanted anyone as much as I want you. When I was human, I was more interested in adventure and satisfying my needs than in any relationships with women. After all, I was a young man and had my whole life ahead of me.

"When I was turned, my entire family was murdered, and I never allowed myself to become emotionally attached to anyone, be they vampire or human. I didn't associate with other supernaturals. It just wasn't heard of. But with you..." Shaking his head, Victor drags his fingers through his hair in obvious frustration and perplexity while sorting out his thoughts.

If this was anyone else I'd probably laugh, brushing aside what he's telling me as some kind of joke, but the moment he started talking my eyes popped open, and I witnessed every emotion flickering across his face.

My eyes lock with Victor's. The intensity in his eyes and the tautness in his body, informs me he's being deadly serious. I stay as still as possible, just in case he changes his mind and stops talking, but I maintain eye contact, letting him know I'm listening.

"You're in my blood," he grinds out between clenched teeth, "and not because I drank your blood either. I can't stop thinking about you, wanting you, needing you. I need you more than I've ever needed anyone else. More than I need blood. And since I need blood to survive, that frightens the shit out of me. But I can't and won't deny it anymore."

He kisses me fiercely, literally taking my breath away. Turning me on my back, he spreads my legs and thrusts himself inside me, pumping hard and fast as if trying to drive out memories and emotions until finally we both come. My orgasm rockets through me so fast and with such intensity I see stars. All I can manage is a gentle kiss before sleep claims me. My last waking memory is the feel of his lips kissing the top of my head as he wraps his arms around me.

Chapter 20

I wake up with my legs tangled with Victor's, and our arms holding each other tight. Even though I only had about five hours' worth of sleep, I feel so alive, relaxed, and happy. I untangle myself from my wonderful lover's embrace, and slowly climb over his sleeping body.

Gathering up my dirty clothes from yesterday, I put them in the laundry basket. I collect my running gear and head into the bathroom. Once dressed, I quietly head downstairs to meet Jasmine for our run. We exit through the back door and go straight into the woods.

Without a word we start off at a jog and run toward the cliffs. The morning sounds of the dawn chorus start up slowly as the birds awake. The rising sun infiltrates the denseness of the trees lighting our path, as a gentle breeze whispers hello, kissing our faces as it brushes past us, lifting the leaves and branches on the trees in a dance of happiness.

As we reach the cliffs, the morning sun embraces us warming our sweat-slicked skin. I take out my camera, and snap photos of the sun reflecting on the rippling water, of the cliffs, and woods. Of birds in flight as they search for food, and of Jasmine, as she stands at the cliff's edge, her hair lifted by the wind, the sun shining on her making her look ethereal in the morning light.

"Do you fancy going to your house?" I ask breaking the silence.

Jasmine turns to me, surprise flitting across her beautiful features. "My house? You mean you were serious when you said…?"

"Of course I was serious," I interrupt her. With a squeal of delight she launches herself at me, thankfully I'm closer to the woods than the cliffs, or we would have both gone over the edge! Instead, I topple backwards and land on the ground with her on top of me. With a laugh I push her off, and scramble to my feet, reaching down, I grasp her hand and pull her up.

Putting away my camera, I give her a big smile as she dances a happy jig in front of me. "So shall we go and see your house?"

"Yes, yes, yes," she squeals excitedly, dancing about.

"Come on then," I laugh, we run back into the woods toward the old ruins. The wind whispers and dances around us, sunbeams flicker in and out of the tree branches, until we arrive in the clearing of the old house.

The sun shines on the ruins and for just a second transforms them into a stunning redbrick two-story house, with slate shingles and flowers on every window ledge. In the blink of an eye, the ruins are back before us. With a gasp I look at Jasmine, realizing this is what she saw the first time we'd come. "We'll get the house signed over to you this morning if you like?"

Shaking her head in denial, she turns to look at me. "We can't do anything until this case is solved. We have too much to do." Sadness laces her voice as she looks at the ruins with longing.

With an understanding smile, I cross to her and give her a hug, and whisper, "I'll call my solicitor, and they can get the paperwork started. We can carry on with the case, and my solicitor can let us know when to sign the papers. This is your house. I don't see a need to postpone the signing, just because of a killer. Come on let's head back. I'm starving."

I turn and jog back to my home, with Jasmine beaming beside me. When we arrive back, we find Victor and Kheda waiting in the kitchen. Without thinking, I cross to Victor and kiss him good morning. He quickly wraps his arms around me pulling me flush against him deepening our kiss.

"Good morning to you, too." Giving me a wicked smile, a look of relief flashes in his eyes, when our lips finally disengage.

Laughing in embarrassment at my wantonness, I wish him a good morning back. "Sorry, I couldn't help myself."

"I hope you never can, because trust me, I like the way you say hello."

With a shy smile, I disentangle myself as my stomach lets out a yowl of discontent at not having been fed yet. "I'd better get some breakfast, or my stomach will eat itself," I laugh.

"We'd better go for our run as well," adds Kheda as his eyes hungrily devour Jasmine. "Where can we safely run without the likeliness of running into anyone else?"

"If you go out the back door and head into the woods, you can follow a path of sorts toward the cliffs. Follow our scents to retrace our path. It's a decent run and is part of my property. Also, you'll see Jasmine's house," I inform them. I notice her beaming smile out of the corner of my eye.

Pouring myself a glass of milk, I drink it quickly. I pour a couple of glasses of orange juice for us as we prepare breakfast. Between us, we have it ready in no time. Crispy rashers, sausages, hash browns, eggs, tomatoes, toast, and a pot of coffee. Carefully removing the photos from the table, we put them in the sitting room. Setting the table, we finally fill our plates. We put Victor's and Kheda's plated food in the oven to keep warm. We're hungrily eating ours when they return.

Getting up I remove their plates and put them on the table, then I carry on eating my food. After washing their hands, they join us at the table to demolish their breakfast. We eat in contented silence. With a laugh of surprise, I realize how at ease we are with each other. At their curious looks, I share my observations.

"You're right, I don't think I've ever been so at ease with anyone in such a short amount of time," Kheda agrees in surprise.

"Especially considering the circumstances that brought us together, though I'm definitely pleased we met," Victor agrees smiling at me. His smile grows bigger, as a pleased blush flushes over my cheekbones.

As a group we tidy up. Looking at the clock, I notice it's ten past nine, so I phone my solicitor, instructing him to start the paperwork to gift the old ruins to Jasmine and the surrounding land from the road to the house, excluding the old grave yard. I inform him to contact me when the forms are ready, say goodbye, and hang up on the bewildered man.

Turning, I head into the sitting room, where

everyone is waiting. With a sigh, I carefully lay out the photos, until the sitting room is filled with images of the cave's entrance and the first three murder scenes. There's not enough room for the final crime scene, and the cave with the stream.

****

Silently, we look at the grisly scene before us. The cold, damp, torch-lit caves illuminate the three victims. Staring at the scene, little things start jumping out at us. Hopefully enough things will add up to help identify the murderer. The faint outline of fingers can be seen on Mrs. Hayes's beckoning arm, due to the pressure and position. Checking the other bodies, we realize each have the same bruising. The female werewolf also has slight bruising on her breasts, legs, and stomach from being kicked and punched.

We switch the photos to the last murder scene and back cave. The female vampire's breasts have slight bruising from being roughly treated. The male vampire's body clearly shows his had been pulled, pinched, and kneaded. The werewolf has the most bruising.

With a grimace of distaste, I notice Victor and Kheda turning slightly green.

"So we're dealing with a psycho witch. These are her collections, which is why she lashed out at the female werewolf, and why she played freely with these three," Kheda said swallowing a couple of times.

We move to the final cave scene. In puzzlement, I stare at the scene before us. Clearly shown is an indentation in the soft mud by the water's edge, where the witch kneeled. The pressure from her knees, legs, and handprint is clearly marked.

"Please tell me that's from getting rid of the blood," I snarl as bile rises in my mouth to greet me.

"Dirty bitch," snarls Jasmine in distaste.

"Fucking hell, how perverse can she be?" Victor mutters in disgust. "Unless it's from draining the bodies?" A note of hope laces his voice, and I hope he's right.

"We've got a handprint," adds Kheda with a triumphant smile. "I'll get a forensics team to meet us, and hopefully she has left us DNA…" He quickly leaves the sitting room to make his phone call. We listen unashamedly to the one sided conversation.

"Hey, Jimmy, it's Kheda. Can you meet me in half an hour at the cave where we found the bodies please? Only bring members of your team you completely trust." A pause as Jimmy replies. "Can you bring a cast mold as well?" A pause. "Thanks, we'll see you then and be safe."

Gathering the pictures, I put them face down in a corner of the room. I notice the relief flashing across Kheda's features, when he spots the pictures in the corner of the room.

"Shall we go if everyone's ready?" he asks.

"I need to go to the toilet first." I raise my hand as if I'm back in school asking permission.

"I'd better go too, or I'll need to go when we get there," Jasmine agrees.

"Right, if it's okay with everyone we'll go in one car, so we'll be together," Kheda informs us to which everyone readily agrees.

We hurry upstairs, and I hear Kheda go to the downstairs toilet. Five minutes later, we pile into Kheda's car. Jasmine and I in the back, while Victor sits in the passenger seat, and Kheda drives.

He zips down my lane, over East Bridge, through the streets till we arrive at Hunters Park, where he stops the car and we all climb out. After Kheda locks up, we hurry toward the cave, duck under the yellow police tape, and carry on to the mouth of the cave, where four police CSI techs are waiting for us.

Kheda greets Jimmy. At only five feet five inches with a slight build, he is a small man with neat close-cropped blond hair, sharp features with lots of angles, and pale blue intelligent eyes. Anyone underestimating him would be a fool, I decide as Kheda introduces us to each other. His handshake is firm, with just enough pressure to show his restrained strength. The other three techs grunt their hellos.

Chapter 21

We enter the cave, passing where the bodies had been displayed. It's creepy the way there's no sign of the horror that recently happened here, until we reach the cave where the two vampires and the male werewolf had died. A trace of the male vampire's ashes remains. We need to collect them before we leave. I can't stand the thought of leaving any part of him behind, in this cave of death and misery. Finally, we reach the end cave with the stream. We guide the forensics team to the area where the witch had knelt, quickly and efficiently Jimmy makes casts of the imprints in the ground.

"What was the person doing here?" A puzzled frown crinkles his forehead as he stares at the area he's casting. I notice his face pale, turn slightly green, and guess his brain is giving him an answer he couldn't contemplate with his knowledge of what had happened.

He turns to us in obvious need of a logical, decent answer, but our grim faces tell him everything he doesn't want to know.

"Can you test the ground in case there are any bodily fluids please?" I ask.

Blanching, Jimmy gives me a grim nod, instructs a technician to test the area, and another to collect the vampire's ashes from the other cave. Once samples, ashes, and the dried cast are collected, he nods goodbye and leaves. We follow them, all of us delighted to leave, and head for the car and the hospital.

When we arrive, we go inside and down to the morgue. During this whole process, none of us has said a single word. After all what is there to say? Once the samples come back, our suspicions will be confirmed or put to rest.

"A word of warning, don't give the doctor any reaction. He will try and get one, especially from you two," Kheda informs us nodding toward Jasmine and me. "Whatever you do, don't react. He has a sadistic streak toward women…"

"We won't give him one, so let's just get this over with, but thanks for the heads-up, Kheda," I reply, silence descending once more as we contemplate what we know and are about to find out. The doors slide open, and we clamber out heading for the door with mortuary above it.

Entering we meet Dr. Sam McKenzie, a fifty-year-old, five-foot, gray-haired man almost half as round as he was tall. His bushy gray eyebrows seem to have a life of their own. They rise and fall with every word and expression. His rosy cheeks remind me of Santa's, and his navy blue eyes sparkle in excitement. If anyone were to describe him, they would probably call him a jolly little man.

"All victims died from exsanguination. The sadistic person mauled and played with them!" he exclaims, while watching Jasmine and me for any sign of weakness.

If Kheda had not warned us this doctor liked seeing people squirm, it wouldn't have taken us long to realize it. His disappointment in our lack of a reaction is obvious, as he tries making us squirm in discomfort by throwing off the sheets covering the female vampire and the male werewolf, fully exposing them, as he watches with bated breath for any reaction. Petulance flickers across his face as his hopes go unrealized.

"The werewolf had extensive bruising on his torso, buttocks, and thighs. The female vampire was impaled with a stake, and her breasts and thighs as you can see show bruising from being roughly handled. Her jaw was forced into this position by being dislocated and both her eyelids were removed. For obvious reasons the stake has been left in her. Apparently there was a male vampire who turned to ashes when removed. Is this true?" He looks highly peeved at our lack of reactions.

"Yes, he was attached to the same stake that was inserted in the female," Kheda informs him.

"I would have like to have examined him," mutters Dr. Sam in annoyance. "Anyway, moving along, next we have the female werewolf." Again he throws off the sheet covering the body while he watches us.

"She was punched and kicked as well as sliced, and she was alive during the stitching of her mouth, and the removal of her intestines. There is also bruising on her arm from being positioned in a beckoning position. She would have been in immense pain as she died." His satisfaction evident, he moves to the next two tables.

"The werewolf was killed in the usual fashion *The Protectors* use, no added bruising, or damage except for the bruising on the arm again. The witch shows the same arm bruising as the young male werewolf and female werewolf, but she also has bruising on her ribs where she'd been punched," Dr. Sam finishes.

"Anything else?" Kheda asks.

"Why, isn't it enough?" demands Dr. Sam.

"It's plenty, thank you, doctor," Kheda replies, gesturing for us to precede him from the morgue.

"Oh, one more thing, before you leave, detective. Whoever bruised the male werewolf and female vampire from the cave, didn't bruise the other three," Dr. Sam adds with immense satisfaction, as finally, he receives a reaction from us even if it is just thoughtful puzzlement.

In silence we leave, retracing our steps into the elevator, and up to the main entrance. Exiting the hospital, we go back to the car and climb in.

"Wow, you were not kidding, were you?"

"No, sadly I wasn't," Kheda replies with a shake of his head. "So where shall we go next?"

"I could do with a coffee, and maybe a light snack," I answer. "I think we should visit places the killer would probably work. Any place where witches, werewolves, vampires, and other supernaturals gather and associate with each other. Victor and Kheda, both of you should write a list of places that meet the criteria. We can visit them, and hopefully identify the witch we're after."

"Okay, we should go straight to Cynthia's Café, down on Carling Street. This way we're killing two birds with one stone. They do great coffee, and it's a safe haven for all species," Victor replies, rubbing his chin. Kheda grunts his agreement and starts the car and drives out of the hospital, onto Sterling Road, left onto Carter Street, and the first right onto Carling Street where he pulls into the first available parking spot at Cynthia's Café.

****

Exiting the car, we go straight into the café. My taste buds spring to life, and my mouth waters in anticipation of the promise in the heavenly smell of the freshly brewed coffee greeting us. I'm surprised how busy it is. Almost every table's full, and there's a large queue waiting to order. Everyone's talking loudly as if competing in a "who can talk the loudest competition."

Victor asks Jasmine and me to grab a table, while he and Kheda order. Jasmine requests a latte and I request a much needed mocha. We snag a table in the farthest corner, so we can watch everyone. I'm surprised at the number of witches, vampires, werewolves, and the odd zombie happily mixing with each other, as if it's the most natural thing in the world. Wonderful to see, but, why aren't there more killings?

As I puzzle over this question, I spot a young couple, a female werewolf, and a male vampire discreetly holding hands under a table. They're sitting a few tables away. That's when I finally make the connection; it's only couples from different species that are killed. That's why places like this are safe for interspecies interaction. As long as you're not in a relationship, like my parents were. Like the two teens obviously are. Just like Victor and me.

Catching Jasmine's eye, I point them out as unobtrusively as possible. Jasmine raises an eyebrow at me as if to say "you can bloody well talk," to which I roll my eyes at her and huff out a breath of impatience. In a room full of supernaturals even a whisper can be heard. Silently I watch the couple out of the corner of my eye, while scanning to see if anyone else is.

Spotting a counter assistant watching us, I recognize her as the woman from my grandmother's shop. I wonder how she is. Maybe I'll phone her later. My grandmother, not the woman behind the counter.

A young werewolf walking in heads straight toward the young couple, and hisses, "Cut it out," to them. He's trying to be quiet, but in a room full of supernaturals everyone hears and turns to look. Jasmine's eyes widen, as she finally realizes why I'd tried to get her attention about them earlier. They practically wore "next victim" tattoos on their foreheads.

The werewolf joining them wasn't helping matters either, until finally he figures out he has everyone's attention. Maybe it's the sudden silence that clues him in, or the fact everyone, and I do mean everyone, is watching! He glares at everyone in annoyance before storming out. An uneasy silence descends upon the customers and staff.

In mortification, the young couple collect their things and knock over their table and chairs in their haste to leave, causing further commotion as the cups and plates smash onto the floor.

With a stammered apology, they rush out of the café as if their lives depend on getting as far away as possible. Sadly, if the killer is amongst us, distance probably won't matter. Everyone starts talking at once, the sudden volume deafening.

Victor and Kheda weave their way toward us, carrying our much needed coffee and some scones with jam and cream. One of the women behind the counter tidies up the broken crockery and rights the table and chairs. We eat and drink in complete silence, as we covertly watch to see if anyone follows the young couple.

****

As the arms of the clock above the counter land on half past twelve, the afternoon staff enter and the morning leave. I notice Kheda and Victor eyeing each other and Jasmine's sudden stillness. We're all wondering the same thing. Is one of the departing staff members the killer? Scrambling out of the café, we pile into the deserted street. In frustration, we go to the Clothes Express shop just in case the teenagers have gone there.

"I can't believe how stupid the boy was, calling attention to the couple like that!" I fume.

"They should be able to go out together without fear," Kheda growls at me.

"I know, Kheda, so don't get testy with me," I snarl back.

"Enough already, don't be taking your frustrations out on each other. It's not helping, and we all want them to be safe, and for them and anyone else to be able to freely date without fear of death," Jasmine sooths.

Sighing, I mutter an apology toward Kheda, and he mutters something back at me, I think an apology, but to be honest I'm beyond caring. All I want is to spirit the three kids somewhere safe where no one will hurt them.

We search the clothes shop and then head toward the college. There's no sign of them, but we find out they attend there which is a bonus. Kheda leaves word for them to stick together, and contact him the moment they get in. We retrieve Kheda's car and go home.

"Does anyone have a map of the town?" I yell making everyone jump at my sudden and unexpected volume, as I jump out of the car.

"I might have a map in the car," Kheda replies.

"Get it please, and meet me in the sitting room," I demand as I rush toward the front door, unlock it, and run upstairs taking them two at a time. I grab a white candle, lighter, and my pendant before scurrying from my room and hurrying downstairs.

****

Kheda triumphantly unfolds an old map of Paradise Falls on the floor. I give him a big smile as I sit in front of the map. Centering myself, I light the candle. Dangling my pendant loosely from my fingers, I ask a simple "yes" question.

"Is my name Candi?" The pendant swings madly around clockwise. "Stop." It comes to a shuddering halt. "Am I male?" To which everyone snickers, and the pendant swings madly counterclockwise. So now I have my yes-no directions. Thinking of the images of the three teenagers, I ask, "Are the three teenagers still together?" The pendant jumps to life and swings counterclockwise, then clockwise.

"What the hell does it mean?" Kheda demands in befuddlement.

"Are the female werewolf and male vampire still together?" The pendant swings clockwise. "Okay, so the young lovers are still together. Is the male werewolf near the young couple?" The pendant quivers on the spot and slowly starts swinging counterclockwise. "Are they all walking?" Clockwise. "Are they near the college?" Madly swinging clockwise. "Has any of them entered the college?" The pendant carries on swinging clockwise, and Kheda's phone rings, frightening all of us.

Answering the phone and covering the mouth

piece, Kheda informs us it's the young werewolf. Jasmine and Kheda leave to go and get him. Victor tells them he'll phone when we find the couple as they hurry to Kheda's car and drive off.

"Are the young couple near the campus?" Clockwise. "Are they going into the campus?" Counterclockwise.

"Fuck, it means no, doesn't it?" demands Victor in frustration, as he starts pacing.

"Are they going to the diner?" Counterclockwise. "What else is around there?" The pendant shudders to a stop. "Victor, what else is around the college?"

"Umm, there's an all-night pharmacy, a pack bar, but they would be stupid to go there, a garage, and student houses..."

"Are they at the student houses?" The pendant springs to life and swirls madly clockwise. As it swirls over the map, it closes in over the student houses and stops. I quickly send up a thank you to the universe, blow out the candle, fish out my phone, and gather the map.

Speed dialing Kheda, I mutter, "Come on, come on," as Victor rushes me out of the sitting room, and the house. He locks the door and hurries us both to my car. Removing my keys from my pocket, I toss them to him. Finally Jasmine answers Kheda's phone, and I inform her where the couple is and that we're on our way.

"Meet us there once you have the boy," I add hanging up. Victor speeds down my drive and through town to the student houses. Screeching to a stop, we jump out causing more attention than I like. Some students turn to glare at us, and I accost one of them.

"Have you seen a young couple enter any of these houses?"

"What of it?" The grungy-looking teen werewolf shrugs, as suspicion and intelligence shines in his blue eyes.

"Please, we're here to help them," I quietly beseech, pointing to Victor who's knocking on doors.

The teenager's eyes widen when he realizes Victor's a vampire, and with me. The tension seeps from his scrawny body. "Yeah, they went into the third house, the one with the green door. They've been in there only about five minutes.

"Sorry, I didn't realize you were trying to help; the last time a witch was here looking for people we never saw the boy again," explains the young man.

"Thank you. Can you describe the witch to me please?" I beg, delighted we have such a lead.

Thinking hard, the teenager shakes his head in denial. "She was female. Nothing stood out to remember her, I'm sorry."

"Who was the teenager she took?"

"Jeremy McKnight. He was a friend of mine and a werewolf."

"Is he dating anyone of a different species, and if so, what's her name, please?"

"Her name's Tina Jameson, and she's a witch. She was around earlier. I saw her in class. When she's not in class, she just wanders around, trying to find Jeremy. No one knows what happened to him. He just disappeared."

"Did the witch take him, or how did he disappear?"

"Nah. She came around looking for Jeremy and Tina, said they'd left something in the coffee shop she works in, and she wanted to return it. So Jeremy, who was leaving on a camping trip, decided to swing by and get it before going. It was the last time anyone saw him. He never made it to the camping site."

"Any chance you have a picture of Tina?" I ask hopefully.

"Yeah, I have one of Jeremy, Tina, and me on my phone. If you give me your number, I'll send it to you, if you like?"

"Please, that would be wonderful." I quickly give him my number, and he sends me the picture straight away. "Thank you so much…I'm sorry I didn't get your name," I apologize, feeling totally mortified.

"Ben Sherman, what was yours?"

"I'm Candi Reynolds, and he's Victor." I nod toward Victor who's heading toward me talking on the phone. "Ben, don't go anywhere alone, and if you see Tina or you're in trouble, give me a ring, please?"

"Do you know what happened to Jeremy?" Fear and dawning realization flickers across his face, and his body slumps into himself.

"I'm sorry, he's dead; we found his body yesterday. His cousin is a friend, and we're all looking for his killer. Please, be safe, Ben." I move toward Victor and indicate the green door, leaving Ben standing looking like a little boy, locked in misery. Quickly turning back to him, I ask him one final question. "What coffee shop does the witch work in?"

"Cynthia's Café. It's on Carling Street."

I watch him as he goes to the house next to the one we're knocking at. A young man, drowning in misery over the loss of his friend.

The door in front of us swings open before Victor

can knock again, distracting me as the young vampire from the café glares at us. "What do you want?" He looks perplexed as he realizes a vampire and witch are standing before him.

"May we come in please?" Victor quietly asks to reduce any further attention.

With a frown and a quick scan to see who's around, the young vampire moves aside so we can enter. Once inside, he shuts the door and shows us into the sitting room, where the female werewolf cagily watches us, while staring nervously out the window.

"Okay, who are you, and what do you want?" the girl demands, her eyes narrowing mistrustfully, her lips pulled back baring her teeth aggressively.

"We want to help get you two, and the male werewolf who was with you, to safety," I inform them bluntly. I watch as their faces blanch, and they instinctively move toward each other.

"We don't know where Eddie is." The teenage girl nervously twitches, as again she looks out the window.

"He went to the college. Our friends have gone to get him and will be bringing him here, but we need to move all of you somewhere safe."

"We're not going anywhere. How do we even know you won't hurt us?" Temper crosses her face, and she narrows her eyes at us again, standing with her hands on her narrow hips and her legs slightly parted in an aggressive stance.

I glance out the window just as Kheda pulls up and parks beside my car. Out climb Kheda, Jasmine, and the young werewolf who'd caused the scene in the café.

Letting out a gasp, the girl rushes past Victor and me and into the hall, where she flings open the front door to let them in. Kheda hustles them in the house and quickly shuts the door behind him.

"Okay, we need to get you all somewhere safe," Kheda informs the three teenagers.

"We also need to find a witch called Tina Jameson; she was dating Jeremy so she will definitely be on the witch's list."

"You're looking for Tina and Jeremy? So, what do you want with Sally, Vincent, and me?"

"Jeremy's dead, and the witch who killed him will be after Tina next, and the scene you three caused in the café will probably put you on her killing list," Kheda informs them his tone so blunt the three teenagers gulp, and pale as his words sink in.

"How do you know Jeremy's dead?" Vincent asks so quietly we wouldn't have heard his question except we all have brilliant hearing.

"Kheda is the detective in charge of his murder; he's also his cousin," I reply soothingly. "We're helping to try and solve the murders."

"Jeremy's dead? Wait you said murders...as in more than one?" Eddie gasps in shock sitting heavily down on the ground.

I look at Kheda and with a grunt he answers, "There's been seven we know of so far. We don't want the number to increase, so we want to get you somewhere safe, and find Tina A.S.A.P."

"No, no, I'm not going anywhere, and you can't make me," Sally shouts.

"Sally, we have to go with them," sooths Vincent softly as he embraces his terrified girlfriend. Pushing him away, Sally shakes her head in denial.

"No, Vincent, we don't have to go with them, and

we can't," she beseeches him, her hands pleading with him, palms facing up as tears pool in her brown eyes.

Looking at Kheda, Vincent shakes his head. "If Sally's staying, then so am I. I'm sorry Jeremy's dead, but can't you do something to help us, so we can stay?"

"Look, if you're staying, don't go out alone. Stick together and stay away from Cynthia's Café. I believe it's where the killer finds her victims. Also, if someone comes looking for you, saying you left something in a shop they want to return, or need help because something is heavy, don't help and don't go and get whatever it is. Most likely it's a ruse to take you, and if it isn't, well it's better to be safe than sorry," I inform them, keeping my voice clipped and to the point.

"But if we know them, or recognize them…"

"No, don't you get it? The killer is stalking and planning how to capture her victims, so most likely you have met and chatted with her. Your lives are not worth giving up just to help someone or retrieve something you might have forgotten. If you genuinely forgot something, tell the person to drop it in at the college. Also, can you keep an eye out for Ben next door, please, and Tina."

Quickly I write down all our names with our numbers next to them and hand them to Vincent. "If you're insisting on staying and feel like you need help, please phone us straight away. If you put us on speed dial in your phones, it'll be faster and easier to ring us. Look, be safe and call if you need help."

Looking at the rest of my group, I shrug and head out the door. There is nothing more we could do for them. The worst of it is, I understand why they don't want to leave. If they leave, they're admitting evil's chasing them, the boogieman, or woman in this case, is hiding under the bed.

With such a lovely thought, I pop next door to see if Ben wants to come with us. I should have asked the poor kid when I was speaking to him earlier, but I just didn't think of it.

****

A grinning Ben answers my knocking, in a menacing parody of his former gentle face, making me feel queasy; the smell of evil surrounds him, in thick cloying waves making me want to wretch. "Are you okay, Ben?" I ask as I back up the path slowly. *Fuck, where is everyone when I need them?*

"Am I okay? Am I?" Ben demands as he advances grinning at me, his eyebrows shooting into his hairline. His head twitched from side to side, and his body jerked in unnatural movements, reminding me of one of those freaky marionette dolls, God, I hate them.

"I'm sorry to have disturbed you, Ben. I'll let you go." Turning I hurry back to the house next door. Quickly dashing inside, I slam the door and throw the dead bolt for good measure. I sink to the ground gasping in much needed oxygen. What the hell has happened to Ben?

Everyone piles out of the sitting room, staring dumbfounded at me. Victor kneels in front of me, gently taking my cold hands between his large ones, rubbing them briskly,

"What happened, Candi?" Concern resonates in his voice, and shines in his beautiful eyes.

Shaking my head in denial, I finally answer, "I don't know. I went next door to see if Ben wanted to come with us, and he was different, really creepy and

218

all jerky, as if his limbs are—he was wrong. God, I want to cry." I shudder in horror.

Everyone stares in silence at me, and then Sally hisses, "Is this some kind of sick trick so we'll go with you? Well, it's not going to work, witch!"

Looking at her in disgust, I give a shaky laugh. "No, princess, you can stay here if you want to. All I want to know is what the hell happened to Ben?" I snarl baring my teeth as a growl of anger rises out of my throat. Sally gives a squeal of surprise, probably shocked at me snarling and growling at her. Shaking my head in annoyance, I take control of my anger and fear, and exhale my frustration in a whoosh of air.

Victor helps me up, and I lean into him gratefully. The sound of the sitting room window smashing in makes us all scream. Sally drags me out of the way, tries opening the door, curses me for dead-bolting it, and as quick as she can, she flings back the bolt and the door narrowly misses hitting me as she runs screaming from the house. Discreet, she obviously is not! The rest of us make a speedy, but quieter exit (no screaming from us). I turn toward the house where I see Ben's lurching body, twitching through the sitting room. The back of his head has been caved in and part of his brains seep out of the gaping hole.

I stumble to a stop, making Victor grab me to try to hurry me along, and Kheda and Jasmine smack into us causing us all to stumble forward. Power fills me in my furry, and balls of fire leap to life in the palms of my hands; silence descends in the little housing area as a wind whips to life. In self-preservation, Victor releases me and backs away hastily with Kheda and Jasmine following swiftly in his wake.

"Necromancer, come here," I call in a deathly quiet voice that holds immense power rippling forth from it. *"Goddess Hecate, Goddess of the witches, Goddess of the crossroads and the underworld, I beseech you. May the spirit of Ben Sherman be released back into the loving arms of you, our Goddess,"* I call, raising my arms. The flames in my hands leap higher.

"I call forth the wronged, Ben Sherman." At this the wind whirls into the house, surrounds Ben, and brings him toward me, his body doing a marionette's dance, while his grin widens and his teeth snap. *"I call forth the necromancer, so she can answer for the crime of this boy's murder,"* I snarl as my lips curl over my teeth in my anger.

The wind howling its fury rushes toward the house Ben had entered alive and exited dead, bursting through the front door. We hear a woman screaming, "No, it's not my fault. No, let me go, please let me go." Sobbing, a woman is dragged from the house, the wind showing her no mercy.

Blood splatters her dress from where she'd smashed in Ben's skull from behind, her gray hair frizzing around her head, as if she had stuck her fingers in an electric socket, her mouth twisting in anger, and her eyes narrowing in hate as she glares at me. "How dare you, you strumpet, call me to account?" she screams, spittle flying from her mouth. When she looks into my eyes, she freaks out. "What are you? It wasn't my fault, she made me do it."

Hecate speaks through me. Her image overlies mine, her dogs appearing at my side to cast judgment and mete it out. *"Enough of your lies, Evelyn. I shall hear no more of them. You knowingly and willfully took the life of one of my children and made him rise to do your bidding."*

Turning toward Ben, Hecate smiles gently at him, her voice turning soothing as she speaks to him. *"Child of mine, I release you from the chains that bind you. Come to me and be at peace, and know your death will be avenged."*

Ben's body ceases its macabre dance and crumples to the ground, with the gentlest of landings, his spirit escaping and disappearing. Hecate turns back toward Evelyn. *"Who are you doing the bidding for, Evelyn? Answer me truthfully, or you shall suffer."*

"A witch. I had no choice. She has my daughter and threatened to kill her if I didn't kill the boy and send him after you. No, not you, Hecate, the strumpet you're inside of," Evelyn whines, as she wrings her hands in front of her.

"Evelyn Morrison, for crimes against my child, I strip you of the magick I gifted you with, and sentence you to the demon dimension, where your body shall be used for eternity."

Evelyn screams a bloodcurdling scream from the depths of her soul, as the hounds attack and drag the magick from her thrashing body. They pull her into a portal as it opens up, depositing her body into its sucking hole, before returning to Hecate's side.

"Justice has been seen, met, and dealt. Take care, my children, for you shall need your wits about you in the coming days."

The wind dissipates, the fire dies in my hands, and I am once more, me.

Carefully I kneel beside Ben's body. With a sigh of sorrow, I send an apology to his soul. "I'm so sorry,

Ben. I should have asked you to come with us instead of letting you go off alone."

"It's not your fault, Candi, and you did go to ask him," Victor sooths, as he wraps his arms around me pulling me against him.

"I've called for Ben's body to be collected. We can go in and search the house." Kheda quietly interrupts, sorrow lacing his every word as he looks at the dead boy on the ground. A shudder of remorse ripples a path through his body. I'm positive he's thinking of his beloved cousin.

"Come on, Candi, there's nothing more we can do, Ben's gone so…" Trailing to a halt, Victor releases a frustrated breath. He tightens his arms around me as we wait beside Ben's body.

****

We don't have long to wait for the police to arrive. We hear the sirens coming toward us, since they're only a couple of streets away. Their speed unsurprising, as this is a college campus and a murderer is on the loose. One whose species-crossing murders gives everyone a vested interest in finding the killer.

As the first police car screeches to a stop, I watch as the passenger door is flung open, and a large muscular witch clambers out. A furious scowl furrows her brow as she narrows jet black eyes in our direction, and a sneer of distaste curls her narrow lips.

She cracks her neck and fingers before slamming the car door making it shudder, almost causing the driver of the car to fall on his face as he exits. I hear Kheda give an almost silent groan, as he watches her stomp toward us.

The closer she comes, the angrier she looks, until

finally in a voice sounding like she eats nails for a hobby, while smoking a pack of cigarettes every hour, she growls, "Who the hell are you three, what are you doing here, McKnight, and what the fuck happened?"

"You know why Detective McKnight is here, Nina," sighs the male officer tiredly, as he shoots an irritated look in Nina's direction. He gives a nod of acknowledgement to Kheda with a simple, "Detective McKnight." To which Kheda replies, "Officer Thompson" with a nod of acknowledgment, before noticing Ben's crumpled body lying on the dirty ground. "Christ on a stick, what the hell happened to him?"

"The back of his skull was bashed in, and he was used as a marionette," I bluntly tell the officers, as I move unsteadily away from the protective circle of Victor's embrace.

"Who are you?" demands Nina as she thoughtfully narrows her gaze at me.

"Candi Reynolds."

"Hmm," snorts Nina distrustfully. "You're a witch. What are you doing here with them?" waving her hand in the direction of the werewolf, shifter, and vampire.

"Excuse me? How does it pertain to the case, and what the hell does it have to do with you anyway?" I growl angrily at the officer. I can feel a headache coming along, and my angry scowl isn't helping as it speeds it up.

"Now, now, witch, no need to be rude…"

"Enough, Nina," exclaims the male officer in annoyance as he glares at his comrade. "If you can't be polite, go and wait in the car. I have no interest in your pettiness or issues at the moment," he snaps furiously as he stares at the dead boy. "Where's the necromancer?"

"Gone," Kheda mutters, rubbing his head in frustration and exhaustion.

"You let the witch go?"

"No, well, not exactly."

"What the hell does that mean?"

"It means, well, she's gone."

"Fuck's sake, now we're going to have to search for her. Please explain to me how the hell you could lose her?"

I watch the emotions flickering across the male officer's face, and almost choke when he worriedly looks at our clothes. Did he think we'd eaten the necromancer? At the sudden relief, I'm guessing the thought must have crossed his mind. Bloody hell! With relief oozing out of him in waves, I watch as three more squad cars pull up along with the ambulance to take Ben's body away. Nina, I notice, has moved over to the three crying kids and is talking to them quietly.

"She might look scary, but she has a kind heart for kids. It's just adults she hates." He informs me when he sees where I'm looking.

I feel the instant Nina tenses and turns to look at me with a combination of wonderment and fear. Her eyes so wide, I'm surprised the skin doesn't rip. Her slack-jawed expression intensified by the paleness of her normally tanned skin.

I hear the officer beside me sudden inhale, as he watches Nina's expression and sudden pallor. Glancing at him, I watch his emotions flicker across his face, confusion and uncertainty, concern and a deep fear, not for himself but for Nina, and finally shock. Looking at him, I wonder just how much he cares about her.

Kheda crosses to one of the new officers, and after a quick word he returns to our little group. "We have five minutes in the house, so let's go and see if we can find some answers." Kheda watches Officer Thompson speaking with Nina, Jimmy, Sally and Vincent. Stifling a sigh, he turns and heads toward Ben's house. With a shudder of revulsion, he hurries inside.

****

The coppery smell of blood assails our noses when we enter the kitchen. Though most of the blood had landed on the necromancer, the smell of it still lingers with an underlying smell of excitement and anger. Closing my eyes, I breathe in the smells, and let them out and repeat my breathing exercise. Once I'm surrounded by the different smells, I speak a simple spell out loud.

"Smells so unique, show us your path,
Show us what happened, this hour past."

I open my eyes as everything turns a ghostly blue. Hearing a gasp of surprise from Jasmine, I quickly indicate they should remain still.

As we watch, we see Evelyn enter the front door, sneaking into the kitchen with a gleeful expression on her face. She removes a hammer from her large handbag. She strokes the hammer in anticipation.

After a couple of minutes, she places it on the table, delves back into her handbag, where she pulls out a little glass vial. Quickly removing the cork, she retraces her steps to the front door and proceeds to splash the contents about, efficiently masking her scent. Once finished, she rushes back into the kitchen, grasps the hammer again, and hides behind the kitchen door, where she waits for Ben to arrive.

Growing bored, she wanders about the place, noticing how tidy it is, and as she enters the sitting room she looks at the photos on display. Ben with his family. Ben with his friends. On the coffee table she sees a book. Reading the title she realizes she has read it.

With this realization she becomes confused. She always believed werewolves to be stupid, messy creatures, but this boy was everything opposite. Apparently he was house proud, smart, and unashamed to have photos of his family, where his friends could see them.

She hears a car pull up quickly outside. Peering out the window, she spots Eve Allhallows' granddaughter and a vampire climbing out of the car. As her anger resurfaces, she watches as the witch walks over to Ben, stopping him on his way to his house so she can talk to him. The vampire who had been knocking on doors joins them.

A couple of minutes later they walk away, and Ben carries on toward his house once more. Quickly Evelyn hurries back to her hiding spot behind the kitchen door, where she waits in growing anger for him to enter the kitchen.

She doesn't have to wait long, and once he passes her hiding spot, she creeps out and smashes his skull in, watching as his body crumples to the floor. She stares for a minute as the anger seeps from her body.

She looks properly at the dead boy lying on the floor. For once she sees him as a boy, not a different species. Her chin wobbles. Shaking herself, she reaches for her bag. Removing a black candle, incense, and a lighter, she quickly reanimates his body before she changes her mind,

"After all, you're already dead. Might as well use you," she mutters to Ben, as if she had stumbled upon the body and decided to use him. On her third try, she manages to reanimate the body.

"Go next door, and kill them all," she crows in delight as she sends Ben jerkily on his mission, just as someone knocks on the front door. Crouching down and hiding, she watches as Ben opens the front door and the witch talks to him. She notices the instant she realizes something is wrong with him. She stares as the witch backs away and runs next door.

In delight she moves into the sitting room where she carries on watching the scene unfold, delighting in their fear, until everything changes. She watches as the witch's eyes turn an impossible shade of violet, and flames erupt from her hands.

In fear, Evelyn runs back into the kitchen, grabbing her hammer and matches, dumping them into her bag. Blowing out her candle, she douses the incense, and clutching them in her hands, she runs out the back door.

She's halfway through the garden, when she's wrapped in an invisible embrace like a steel trap and dragged back through the house and toward the witch.

Screaming her hatred, she shakes in fear as Hecate speaks through the witch, strips her of her powers, and Hecate's hounds drag her into hell.

The ghostly blue fades, and once more we're in the blood scented kitchen. Quickly I head into the garden where I spot Evelyn's bag in the grass. Calling Kheda, I point it out, and we go toward it. I photograph the area, the position of the candle, drenched incense, and the bag. Kheda retrieves all the items and brings them back into the kitchen where we search for any clues. There is nothing obvious, just the usual items you would expect to find in a woman's handbag. It holds a comb, pen, shopping bag, phone, knitting (probably for knot spells, not for actual knitting), old receipts, keys, and different color candles and incense. With an annoyed huff, Kheda puts the phone on the table.

"Nothing of use in there. I don't think she used it often," he grunts in annoyance.

I look at the contents on the table in confusion. I know it's quite a lot she has in her bag but…

"Is that all?" Jasmine asks as she looks at the contents in front of her.

"Isn't it enough?" Victor laughs. "I mean, the only thing she's missing is the kitchen sink!"

Shaking my head, I pick up the bag and shake it. Something inside shifts, keeping the bag just the tiniest bit heavier than it should be. Quickly, I turn the bag inside out and feel for a pouch small enough to go unnoticed, but large enough to hold something inside.

It's Jasmine who finally notices it, a slim pouch in the lining near the seam. Easily missed, if you didn't know it was there or looking for it. She slips her long slim fingers in nervously as she doesn't know what's inside, or if it's bespelled. Finally she extracts a slim leather-bound black book.

Her personal space a thing of the past, I stare over her shoulder, so I can read what's in the book. Opening it up, she finds spells and some names. Farther into it she sees Ben's address, who to send him after, and finally directions to another location. Silently she hands the book to Kheda.

Taking it from her, Kheda flicks through it stopping at the directions. His brow furrows in concentration as he looks at the diagram, reading the directions. "I can't for the life of me think where this is," he mutters.

Victor and I peer over his shoulder so we can see if we recognize it. The next thing Victor whips out his phone. Speed dialing a number, he harshly informs whoever answered to get out, get everyone out now.

Chapter 22

In a flash, Victor hangs up and dashes out the back door.

"What is it, Victor?" I yell.

Looking back at me, Victor pauses to reply, "My bar." He reaches a hand out to me, which I take willingly. Victor pulls me against him and shoots up into the sky, leaving Kheda and Jasmine behind. I tuck my head into the crook of his neck, inhaling his warm musky sent which reminds me of spices, and hot summer nights in the desert, even though I've never been to the desert. I cling tightly to him; a second later, we land in the woods behind Victor's bar.

The screaming and scent of terror assails our senses, as we dash to the back of the building. Peering in the nearest window, we stare at the scene before us. Blood decorates the walls and floor of the pub.

We spot Simon lying on the bar, his head facing the door, eyes open wide in terror. Ropes have been wrapped tightly around him, holding him down, preventing him from rolling off.

A tube inserted into his side is draining him of his blood; the tube I notice, leads to the bathrooms, if I remember correctly. Tears flow down his bruised face as he cries helplessly, unable to save himself.

A shudder ripples through him, as his eyes stray to a decapitated head in front of him. I look at the head and gasp in shock as I recognize the quiet witch from the cave, and my grandmother's shop.

Bloody hell, what was her name? Peter Rabbit...Beatrix something or other. Crap, I'd begun to think she was the killer; after all she kept turning up everywhere. I feel guilty of suspecting her, even if only slightly, but to be honest she did fit the profile.

Glancing at Victor, I reach for his hand and squeeze it gently. The look of anger in his eyes is frightening, yet I'm not afraid. I understand it completely, I feel just as furious. I twirl one finger around, raising an eyebrow in enquiry. Giving me a puzzled look, Victor realizes I'm asking if he wants us to continue to look around.

With a nod of agreement we separate, circling the building. Every window I come across I peek in, but apart from finding the staff's bodies, there's nothing else to see. At my final window, I spot Victor glancing in a window opposite, and wave at him in warning. A cloaked figure is approaching him from behind.

He turns, just as the figure whacks him, knocking him unconscious. Staring helplessly, I quickly duck, covering my mouth as I stifle a sob. Anger floods me. A second later peeking once again, I see the cloaked figure drag Victor's unconscious body to the front door.

Quickly I hurry back to the bathroom window. Jimmying it open, I heft myself up straddling it before slipping silently inside. Listening, I creep toward the door, pausing as I hear Simon crying.

Pushing the door open a crack, I gasp in shock then anger, as the cloaked killer strips Victor's shirt from his body, running her hands over his muscled torso. No way in hell is this bitch getting away with touching my man.

Flinging open the door, I step in to face the woman underneath the cloak. At my sudden entrance, she falls back in shock, dropping Victor. His head bounces off the floor at the sudden impact.

"Get away from him!" I growl.

Clambering to her feet, the cloaked witch throws her cloak back dramatically, showing me her face. I stare in puzzlement at the waitress from The Olive Tree.

"Why?" I demand.

"Why? How can you ask me why? It should be obvious, especially to you. The question is, how can you associate yourself with the likes of him?" Sally Jensen demands as she curls her lip in disgust. "Filthy whore, you will be next, once I've taken care of him," Sally cackles.

"Behind you," gasps Simon in warning, as slim feminine arms wrap around me, clamping my arms to my sides with surprising strength.

"Hold her, and make sure she watches while I take care of her lover," sniggers Sally. I struggle to free myself, slamming my head back into my assailant. As my head impacts with hers, her arms loosen enough for me to break her hold. Quick as lightning I twirl around, recognizing the waitress from Hal's.

Shooting electricity from my fingers, I electrocute her. Her body shakes and hums before collapsing in a heap. Growling, I turn back to Sally, as she hits me with a binding spell, trapping my magick and preventing me using it. This explains how she is able to kill other witches. My eyes widen in mimicry of fear, as she pulls me magically toward her.

"Stupid witch, you're helpless, and now you will watch as I take care of him." She gloats pointing at Victor who's waking up.

"If I was only just a witch, you would be so right," I calmly reply getting her attention. I pounce, shapeshifting into a wolf, ripping her throat out mid scream.

Victor is gaping at me, with a stupid but quite endearing smile, as the front door bangs open. Kheda, Jasmine and some officers pile into the pub. Padding over to Victor, I give his face a lick and plop down beside him as he scratches behind my ears, making me wiggle in satisfaction and give a happy tail thump. Jasmine and Kheda hurry toward us.

"Where's Candi, and who's this?" Kheda asks as he eyes me in confusion. It's only when he looks at me again, a gasp of shock escapes from him, as he recognizes my laughing eyes. In the split second it takes to draw in a breath, I transform from wolf to witch, with Kheda gaping in shock, his jaw hanging loose.

Chapter 23

Kheda finally stops gaping at me, to untie Simon. The EMTs carefully take him off the counter and onto a stretcher, rushing him to the hospital.

Victor informs the officers he has security cameras. Except for an officer standing guard over the unconscious Savannah, we all pile into his office to watch the recording.

Savannah wakes with her arms handcuffed behind her. She tries playing the victim; with her broken bloody nose, she looks the part, I grudgingly admit.

"What, what's going on?" she stammers, forcing out a couple of tears for the added benefit of the officers, superstitiously looking around. "Why am I handcuffed? I don't understand, I was attacked," Savannah sobs. Spotting me she starts screaming hysterically, "It was her. She attacked me. I was just minding my own business, when she came in and…oh it was so horrible," Savannah cries.

Blimey, if I didn't know for a fact she was speaking the biggest load of bull crap I have ever heard, I would believe her! Seeing an officer move toward me, I roll my eyes in disgust. "Did you not just watch the security video?" I demand, to which the officer has the grace to flush in embarrassment and step away.

"What security video?" Savannah demands, all pretenses of tears vanishing as she looks around at the grim-faced officers. For a second she gives up, sagging forward in defeat.

"The one clearly showing you and Sally, entering the bar and brutally murdering and torturing all these people," Kheda informs her in satisfaction.

Furiously, Savannah glares at Victor as if this is entirely his fault.

"Security cameras, really? It's a pub, why are security cameras necessary?" Savannah shrieks, as she unsuccessfully tries to clamber to her feet.

"Well, apparently they are necessary," drawls Victor as he looks at the death and destruction in his bar, before turning his furious gaze back on Savannah.

"I take protecting my staff and customers very seriously, and obviously I was right in having them, or you would have probably gotten away with these murders judging by your excellent acting skills."

****

During this conversation, I sit on a bar stool staring in disgust at Savannah. My eyes keep skittering toward Beatrix's decapitated head. With an exhausted huff, I shift, almost falling off the stool before righting myself to settle more firmly. Again I exhale noisily, as my brain sluggishly processes everything around me. Once more my eyes are drawn to Beatrix's head. A perplexing frustration settles over me as I find myself staring yet again at it, with a further sigh I give in, going to it for a better look. Crouching down I cock my head, studying it, the more I study it, the more puzzled I become.

"What the hell are you doing?" demands Nina as she stares at me in puzzlement.

As realization dawns on me I give the head a poke,

watching it as it topples over. Numbers counting down flash at me. Someone screams at me. My face blanches, and I scream at everyone to get out as I fall on my ass.

"Leave the head alone, you sick bitch," a young officer screams at me in anger.

Scrambling to my feet I shout again, "Get the fuck out. It's a bomb, for crying out loud." Finally my words sink into some of their heads. Victor grabs me rushing us outside, with Kheda and Jasmine on our heels. We hear Nina screaming "Bomb," and everyone starts running for the exit. We reach the road's edge when the bomb explodes. Fire and debris rain down around us as we rush out of harm's way, before turning to stare in shock at the fiery ruins of Victor's bar.

"I'm so sorry, Victor." Staring at his pub in horror, I squeeze his hand that's linked with mine.

"It's just a building. Thankfully, we all got out. How did you know?"

"What?"

"How did you know there was something wrong with the head?" Victor repeats curiously.

"I couldn't remember seeing her in the pub before Savannah and Sally came in on your security tape, yet her head was there. I kept remembering how Simon had kept staring at the head in fear. I had assumed it was because, well, a decapitated head was staring at him, but the body parts weren't adding up either, and I just had a feeling all was not right with the world.

"I couldn't stop looking at the head, so I had a proper look, and the rest is history," I finish as I nod toward the destroyed burning pub.

Kheda, Nina, and some other detectives and officers had listened to my answer. I saw the instant their brains realized my observations had been correct. None of them remembered seeing Beatrix, with or without a body, before her head was on the floor!

We hear the fire engines zooming through the streets, their sirens blaring. I wonder if one of the officers had phoned them, or if it was the loud boom of the bomb going off which had attracted them. In the scramble out of the bar, I hadn't noticed.

With a groan of exhaustion, I sit heavily on the ground, leaning my body into Victor's muscular legs. The officers decide to hustle us to the police station, to book Savannah and take our statements for both the murder of Ben, Evelyn's disappearance, and how we knew to get to the bar and what happened. Thankfully, Victor had passed over the security tape. Victor picks me gently off the ground, and I wrap my arms around his neck, before snuggling into him.

Feeling the gentlest of kisses brush across my forehead, I close my eyes, just to rest them for a minute. I'd only just closed my eyes when I'm getting told to wake up. Grumbling unhappily, I open my eyes to inform the annoying person I'm not asleep, when I notice we're at the police station. Huh, when did that happen? One by one, we're dragged in to a little room to be grilled.

"Why were you looking for Sally and Vincent?" demands the questioning officer. What did he say his name was again?

"Because there was a murderer on the loose, and after the scene caused in Cynthia's Café, we thought it best to make sure they were okay," I reply as I try to remember who the officer is.

"What happened to Ben Sherman?"

"He was murdered, and brought back to life by a necromancer. Look I've already answered your questions, and I am tired, so unless you have a new question to ask me, not just the same question asked in a different way, I'm going home," I inform the officer in annoyance. He has been questioning me for almost two hours and I'm ready to drop. I'm not sure if exhaustion or hunger will claim me first.

"How did you turn into a wolf?"

Looking at the officer, I give a snort of derision. So we're finally coming to what he really wants to know. Leaning forward, I look him straight in the eyes and continue staring until he starts fidgeting nervously. I let a smile twist my lips. "How do you think I turned into a wolf, officer? You obviously believe you know the answer."

"I think you're the one from the prophecy. My grandfather told me about it, and I think it's you he was telling me about," the officer whispers. His eyes hold a well of curiosity, excitement, and some doubt.

"If you have nothing else to ask me pertaining to the case, I'm leaving," I repeat, as I eye him thoughtfully. "What did you say your name was again?"

"My name is Officer Jesse James, Miss Reynolds, but you can call me Jesse."

A smile slips across my face before I can prevent it. "You can call me Candi, Jesse," I reply as I head toward the door.

"Wait, Candi. If you think of anything else, please call me." He passes his card to me while showing me out.

****

I watch the witch leave the police station, and hurry down to her waiting vampire lover. She hasn't noticed the young officer watching her. But I do. I watch him, watching her, and am astounded at how envious he looks. Turning, I look at the witch in time to see the breathtaking smile she bestows on the vampire, and anger rolls inside of me.

The young officer and I both watch as she says something, links hands with the vampire, before they walk off without a backwards glance, heading toward the college campus. Quickly I go in the opposite direction, leaving the officer behind as he watches the couple walk away.

****

I'm the last to be released. Leaving the police station, I spot Victor waiting patiently for me. I hurry toward him, drinking in the wonderful sight of him.

"The others are at the campus diner ordering food. I told them I'd wait for you. You okay?"

"I'm fine, thank you, just starving. How are you?" I beam as I lace my fingers through his and we head toward the diner.

"Better now you're with me." Victor smiles as he gently squeezes my fingers.

It doesn't take us long to reach the diner, and we spot Jasmine and Kheda in the back booth. I think we're all thinking of it as ours. I reluctantly release my fingers from Victor's to slide in. Victor sits beside me, so close we look glued together, and I don't care. Lacing my fingers back through his, I give them a squeeze. Jasmine and Kheda are sitting opposite us, and I'm delighted they're sitting pretty damn close, too.

"So, you literally are double magick," Victor states

grinning a very sexy, lopsided grin at me, as he traces a pattern on my hand.

"Yeah," I reply, grinning back at him, "I literally am."

"So what happens next?" Jasmine enquires.

"Next we order our food, before even thinking of doing anything else," I laugh.

"Already been taken care of, and it should be arriving soon," Jasmine informs me. "What did they ask you?" she enquires quietly, leaning forward to catch my answer.

"Probably the same as the rest of you, over and over again, and in different ways, until at the very end when I was asked how I changed into a wolf, and if I was really the double magick from the prophecy," I inform them.

"Holy cow, who was questioning you, and how do they know about the prophecy?" Kheda demands in shock.

"Jesse James, and apparently his grandfather told him," I answer trying not to smile again at his name.

"Jesse James? Seriously, that's his name?" Jasmine asks her lips twitching.

"I have to ask, how do you manage to keep your clothes on? Every shifter and werewolf I have ever met has to strip, or get their clothes destroyed in the change. What makes you so different?" Curiosity laces Kheda's voice. He leans forward to make sure he catches my answer. Looking at his puzzled expression, I try not to laugh.

"I don't know how to explain it, to be honest. It's the way I've been since the first time I transformed. It's part of my magick. It's like my witch magick and wolf are separate. My clothes in that sense belong to the witch side of me. It's why when Sally put the binding spell on me, it only worked on my witch magick, so my wolf took over."

The waitress turns up with our burger, chips, and sodas, and receives grateful smiles from all of us. We dig into our food. Turning to Victor, I ask a question which has been bothering me for a while now. "What happened with the demon, and why was she impersonating my grandmother?"

"Apparently, Savannah had sent her to find out what you knew about me. My sitting with you at the booth spiked her interest. She couldn't understand why I willingly met you but wouldn't associate with her. She was also confused about Jasmine, though she hadn't realized she was a shifter, just why you had a dog, being a witch and all," Victor replies. "The demon is still with Big Michael, he believes she's still withholding information."

"Okay, but what was with kidnapping George Seabast the Fourth?" Jasmine asks.

"He dumped her after dating her for a month, with no reason, so it was simply a little revenge thrown in for good measure," Victor answers, with a shake of his head at the oddities of people.

"Wow, talk about a harsh lesson," I mutter thinking of the state we'd found him in.

"So the only thing we don't know, is why your grandma is practicing black magick, and who else is practicing with her," Jasmine states, as a frown creases her beautiful face. Kheda rubs the frown away from her forehead making her smile at him, before kissing him gently on the mouth.

I lean into the wonderful man beside me, resting my head on his shoulder, and feeling contented.

"We'll find out sooner or later, hopefully sooner. But it's not the only thing we don't know the answers too. I'm going to give my gran a ring and see if we can meet up. Hopefully she will tell us why, and who else is practicing black magick, but to be honest, I doubt it. Practicing black magick is a personal choice and frankly none of our business. I might not like the choice, but I have no say in the matter."

Victor wraps an arm around my waist and drags me even closer to him.

"What did you do to piss off Savannah so much?" I ask curiously.

"Nothing, I didn't even know her. She's a customer in my bar and has waited on me in Hal's, but otherwise I didn't pay her any attention." Victor shrugs his powerful shoulders in puzzlement.

"She obviously wanted you. What about Sally, did you know her?" I inquire as jealousy ripples through me as I remember her touching him.

"She hung out with Savannah at the bar, but I paid them no attention," Victor answers with a delighted smile as he senses my jealousy.

"Okay, but where is the body of the decapitated witch?" Jasmine asks. "And did Sally and Savannah kill all those in the cave, and the man in the woods, because their murders were definitely on a whole different level. They were the work of *The Protectors*, and nothing like the bar massacre."

We all stare in horror at Jasmine, as the truth of what she says ripples through us.

"Flipping hell!" I exclaim in disgust at myself.

"You're right. Their murders are nothing like the bar. How the hell did I not see this earlier?" I grumble in annoyance.

"None of us did, well, except Jasmine," Kheda adds looking at her in admiration.

"Look, there's nothing we can do about it now. We're all knackered and need to rest. How about tomorrow, we look at everything with fresh eyes, and see what we come up with," Victor states.

With a happy sound, I snuggle into him and enjoy the moment. Feeling my leg vibrate, I realize it's my phone. Removing it, I read the message. Reading again, I draw in a sharp breath.

"She's left," I exclaim.

"What? Who's left?" Victor demands in concern.

"My grandmother. She says she needs to sort some things out, and she can't do it here. She doesn't know where she's going, or for how long. She also says for all of us to be careful."

I trail to a stop staring at my phone, until Victor, who'd been gently rubbing my back, finally asks, "What else did she say, Candi?"

"She said, a change is on the way, and darkness follows it swift and fast. We had better call in help, and find the answers we seek, but we won't find them here."

"Where are we meant to find these answers?" Jasmine asks quietly.

"I don't know," I reply shaking my head. "It's all she wrote."

Quickly we pay for our food, and as one we hurry into the night. A rumble of thunder breaks the quietness surrounding us, followed by a distant flash of lightning.

We dash back to the student houses where I'd left my car and pile into it.

Once we're buckled up, I reverse and head home. Thunder rumbles once more followed swiftly by another growl and grumble, and the smell of raw electricity permeates the air sharply, just before a bolt of lightning flings itself from the sky, ripping it open, and rain pours from the open wound in a heavy downpour. Thunder crashes and booms angrily above us; louder this time, deafening in its intensity.

I drive quickly through town and up the lane to the old Winters' house, where in relief I stop. We scramble out, running to the front door. Jasmine unlocks it, and we all feel the welcoming warmth of the house embrace us. Turning, I lock the door. We trudge toward the kitchen to grab a drink.

Finishing one drink, I fix myself another. Looking enquiringly at Victor with a small smile, I raise my eyebrows and waggle them suggestively, making him laugh as he reaches for me, dragging me against him before kissing me soundly on the lips.

We deepen our kiss, finally separating, leaving me panting, as desire tingles and anticipation shoots through me, pooling in my belly. Tangling my free hand in his, as my other hand keeps its death grip around my spilling drink, I pull Victor out of the kitchen and upstairs.

With a saucy grin, I lock my bedroom door behind us, taking a sip from my drink. I sashay to my desk, placing my glass carefully down. Turning to face Victor, I watch him move with infinite grace and fluidness toward me. Slowly unbuttoning his shirt, he reveals delicious skin, soft as velvet, encasing muscle and bone as hard as marble. With a moan of anticipation, I cross the room, meeting him halfway.

Tonight I will let nothing come between us, and tomorrow, well, tomorrow we have a killer to find. Tomorrow can wait, for tonight is ours. Reaching up, I run my fingers through his luxurious hair and drag his head down to meet my waiting mouth, in anticipation of his kiss.

His arms anchor me to him, lifting me off the floor. Wrapping my legs around his lean waist, I hold on tight. We make love slowly, and with so much emotion, I feel like crying.

I fall asleep curled around him, his arms like steel, holding me tight, as if at any moment I might vanish, his embrace, the only thing keeping me here. I'm okay with it. I don't want to go anywhere, or for him to either. The last thing I remember before sleep drags me into its world is Victor's voice, whispering on the breath of a kiss, "You're mine, always and forever, my Double Magick woman."

Chapter 24

The next morning I awake, wrapped securely around Victor's lean body, as he gently strokes my back, tracing patterns along my spine. With a contented sigh, I kiss his muscular chest, allowing my fingers to explore the silky skin containing his raw power. My fingers trace the hills and valleys that make up the sculpted beauty of his chest and stomach. But before I can explore further, I'm rolled onto my back, my hands captured securely by the wrists in one of his large strong hands.

The muscles of his arm sit just above my head in tantalizing reach of my mouth. Lifting my head to gain easier access to his arm, I open my mouth allowing my tongue to escape, licking the corded strength of his arm before wrapping my legs around his. I slowly drag one up and over the muscled masterpiece of his ass.

Wrapping my leg around his narrow waist, I bring his body back to mine. We make love again, exploring every inch of each other, before finally collapsing in a sweaty satisfied heap of tangled arms, legs, and sheets. Grinning in satisfaction, I kiss him on his left, very impressive pec. A rumble of laughter vibrates under my head. I glance up at Victor in enquiry. "What's up?"

"Nothing, my beauty is up, you insatiable minx. Well, not yet anyway," Victor replies with a wicked grin, as he grabs my ass pulling me up his body, my legs draping to either side of his waist. He looks into my flushed face, and gently kisses me, wrapping his arms around me, holding me firmly in the circle of his embrace. An hour later, I finally drag myself out of bed to have a shower.

Victor finally relented after my insistence and drank some more of my blood. With everything going on, it's imperative he's at full strength. Pulling my housecoat on, I hurry to the bathroom where I have a quick pee, brush my teeth, and turn on the shower.

Stripping off my housecoat, I climb in. Standing under the hot spray, I let it drum its rhythmic tattoo onto my head and shoulders. I close my eyes and enjoy the surrounding warmth. I wash and rinse my hair and reach for my shower gel only to find Victor's hard body. With a gasp of shock I jump back, skid, and knock my arm against the wall tile before Victor can grab my flailing body to steady me.

"What the hell are you doing?" I demand hitting his shoulder, which stings my hand and doesn't move him an inch. "You scared the hell out of me!" I pant trying to steady my poor racing heart.

"I'm sorry I thought you heard me. Since you were taking so long, and I also need a shower, I decided to come and help you," he informs me with a cheeky grin, as he squirts a liberal amount of shower gel into his hand, before slowly washing every inch of me.

By the time he's finished, I'm trembling so badly he has to support me. Propping me against the wall he washes himself. As I watch him, my breathing hitches, and I'm surprised I don't pass out from hyperventilating. Sadly he won't let me help, maybe because I'm drooling so much, or maybe because I'm finding it so hard to breathe. Whatever the case, he finishes much too soon for my liking, until he decides it's best for him to dry me. I have never realized a towel could be so sensual.

Finally dressed, we head downstairs for brunch. Walking into the kitchen, I notice Kheda leaning against the counter, staring into his mug as if it's a crystal ball. Jasmine gives me a look and a waggle of her eyebrows; the girl wants details. What she gets is a blush from me as I head for the kettle; I so badly need a coffee. Finally I sit, my hands clutching my coffee mug as if it's my life line, and munch some toast. Victor sips from one of his little blood baggies he'd heated up, his lips curling in a grimace. Raising a questioning eyebrow at him, he gives me the barest shake of his head in answer.

"So what's next on the agenda?" Jasmine asks looking at Kheda, Victor, and finally me, guzzling my coffee as if it's oxygen.

"We find out if Beatrix is alive," Kheda answers softly as he twitches. "Full moon's tonight, and I feel it crawling through me," he answers Victor's unspoken query.

"I'll summon the others tonight. We'll need them. I'll also go over to The Witches' Brew in a minute, and ask some questions about Beatrix. Find out where she lived and worked, in case she worked in two places," I mutter, finishing my toast and looking with longing at my empty mug. With a final look, I put it down; staring at it will not make it refill itself.

"Because I'm going to the witch's bar, I'd best go on my own. None of you would be welcomed there, or be safe if caught on your own outside." I ignore everyone's objections. After all they know I'm right.

Getting up from the table, I tidy up after myself and head out the back door where I change into wolf form and run into the woods. Staying in the woods, I run to the pub. It should just be opening and hopefully I can have a private word with Nici, before anyone's around to overhear.

Once I'm behind the pub, I sit for a second sniffing the air. Finding nothing troubling, I change forms and enter the bar. Spotting me, Nici flings her arms around me. In shock, I stand there with my arms stiffly at my sides and my back poker straight. I am so not a hugger. "Um, Nici, can you let me go please?" I ask, as I awkwardly try wriggling out of her embrace.

"Sorry, I'm just so happy. Everyone is so much happier since you destroyed the hex on the door, and my business is booming." Nici grins dragging me toward the bar. "Now, how can I help you? I'm gathering you're not an early drinker?"

"You gathered correctly." I smile back. "I need your help in finding a witch. Her first name is Beatrix. I don't know anything else about her." With a grimace, I realize how unhelpful that information is. Scrunching up my face in thought, I remember something else. "I think she lived either next to or near Mrs. Hayes."

"Oh, you mean Beatrix Sullivan. Yeah, I know her. She's...odd," Nici replies, bobbing her head. "I think she works at Sterling Nightclub and Cynthia's Café across the river. She lives in one of the river cottages. I'm not sure which one though," Nici informs me with an apologetic shrug.

"Thank you so much, Nici, you've been amazingly helpful." My brain starts running away from me.

Quickly I get up, leave the pub, and enter the forest. I shift back into my wolf and run toward my grandmother's house.

When I reach her property, I change back and walk slowly toward her house. Her car is gone, so I let myself in to search for some sign of where she's gone. The only thing I find is a note saying, "I'm sorry."

Taking one last look around, I leave locking up her house, and slowly walk home. On returning I find Kheda and Victor gone, and Jasmine climbing the walls. With a chuckle, I ask if she fancies coming with me to try and find Beatrix's house.

"Of course I do, but you must give me details on Victor. I want to know everything," she exclaims. "Do you think Kheda…"

"If you're going to ask if he likes you, I'm just going to say, duh, of course he does. Hell, he can't keep his eyes off you, and he touches you at every opportunity he has." I laugh at the relief flittering across her expressive face.

"Come on, let's go search Beatrix's house and maybe find her body!" God only knows what someone is doing with it. We leave a note for the guys telling them where we've gone.

Leaving on foot, we stroll in contented silence for a while, before Jasmine finally breaks it, asking with a cheeky grin, "So you and Victor, how's things going? Come on, Candi, I want details, and you're holding out on me!" She laughs in delight, as she witnesses the flush creeping up my cheeks.

"It's new and wonderful, and so amazing, but I don't know where we're heading, and I don't want to talk about it."

With a nod of understanding, she thankfully drops the subject. What I don't tell her is I want Victor with every fiber of my being. I haven't felt so alive in ages. Scrap that, I haven't felt this alive ever, and to be honest, it scares the shit out of me. And after he was brave enough to admit how he feels, I feel almost ashamed I don't have the courage to admit how I feel. After all, how can anyone affect me so completely, in so short a time?

Reaching the river cottages, we decide it'd be best if I find Beatrix's house, and then meet her in the alley behind them and enter from the back gardens. It doesn't take me long to find Beatrix's house. It's surprisingly easy. In fact it's so easy I almost have a heart attack.

Quickly I run back to Jasmine and drag her into the alley. I shove my hand over her mouth preventing her saying anything, or letting her muffled scream of surprise out, as we hide in the shadows.

A second later Beatrix walks by, heading toward East Bridge whistling a happy tune, her head securely attached to her body! Jasmine gasps, it could be from shock, or lack of oxygen, either reason plausible. Taking my hand away, Jasmine sucks in oxygen as if it's going out of fashion.

"I found out where she lives," I whisper to her, receiving a what-the-fuck look. In reply, I give her a wicked grin and a shrug of my shoulders before heading further into the alley to reach the fourth house along.

Jasmine keeps looking back, shaking her head as she follows behind me. With a final look to make sure the coast's clear, we sneak through the back gate, silently closing it behind us. Spotting a large shed with windows, I wander over to it. Peeking in I see a mini gym, with a punching bag, treadmill, weights, a leg machine, as well as a bike.

"Holy crap," mutters Jasmine gawking at the equipment.

"I so must get one of them," I grumble. I have to admit, I feel kinda envious as I stare at the punching bag. We move to the back door, turning the handle. I'm not surprised to find it locked, so I let Jasmine pick it. She did teach me, but she's faster and let's be honest here, with a dead witch walking, time's not on our side. Especially if the undead witch is a possible serial killer!

In less than two minutes the lock is picked, and we enter the silent house. Bright orange walls and hot pink doors greet us, with a neon brightness that almost blinds me. "Yikes, I do not like her color theme," I mutter shielding my eyes, wishing for some sunglasses.

"She's obviously making sure people don't want to come in, or…heck, I can't think of any reason someone would deliberately color their home these colors." Jasmine winces, looking in horror at the bright walls and doors.

Searching the house, we find the bad taste in color scheme and furniture appears only downstairs. Upstairs, the colors are warm and inviting, the furniture's rich dark woods beckoning you to relax and enjoy. If I hadn't believed Beatrix probably is the killer before, I sure as hell do now. What other reason could anyone have for the literal split-personality house?

Quickly and efficiently, we search the house, but find nothing. Nothing stands out, apart from the decoration, no trophies from the murders, or a reason for killing them. Glancing at Jasmine, I see she's as puzzled as I am. Nothing makes sense. We decide it's time to leave and move toward the stairs, when we hear the front door opening.

Hugging the wall, we watch the door slowly swinging open. Catching a glimpse of someone with red hair entering, we stare in puzzlement. *Who the hell is it?* Snapping out of our frozen state we return to the back bedroom. The only thing we know for definite is, it's not Beatrix. Her hair's brown!

As silently and quickly as we can, we enter the bedroom closing the door behind us as the footsteps ascend the stairs. "Hide," I mouth, as my eyes widen in alarm.

Glancing around the room, I groan in annoyance. It holds a double bed, night stands, chest of drawers, and a wardrobe. We contemplate hiding under the bed, but it's a divan and so no space there, and the wardrobe won't fit us both. I think about hiding behind the curtains, for just a second, before with a grimace I head for the open window. Hefting myself up, I climb out. Grasping the gutter, I swing myself onto the roof and move over to give Jasmine room. A second later, she climbs out and eases the window back into position, joining me on the roof just as the gutter gives a groan of strain. Glancing at each other, we grin. I haven't had so much fun in ages.

We inch toward the drainpipe to shimmy down, when we hear someone enter the bedroom we'd just left.

The window swings open, and a head pops out. We both freeze, gripping the roof. We hear muttering, and then the window slams shut.

As quietly as possible and with our hearts racing,

we reach the pipe. I slide down it and jump on the wall separating Beatrix's garden from her neighbors. Crouching down, I crawl a few steps forward, making sure no one sees me. Glancing up, I incline my head to Jasmine, who swiftly follows my path.

I'm about to move forward again, when I feel her place a steadying hand on me. Turning, I raise an inquiring eyebrow at her. She points toward the back door mimicking turning a lock. With an inward groan I know she's right. There's no point in slipping away quietly, if we let the occupants know someone's entered the house by leaving the door unlocked.

With a grimace I give her a nod. She lowers herself down and swings her legs over the side, grasping my hands. I help her lower the rest of the way.

Once she's on the ground I straighten, turn around and crawl backwards until my back is against the wall so I can keep an eye out. I hear movement from both next door and Beatrix's house.

Tapping two fingers against my leg, I catch Jasmine's eye and twirl them around in a "wrap it up motion," before tapping my wrist where I should have had my watch, if I'd remembered to wear it.

With a curt nod and a final twist, she locks the back door and crouch runs toward me, where I once again straddle the wall, lean down grasp her proffered hand, and swing her up. She runs to the end of the wall and jumps into the alleyway with me on her heels.

I've just cleared the wall when I hear the back door rattle. Stifling a laugh as Jasmine goes sprawling, I half land on top of her. I jump off her and help her up. We head toward the mouth of the alley with me still laughing.

"It's not funny, Candi, so stop laughing!" she hisses in exasperation.

With a snort, I try valiantly to get a hold of myself, sobering up quickly as I spy Beatrix heading home. We slip further into the alley's shadows, silently watching Beatrix talking on her phone, gesturing in annoyance at whatever she's hearing. For a split second, I think she's coming into the alley. Glancing around for an escape route, I notice Jasmine looking just as wary as me. We have nowhere to go.

"Beatrix, what are you doing?" a female voice hollers in annoyance, making Beatrix hesitate before she bypasses the alleyway to move toward the voice at the front of the house. I don't hear her answer. Instead Jasmine and I turn heading as fast and silently as we can farther into the alley and out the other side, along the back of the mall's car park toward West Bridge, and the long way home.

An hour later we arrive starving, tired, and in desperate need of a drink and the bathroom. Once finished I go to the kitchen feeling more relaxed. On entering Jasmine hands me a mug of coffee. With thanks I accept, taking a reviving sip. Contentedly, I curl my hands around the mug and drink deeply.

"You know, I had wanted something alcoholic to drink, but this coffee is definitely doing the trick." I grin happily, as I lean against the kitchen counter.

"Glad to hear it." She smiles. "But what I want to know is, what are you making us for lunch?"

Frowning at her, I try to remember what we have, foodwise in the house. With a grunt of annoyance, I put my mug down and rummage in the fridge, pulling out butter, mayo, ham, and lettuce. Grabbing a loaf of bread from the bread bin, I start making us a sandwich each.

"Someone is going to have to go food shopping," I mutter as I finish the ham. "And it's not going to be me," I add for good measure. I hate food shopping. I pass her a sandwich. Retrieving my coffee and sandwich, I move to the sofa which is still in the kitchen, and plop myself down almost spilling my drink. In silence we eat and once finished, I release a long groan. *What the hell is going on around here?*

"You know, when I decided to move back here, it was meant to be easy and straightforward." I continue without waiting for a reply. "No murders, no Grandma going bad, and do you realize how weird it is to say that?" I demand. "And most definitely, no headless corpses, or corpseless heads walking about the place! Oh God, maybe I've just gone crazy, and this is some majorly fucked up dream?" I ask hopefully, as I cradle my throbbing head in my palm.

Her laughter interrupts my pity party, and raising my head I send a "bitch, please" glower at her, which only makes her laugh harder. "What are you finding so Goddamned funny?" I growl in frustration.

"Your pity party is what I'm finding funny. Are you seriously trying to say you would rather be crazy than…yeah, okay…well, what about Victor, hmmm?" she demands in obvious relief at finding something good to come out of these admittedly bizarre events.

Looking at her, I study her closely. "Having you back has definitely been worth everything that's been happening, and yes, meeting Victor has been a most wondrous experience, and I wouldn't want to not have met him," I quietly agree with a small smile.

"He really is amazing," I whisper as a breathless

laugh escapes me. At her enquiring look, I smile and admit, "He makes me feel."

"Feel what apart from the obvious?"

"Just feel. I don't know. I feel alive and complete. I feel breathless, and as if for the first time I can breathe."

"Wow, is that all?" she laughs. Then with a look of curiosity reflected in her voice, she asks me, "Does he feel the same way?"

"Yes." Dragging my feet onto the sofa, I wrap my arms around my knees and rest my chin on top. With a shaky laugh, I admit, "Yes, he does, but I'm not ready to admit how I feel about him." Seeing my friend's incredulous look, I smile.

"I'm being serious. I know I'm feeling these emotions because of him, but they're my emotions, and I'm not ready to share them, and to be completely honest, it's not as if we really know each other, other than in the biblical sense, you know? What if...what if I get hurt or he changes his mind? I'm not ready to put my emotions on the line."

"But...Candi, I don't know how to tell you this. He has a right to know, especially if..."

"Who has a right to know, what?" enquires Victor, as he and Kheda walk into the kitchen, scaring the crap out of me.

I notice the guilty look flashing across Jasmine's face, and wonder if she'd heard them coming in. Narrowing my eyes at her, I arch one eyebrow in a silent demand. Shaking her head in silent denial and flushing slightly pink at the same time, makes me wonder if she had indeed heard them. I decide to ignore the question for now, and instead turn to Victor and

Kheda and change the subject. "Beatrix is alive."

"What? How is this possible? We saw her head, for crying out loud," Kheda exclaims in vexation as he dumps his shopping bags on the counter, and turns toward us as if to make sure we're not telling some sick joke.

Victor places his shopping bags on the kitchen table and slowly unpacks them. Every now and again he flicks a glance toward me, while I just sit hugging my legs, contentedly watching with a silly half smile on my face.

Finally, he's unpacked and put away the shopping. "What exactly happened?" Victor finally asks before Kheda explodes from gaining no information.

"Well, we went to check out her house, and she was leaving it," I reply with a shrug, as I watch Victor move toward me. With a sigh of appreciation, I finally blink and rouse myself enough, to tell Victor and Kheda everything.

"Are you two crazy?" Kheda demands in horror.

I laugh at his question as it reflects so closely what I had been thinking earlier, but receiving a withering glare from him, I quickly sober enough to say," No, we're not crazy, what we are is determined to find out what is going on. I think we should go to the club tonight," I add for good measure.

"Why?" Victor asks sitting down beside me.

"Because, it's where everything is centered," I explain slowly as I work things out in my head.

"The night after the first murder, everything was silent, except the club. You said the two vampires who happened to turn up dead, went missing from outside the club. Also Beatrix works at the club, and what with her head turning up at your pub, turning into a bomb, but not really, as it's on her shoulders very much attached, I think we need to check it out." Taking a deep breath, I look at everyone. "How many coincidences can there be?"

Chapter 25

Deafening silence greets my final question. With a tired smile, I decide to go for a nap. "Tonight is the full moon. I'll be able to send out a request to the rest of the girls from the army, and I think we should go to the club." Kheda and I will have to go for a run. Well, Kheda more than me. Though both of us can change outside of the full moon cycle, normal werewolves have to answer the moon's call; I'm not as much of an emergency, as my witch magick acts as a buffer to the moon's call.

The magick of the full moon is powerful; it calls to the wolf in us, and demands our change. The call starts a couple of days before the full moon, becoming stronger and irresistible, making the werewolf want to crawl out from beneath the skin. The need to run and hunt becomes all consuming. Then the moon call's power wanes over the days after it.

Getting up tiredly, I tidy up my dishes and go upstairs. I can hear and feel my bed's siren song calling my tired body. I manage to drag off my outer clothes and crawl into bed in my bra and panties. I don't remember anything else of my waking moments, but I do remember my dreams, or at least I think it was a dream.

I'm walking through the woods at the back of the pub; but this time the pub is in ruins. Something silver glitters at me, as if winking. Moving silently toward it, I reach down and retrieve a shiny silver disk. Without looking, I curl my fingers around it, half noticing it fits perfectly in the palm of my hand. Sniffing the air, I inhale the burnt wood and flesh, yet the barest scent of perfume wafts on the air, as if a woman is near.

Silently I return to the woods, keeping close to the ground. I crouch, watching. I'm just getting restless, and about to move when a noise to my left makes me pause. I flatten myself completely to the ground. My right leg stretches out behind me, as I bring my left tight into my body. My hands curl into fists, which I lean on for support. My body strains in readiness to pounce. I watch silently. The redheaded witch from Beatrix's house searches for something within the ruins. In puzzlement, I wonder what she's looking for.

Then the burning starts. My hand feels like it's on fire. Smothering a scream of pain, I glance down and realize my hand is bright red. Heat and flames erupt up my arm and crawl to my elbow. Along its path my skin is unhurt, but laced with a delicate black lace tattoo interspersed with red roses.

I stare in shock. Uncurling my palm, I discover the silver disk is gone but a pentagram is burnt into my palm, laced with the same black web and red rose tattoo. But with a fine silver thread weaving in and out of it.

I touch it gently with my uninjured hand, and the pain jumps swiftly up my other hand to my elbow, leaving the same delicate design. Biting back my scream, I decide it's best to not touch anything else, just in case I gain any more tattoos. When I look up, the red-haired witch is gone. There is no sign of anything strange having happened, except for my newfound tattoos that cover my hands and arms.

I wake up to being roughly shaken. Groaning, I try to push away the strong arms, but they don't cease their annoying manhandling.

"What is wrong with you?" I groggily demand. Opening an eye, I catch sight of Victor's face and come wide-awake. He looks like all the blood has left his body! Reaching a hand out to him, I notice a delicate black lace tattoo with red roses.

"Holy shit, it wasn't a dream," I whisper in shock.

"How did this happen?" Victor demands. In wonderment, he reaches out tracing the pattern on my arms. "How is this possible?" He asks so quietly, I only just hear him.

"I don't know. I dreamt of the pub, of finding a silver disk, and the red-haired woman from Beatrix's house. I felt my palm going on fire, and this happening," I tell him, waving my arms to indicate their new design. "You woke me up…She was looking for something, the red-haired witch. I wonder if it was the silver disk?"

Turning my palms up, I realize each palm has a different pattern; the pentagram in my right hand is laced in the silver thread. My left hand has a wolf's head, also laced in silver. Sucking in a breath, I look up at Victor. "My two forms of magick," I whisper in awe, offering my palms for inspection.

"How is this possible?" Victor whispers again. "They are magnificent. You are magnificent," he whispers before claiming my mouth in a gentle kiss.

I kiss him back, savoring every second of it, and drinking in the emotions he offers, giving mine in return. Finally we part and just stare at each other. I reach my fingers up to his beautiful face and trace the full contours of his talented mouth with the tips of my fingers. Victor gently nips them while staring intently into my eyes.

Giving a shaky smile, I retract my fingers, finally climbing out of bed. It's time to start getting ready for the busy night ahead. I pull on the clothes I'd worn earlier and give Victor some candles to carry downstairs. I bring down my box of matches, a crystal bowl, and some white sand I use in spell work. I follow Victor down to the sitting room, where we put them on the floor. We seriously need to get the furniture back in there. This is getting ridiculous.

"Dinner's ready. What the hell happened to you?" gasps Jasmine in shock, catching a glimpse of my arms. She grabs my arms, running her hands over the beautiful design. "Wow, how did you do these, and when?"

"Happened in a dream. They got burnt on sort of," I explain.

"Seriously?" She laughs, seeing Victor's and my expressions. She looks at the designs again and rubs them, as if to wipe them off. "Bloody hell, you're being serious!" Puzzlement and concern flash across her face, as she gently traces the designs on my arms.

"I don't know, but they seem to represent my two types of magick," I reply showing my palms.

"Wow, they're seriously cool," she murmurs. "They're beautiful and strangely suit you. Now, let's go eat dinner before it gets cold." Smiling, she drags us into the kitchen.

Kheda's serving steak and salad with baby

mushrooms and sundried tomatoes. Turning around in curiosity to find out what is taking us so long he drops the serving spoon he's using when he catches sight of my arms. "What, how...what?" stammers Kheda in shock, unable to formulate a sentence. Rubbing a large hand over his face, he takes a deep breath and starts again. "What happened to you, and how?"

Sucking in my lips, I drag in a deep breath, and once again explain what happened as best I can.

Bending down, Kheda picks up the dropped spoon and dumps it in the sink while he listens to my unusual story. "So you dreamed it happened, and you woke up with them?"

"Basically, yeah, that's exactly what happened." I laugh.

"I think we should go to the ruins of your pub after dinner, see if there is anything there, but I also think we should be careful, in case someone we don't want to meet is actually looking for something," he instructs, looking thoughtfully at my arms.

"So basically, you want us to take my dream seriously?" I ask doubtfully.

"Candi, you have tattoos you dreamed of on your skin, as if you were born with them. So yeah, we're taking your dream seriously," Kheda answers. I spot the moment Kheda realizes it isn't doubt of my dreams, but fear of them that causes my question.

These markings had burnt themselves into me, through a dream! They had hurt like hell, and going by Victor's pallor, he had seen it happen and was feeling helpless at not being able to stop it. Silently Kheda brings over our dinner, giving Victor a bloody steak.

We sit and eat in silence, each of us thinking about

what the night might bring. I hope we'll all be okay, and that no one will be hurt. Mind you, I also hope I'll win the lotto, so what I hope for means diddly squat when you really think about it. On such a happy thought, I finish my dinner.

One by one we all finish and tidy up after ourselves. I give a big stretch. I can feel the moon's pull, glancing at Kheda I know I'm not the only one, his muscles twitch, and crawl under his skin, and his eyes turn green.

The werewolf within him looks at me curiously. Sniffing the air as if trying to figure out what exactly I am. The change comes over me instantly, transforming me from human to werewolf in the space of a breath. I let out a little chuff of a laugh, as I look at the surprise in Kheda's wolf eyes, and realize even though Kheda has seen me as a wolf, his wolf hasn't. And with my witch magick allowing me to keep on my clothes, I'm definitely unique.

"I've never seen a change so effortless," growls Kheda just before his body goes into the most painful transformation I have ever seen in my life. His body bows in sudden rippling, bone-crunching viciousness. I back up with a little yelp into Victor's legs.

Quickly Kheda strips, hunkering into a crouch, just before his legs shoot out from underneath him, his body rippling and distorting, bones breaking and reconnecting differently. His face elongates, distorting and transforming until finally he turns into a wolf, panting in agony before our shocked faces.

None of us realized how much pain and agony werewolves, normal werewolves, I amend, suffer. After all, other shifters don't, so why werewolves? Maybe it's to do with the moon's pull? I'll have to ask him about it sometime. I've never seen another werewolf shift before. A couple of the girls from the army are werewolves. They always transformed in private. Looking at Kheda, I understand them wanting to do so privately! Jasmine strips and transforms into her dog form and curls up beside Kheda, offering him comfort and a warm lick of her tongue.

"Holy shit," Victor whispers, as he scratches me behind my ears making me shiver in great satisfaction, my tongue lolling out as I look up at him, giving him an adoring look.

After about three minutes, Kheda finally gives a satisfied grunt and licks her back, slowly standing up so as not to disturb her. I get up as does Jasmine. We exit through the back door which Victor opens for us, and as one, we run silently over the bridge, into the woods until we come out behind the back of the burnt out shell of Vlad's Bar.

In the ashes, I notice a silver disk glinting at me. I quickly transform into my human form, hurry over, and grab the disk. It fits perfectly in the palm of my hand. Curling my fingers around it, I slink back into the cover of the trees where Victor, Jasmine, and Kheda are waiting for me. Victor's just about to speak when we hear the sound of someone rummaging through the ruins. Quick as lightning, we flatten ourselves against the ground and watch as the red-haired witch from Beatrix's house emerges.

As in my dream, I wonder if it's the disk she's searching for. Silently we edge farther into the woods and hear a scream of rage, as the witch kicks at a fallen burnt plank of wood. She lets out another curse, I'm guessing from hurting her foot. We don't wait to find out the reason, but instead retreat further back. Victor indicates for us to follow him, leads us through the woods, and to a house near the pub, but set on the other side of the car park.

The house is enchanting, old stone walls with dark mahogany wood for the door and window frames. The roof has black slate and a stone chimney. I look curiously at the door, for I can't see a key hole anywhere. On silent hinges, the door swings open after Victor runs a single finger down its center. I stare doubtfully at it and then back at Victor.

"It's okay, Candi, this is my home," Victor whispers before entering. With a final look behind me, I follow Victor inside, with Kheda and Jasmine on my heels. Once we're all in, the front door closes behind us, as silently as it'd opened.

Looking around, I notice the hallway is sparsely furnished, holding only a coat stand and a hall table with a phone on it. Following Victor into the sitting room which is decorated simply, the walls painted cream, apart for the fireplace wall and carpet which is a rich chocolate brown.

The two sofas are dark green leather recliners. A heavy redwood coffee table and two large bookcases in the same wood filled with books frame each side of the fireplace. The only other furniture is a drinks cabinet and a TV in a corner. Apparently Victor doesn't watch it very often.

"What did you pick up?" Victor asks me, snapping me out of my perusal of his home. Opening my palm, I look at the silver disk. The head of a werewolf stares back at me, but it has blue eyes unlike the wolf burnt into my palm. Turning it to the other side, I notice it has the same pentagram that is burnt into my palm. I show Victor and inform the others of my findings.

"It's quite literally the disc from my dreams," I say showing my tattoos and the silver disk.

"The werewolf has blue eyes," Victor puzzles. "Werewolves don't have blue eyes, and your eyes are violet in your werewolf form."

"Not everything is about me," I tease Victor. "Anyway, it's the only difference between the disk and my imprint. Mine has violet eyes.

A loud silence descends upon us at my statement, as all stare at me.

"Are you sure?" Victor demands reaching for my hands. "How can this be, and what the hell does it mean?" He traces the wolf's head on my palm.

"I don't know, but I have to get home to do my summoning spell, before we get ready to go to the club tonight," I admit, removing my palm from his wonderful hands. I head toward the door, pause, I come back to Victor.

"How the hell do you open your door?"

"It's an imprinted door, so no one, other than those who live in the house, can open it," Victor explains. Seeing the curious and puzzled expressions on everyone's faces he adds, "Vampires have had imprinted doors for centuries, for protection."

"Huh, never heard of it. Clever though, but does it mean you have to constantly open the door for visitors when they're leaving as well?"

"Yes, but that is also part of being a good host."

"But what about if you have a house party? Doesn't it get annoying? Or what if there's a fire and no one can get out until you open the door or what…?"

"Candi, vampires can always remove the imprint on the door. Well, we can switch it off at least, if needed."

"Oh, okay, that makes sense."

"Now, let's get back to yours, so we can get what needs done tonight, done." Victor smiles as he brushes his fingers along my arm before sliding past me to run his fingers along the centre of his door, stepping back as it swings open.

We follow Victor out and the door shuts behind us, locking us out. We move into the forest just as an arrow whistles through the air. Tackling Victor, I knock him to the ground landing on top of him.

Running my fingers over him and finding no injuries I roll off him, bringing flames to my hands and sending them in the direction the arrow came from."Do not injure, just restrain," I mutter. I hear a squeal, as my firebomb hits its target, transforming into bands of fire holding a prisoner in their grasp. Warily I creep to the area lit up by the flames, holding the would-be assassin.

Peering down, I'm surprised to see Sally, the young werewolf we had tried to help a couple of days ago. She is shaking, her muscles twitching like crazy, fighting off transforming.

"So Sally, we meet again."

Kheda and Jasmine arrive, standing on either side of me, baring their fangs in a silent but deadly snarl. I feel Victor standing behind me. His fingers press and prod me as if to make sure I'm uninjured. I call back my bindings. Sally's not going anywhere.

"I'm sorry, I had no choice," Sally pants, tears running down her face, her body shaking uncontrollably.

"What do you mean? Who are you helping, Sally?"

"I, I don't know who—I ahhhhhhhhhhhhhhhhhh!" Sally screams, a blood curdling scream of terror and pain. I jump in shock. To our horror, she rips apart in an explosion of body parts, drenching us in blood. A piece of bone hits me in the forehead making me wince.

"Christ on a stick, what the hell?" I demand, as I wipe blood and gore from my face.

"Come, let's all get back to the house and get cleaned up," Victor interrupts.

"All of us?" I say, turning to look at Victor who's spotless. "Huh, how the hell did you manage to stay clean?"

"I was standing behind you, checking to make sure you were unhurt at the time she…exploded. You protected me from the majority of the gore…" With a grimace he picks something out of my hair and swipes at the top of his head, where I now see some blood, and what looks like gristle. "What caused her to blow up?"

"Black magick. God, I feel dirty."

Leaning closer to me, he whispers in a gruff voice, "I can wash you clean if you like?"

A shiver ripples through me, and a smile twitches at the corner of my mouth as Victor wiggles his eyebrows suggestively at me.

"Come on, let's get back home, and hopefully no one will see us."

****

I'm glad Victor isn't offended by my turning down his offer. But with how gross I feel, the thought of intimate contact just feels wrong. An hour later, I'm still scrubbing myself clean, and I've run out of shampoo. Finally I switch off the shower, climb out looking more like a prune with raw skin, than a human. I dry myself, put on sweats, comb my hair, and jog barefoot down to the sitting room to do my summoning spell.

I take a few moments to myself just to breathe, clearing my thoughts from everything that is happening. Once all is quiet, I light the candles, scattering white sand in a circle around me. I call my power to me, placing my hands flat on the ground drawing the earth's energy into me.

Normally for spell work I'd use salt, but for a summoning like this, I use sand as it's part of the earth. The sand glows pink, then gold, until it turns into a shimmering bubble of golden energy with a pearl tinge, surrounding me in a bubble of protection. Bringing the bowl to me, I circle my fingers around it faster and faster, until it sings.

I summon you, my family of warriors,
I summon you, on a quest of mine,
Come to us, my sisters in arms,
Come to us, your sisters in arms!

With a clap like thunder, the bowl rises into the air, spinning its song, before slowly lowering back to the ground, until it stops spinning and grows quiet. I place a palm on my forehead, and the other flat on the ground, returning the borrowed energy to the earth with a quiet thank you. The golden bubble retreats, until finally sand is all that remains. I send the sand back into its container. Taking a deep breath to centre myself once more, I look up to see Victor in wide-eyed surprise.

"You okay, Victor?" I've never seen him look so, so flabbergasted before.

"I've never seen anything like it before," Victor finally manages, while walking into the sitting room. His lean body moving like a large jungle cat, all muscle and power, in a divine wrapping. "Sorry, did you say something?" I blush, realizing Victor was still talking.

"Do you want to grab a drink from the kitchen, before getting ready for tonight?" Victor repeats grinning.

"I'd love one." Clambering to my feet, I leave my candles and stuff behind; we leave the sitting room to join a clean Jasmine and Kheda, who are both in human form. With a contented smile of gratitude, I accept the rum and soda I'm passed. Leaning against the counter to support myself, I take a fortifying gulp.

We have a couple of drinks and get ready for a night on the town. Hopefully tonight will just be a nice night out, no murder involved. Two hours later we're all finally dressed and ready to leave. I'm in a gold tie back PU top and a pair of black trousers with black heeled boots. I've twisted my hair up and secured it with a clip in the shape of a black and gold butterfly. A bit of eyeliner, green eye shadow, and a little lip gloss, and I'm ready to go. Leaving the bathroom where I'd applied my makeup to retrieve my purse, I spot Victor.

I come to a screeching lust-filled stop. Dressed all in black, he looks like a sultry dark God, come to wreak pleasure and decadence upon me. I suck in a breath as I gaze at him. My God, he's divine! His black shirt hinting at his muscular torso is open at the throat. Such a tiny glimpse, but I want to lick the barely visible skin. His black trousers mold to his muscular legs, making me jealous of their close proximity. I blink, a smile twitching at the corner of my mouth. His shoes are the most comfortable-looking trainer boot I have ever seen. I have no idea what they're called, but I want a pair.

"You look stunning," Victor states, crossing to stand in front of me. "I want to strip off your clothing and make love to every inch of you."

I turn shy at this statement, looking down, then back up at him through my eyelashes and finally away, smile and back at him.

"My God, have you just gone shy?" demands Victor in amazement.

"Apparently, and I have no idea why," I mutter as I grab my purse and turn to leave.

Victor stops me by wrapping his arms around my waist, pulling me against his rock-hard body. "If it wasn't for the fact we have to leave, I would take you right here, and savor every inch of your delectable skin, before making you come over and over again," he whispers into my ear, before nibbling at the side of my neck and sinking his fangs into me. A moan of desire ripples up my throat, escaping me as Victor drinks.

Extracting his fangs, he places a kiss on the now healed skin of my neck. Releasing me from the circle of his arms, Victor takes my hand and leads me into the hallway, down the stairs to await Jasmine and Kheda.

Chapter 26

The music vibrates through my body, as we enter the club. God, I love dancing. Jasmine and I head straight for the dance floor, joining the writhing bodies moving to the beat. I let the music enter me and dance to its pulse, my body becoming one with it, as I move my hips and legs in fluid motions. My arms and shoulders sway with the tempo.

Victor and Kheda have gone to the bar to get us drinks, but apparently change their minds as they watch us dancing. The scent of lust is strong in the club, as people writhe and grind against each other. A couple of men try to reach for us, but we ignore their sweaty hands, and they soon turn toward others willing to dance with them.

Suddenly, Victor's in front of me, his hands on my hips as he moves his body to dip and move against mine. I move one of my legs around his and our bodies move in a sensual dance. I wrap my arms around his neck, and as one we move in beautiful sync with each other and the music. Eventually we pull apart to get a drink. Every nerve ending in my body thrums in happiness. As I look at Victor, I see his expression, one of such raw desire, and something else, causing my heart to take joyous flight.

****

Looking at the vampire maul the witch, I feel

hatred for him erupt through me. I'll liberate her from him soon. But first, those troublesome sisters are at it again. Seeing them zero in on a young couple, I decided to phone the police.

The Protectors *do not keep trophies! They were warned, and yet they still disobey. Stupid bitches, tonight the police will arrest them. Feeling smug, I leave the club to make my phone call. After all, there is only one place they'll be heading with their prize.*

****

All four of us are standing at the bar when feelings of anger, hatred, and jealousy bombard us in a rush of malevolence. It leaves me shaken. Catching sight of Jasmine, I see I'm not the only one. Victor puts a protective arm around me, drawing me close to his side as he casually looks for the source of the hatred filtering through the club.

I spot the red-haired witch first, prowling around the outskirts of the dance floor, watching the dancers. Every now and again she looks back as if seeking an unspoken answer.

"Who is she looking at?"

"I don't know, but I think we need to find out fast," Kheda answers, as he watches the red-haired witch give a slight nod of acknowledgment. She starts dancing toward a young couple on the dance floor.

We separate. Jasmine and Kheda head to the left, Victor and I toward the right. We join the dancers and slowly spin, dip, and twirl our way around the dance floor. Each time, getting closer to the back of the room where the red-haired witch had looked. To my eternal frustration, I don't spot anyone watching the dancers in an obvious way. Victor spins me, just in time to witness

Jasmine and Kheda being led outside by the red-haired witch and someone else.

"Christ on a stick, what the fuck!" I exclaim in panic, as we come to a screeching stop, knocking over a couple of other dancers. With a muttered sorry, we rush outside. Looking about, I realize there's no sign of them.

"Oh my God, oh my God, where are they?" I panic.

"Breathe, Candi," Victor sooths me, rubbing my back in comfort while searching for any sign of our friends. Anger ripples through me, so strong it knocks Victor back a step. Power zips up my arms and lightning hot and strong ripples across the sky. My eyes turn violet; the intensity of the sudden change turns everything violet for just a second, before settling. I feel the change as power vibrates through my body, and sparks shoot from my fingers into a trail of violet fire. *"Follow the trail and protect your brother and sister."* A voice like thunder erupts from the sky, into me, and then out my mouth.

A couple of partygoers scream in fear, then giggle, as if to pretend they're only messing at being scared. Victor and I ignore them; I transform into my wolf, running after the violet trail with Victor keeping pace at my side.

****

I watch as again he lays his hands on her. Her eyes turn violet and all hell breaks loose. Some stupid girls scream and giggle away their fear, but all I can do is stare, transfixed as power, so much power surrounds the witch. Trailing violet lightning, she transforms into a wolf and chases the trail to the caves. "I have to tell the high council," I mutter in shock as I realize the

Double Magick one is alive. As the silver wolf and the vampire disappear into the night, I grimly stare at the spot I last saw them, knowing a war is beginning, and her death will come at the hands of The Protectors.

****

The trail leads us through town toward Hunters Park. With a howl of anger, I run harder toward the caves where we found the bodies. Outside the cave I stop, transforming back into my human form. I turn to Victor. "Can you get through the roof of the cave?"

"I could, but it will take too long and they'd hear me coming," Victor apologizes. With a frustrated nod, I transform back and slink into the cave. Victor creeps in, hugging the other side of the wall from me. As one, we prowl through the cave, until we reach the back. I spot the red-haired witch shivering on the floor.

The moment she spots me, she gives me a pleading look, and without speaking, she turns toward the main cave, where the two vampires and the werewolf had been. Creeping closer, I spot a figure cutting off Kheda's clothes; Jasmine's have already been removed.

I can hear their heartbeats, slow and sluggish. I have no idea what they've been drugged with, but it's fast.

A silent growl vibrates through me as I watch my helpless friends. Fury explodes through me as I realize this unseen person is going to use my best friend as her plaything. A deep, hate-filled roar erupts from me as I pounce. The witch swings around to face me, raising the scissors she's holding to stab me.

I open my mouth to howl in fury when a ball of violet power erupts from me. It shoots straight at Beatrix. A yelp of fear escapes her as she dives out of the way only to be tackled by Victor. My power bubble smashes into the wall sending shrapnel flying.

I hadn't even seen Victor move. He punches her in the face, knocking her unconscious. Quickly I swing around to face the red-haired witch, sending a snarl of warning to her as she tries to escape. Transforming back into my human form, I go to Jasmine, checking to make sure she's okay.

"I'm heading out to the entrance, so I can call this in," Victor informs me as he puts a gentle hand on my shoulder, before heading out of the cave with his phone in hand. Looking at the red-haired witch for the first time, I realize just how young she is. Probably eighteen years old, if not younger.

"What's your name?" I demand.

"S-Sarah, Sarah Sullivan," Sarah stammers in fear.

"Are you related to Beatrix?"

"S-she's my sister."

"How long has she been killing, and how long have you been helping her?"

"She—she has been killing always, I think. W-when I was ten, our parents died. I t-think she k-killed them, too. S-she made m-me h-help from then on," Sarah stammered.

"Christ on a stick," I mutter in shock. *How many more bodies are out there, and where are they?*

Victor arrives and obviously heard what Sarah had said. He looks rather pale. It's unusual; he normally looks so healthy.

"The police and ambulance are on the way," he informs me. "The thing is…they were already called." While he keeps an eye on Sarah, I try to cover up Jasmine as best I can. She's so not going to be happy at the state of her clothes when she finally wakes up. Ten minutes later, the ambulance arrives with the police hot on their tails.

Beatrix has already come to and is throwing insults at Victor and me. She has such a potty mouth. I'm actually quite shocked. Jasmine and Kheda are rushed to the hospital. Words like "IV" and "drip" are mentioned as well as flushing out their systems.

The police arrest Sarah and Beatrix. I think they also wanted to arrest Victor and me, too, not sure what exactly for, but thankfully Nina of all people stands up for us. Victor and I are taken down to the police station so we can give our statements. We're given a lift to the hospital, which I'm grateful for. I'm so exhausted by this stage, I just want to collapse.

****

Reaching the hospital, we find Jasmine and Kheda easily enough, though they're in different rooms. Hospitals can be so fussy at times, and very inconvenient. Don't they know we need to visit both of them?

"I'll stay with Kheda tonight to keep an eye on him," Victor informs me, pushing me gently into Jasmine's room. I'm horrified at how small she looks, as she lies still in the hospital bed. Sorrow shudders through me, as I acknowledge how close I came to losing her again.

"Oh Jasmine, I'm so sorry," I whisper, as I run my hands over my face in exhaustion. I plop down on the nearest chair, dragging another over to prop my feet up. I must have nodded off at some stage, because I wake up stiff and cold on the floor, with Jasmine peering over the side of the bed laughing at me.

"Hello, sleeping beauty. Are you comfortable down there?" She snickers as I rub my eyes blearily, climbing stiffly to my feet. When I finally register she's not only awake, but talking to me, I let out a squeal of delight, flinging myself at her.

"You're okay?" I demand, bursting into tears.

"I'm fine, just so glad you found us. How did you?" she asks as she hugs me in relief. Sitting gingerly back down on one of the chairs, I explain how we found them, and about Sarah's role in the situation.

"She believes Beatrix killed her parents and has apparently been helping capture people ever since. I'm not sure how much was involuntary, to be honest. But, God, if you or Kheda had died, I'm so sorry." My eyes well up with tears again. Placing a hand over my mouth to compose myself, I give a slight nod and look at her. I'm ready for whatever she says to me. I just hope she will forgive me.

"You have nothing to be sorry for, Candi. You did nothing wrong, and you saved my life," she reassures me, surprise and confusion in her voice at my feelings of guilt.

"If I hadn't moved back here, you wouldn't have been in this situation," I explain, as if it automatically made me responsible for the killer's actions.

"But Candi, if we hadn't moved here, we wouldn't have met Kheda and Victor. I wouldn't change that for anything. And the killer wouldn't have been found, so more people would be dead. I don't regret moving here, how could I? I'm back to myself and feel better than I have in years. So don't you dare apologize for bringing me here," she finishes fiercely.

"Okay, outside of you and Kheda being kidnapped,

and almost killed, I'm also happy to have met Victor and Kheda," I admit.

"I'm glad to hear it. I would hate for you to wish you had never met me," Victor informs me from the doorway, making us jump.

"Bloody hell, Victor, do I need to get you a cow bell, so we can hear you coming?" I demand, placing a hand over my racing heart.

"I know a much more interesting way for you to know I'm coming," Victor answers with a wicked grin on his face, as he prowls into Jasmine's room, with a wicked gleam of dark promises in his eyes. "I just came to say Kheda's awake and restless, he'll also be in to see you in a second, once he can find some clothing to cover up his ass that is." Victor laughs. "Detective Nina was just in. Apparently, both sisters deny killing the human in the woods, Kheda's nephew, the female werewolf, and the old witch. The sisters did recognize the human; he worked with *The Protectors.* They don't know why he was killed, but they did say he must have gone against *The Protectors* in some way for him to be murdered. Most likely he warned someone they'd made the list. It appears *The Protectors* sent someone to stop them from taking trophies. They believe there is another killer out there, so there will be a guard on duty to watch over you and Kheda while you're here."

"They do believe the killer has left, after phoning the police to have Beatrix and Sarah arrested. Now I've come to take Candi home, so we can get some sleep. We need to rest, for tomorrow, we have a prophecy to find, and we also need to gather more allies to our cause."

Giving Jasmine a quick hug, I tell her we'll be back

later to check on both her and Kheda. Victor and I leave the hospital arm in arm. As the breeze whispers around us, I hear the voices of my sisters in arms whispering, *"We're coming, sisters, we're coming."* I look at Victor and realize I hadn't imagined it. Victor is right, tonight is ours, for tomorrow, we really do have a prophecy to find.

Hand in hand, we walk into the dawn, heading toward Victor's home. A new day for new beginnings. After the trouble we've had, our adventures are just beginning. Thinking of the cards I'd drawn, I realize, they really do make sense.

Seeing my smile, Victor turns me and pulls me into his arms. "I am falling so much in love with you, my Double Magick woman, it scares the shit out of me."

He kisses me so soundly, words and thoughts fly from my head. All I can do is kiss him back and enjoy the moment.

A word from the author...

Born in Dublin, I moved to England, and then finally back home to Ireland. I now live in West Cork but want to move to Montana, America.

In October 2010, I self-published a book of poetry called *Different Kinds of Emotions.*

But I always wanted to write down the stories in my head, and finally I wrote my first novel, a paranormal fantasy called *Double Magick in the Falls*, Book 1 in the Candi Reynolds series.

When I was a child I fell in love with books, amazing stories filled with mystery and intrigue, danger and fantasy. This love has progressed into a passion for me. I also like photography and cemeteries—the older the better.

You can connect with me through the following places.

Website: http://aprilhollingworth.wix.com/april-hollingworth

Facebook: https://www.facebook.com/aprilhollingworthauthor

Twitter: https://twitter.com/No1Bitchmaster

Goodreads: https://www.goodreads.com/author/show/4759078.April_Hollingworth

Amazon: http://www.amazon.com/April-Hollingworth/e/B00H48PPAG/